HAUNTED HALLWAYS

EDITED BY MAY SELESTE

THE MALLORY THORNE
SCHOOL OF EXCELLENCE

Published by Outland Entertainment LLC
3119 Gillham Road
Kansas City, MO 64109

Founder/Creative Director: Jeremy D. Mohler
Editor-in-Chief: Alana Joli Abbott
Senior Editor: Scott Colby
Project Director: Anton Kromoff

ISBN: 978-1-954255-80-7 (print), 978-1-954255-81-4 (ebook)
Worldwide Rights
Created in the United States of America

Editor: May Seleste
Copy editor: Alana Joli Abbott
Proofreader: Scott Colby
Cover Illustration: Anne Marie Cochran
Cover Design: Jeremy D. Mohler
Interior Layout: Jeremy D. Mohler

Printed and bound in the United States of America.

Visit outlandentertainment.com to see more, or follow us on our Facebook Page facebook.com/outlandentertainment/

TABLE OF CONTENTS

INTRODUCTION
A YEARBOOK OF HAUNTINGS

AI JIANG

There is something about schools that makes them particularly primed for ghosts and hauntings, and sometimes I wonder if it's because they're a place where many leave behind regrets—a space that holds onto them whether students move forth from their memories and experiences or not. School is a place where our younger selves linger, where many of us make our closest friends and most dreaded enemies, where teachers might make or break our love for learning. Parents, too, though they seldom walk the halls, haunt their children's every breath, whispering in their ears, judging their answers and behaviors, waiting with stretched smiles when their children return home to the extent that sometimes it feels like school doesn't leave us when we exit the building. As though school follows us home—and often, it does.

What I love about this anthology is the core resonance of each story and the stories as a collective in capturing the different interpretations of what haunting might mean. There are stories centered on identity and belonging, the pressures of school, performance, and competition—both between fellow students and within us. Many have felt the need, or perhaps this thought process has been so deeply ingrained into us throughout childhood, to be the perfect child and student, to achieve high grades so we can become the pride of our parents and the envy of our friends. But to reach this far-stretching goal post, there might be hefty sacrifices that students feel justified to make—no matter how horrid the consequences.

Not only are there stories about the experiences of students, but there are also tales focusing on the way expectations differ between students and teachers in educational institutions, and also between different cultures. Schools can shape our paths, make or break us as people, and influence the rest of our lives if we allow it—or even when we don't. This reminds me of my own experience in schools and similar places: swimming instructors who dunked our heads into the water when we didn't learn fast enough; teachers who threatened to lock us into closets when we wouldn't sleep during nap time; teachers who didn't offer guidance but insistence, impressing on our pliable minds the idea that their thoughts and beliefs were the only correct ones.

But schools aren't only places of darkness; they also have the potential to foster great learners through empathy and compassion. Here, I think of the teachers who bought me my favorite book as a gift and a Halloween costume of my favorite cartoon character; teachers who took me to McDonalds after school; teachers who befriended my parents, and the one who had almost married my uncle; teachers who allowed us to take naps in class because to them, our wellbeing was above our studies.

In this anthology, there are stories of body horror, of the way the school system might force rigidity and regurgitation, of bullying and harassment (and the way it completely changes the dynamics of a school and students' livelihoods and consequently their futures), of privilege and competition, of access and scholarship and financial need.

More often than not, educational institutions favor those more fortunate and make those with fewer resources compete with those who are already several steps ahead of the starting line. The stories highlight the reality of the lies we might tell to rise above others— on applications or in papers, even if they are things we ourselves are not, and things we ourselves do not believe in. But for these institutions, we make ourselves fit into checkboxes of diversity, feel the need to flaunt identity, culture, background, as though it is the group we are part of that matters and not ourselves as individuals. Yet, there is the need to hide these very things for the very same reasons.

School culture can be toxic in its deadlines and stress-driven productivity, the way institutions might teach us to avoid failure, or instill a fear of failure, so we do not challenge ourselves or take risks, but reach for what might be easiest and what would guarantee success. And this same fear of failure stops us from trying hard because we are afraid we might still fail, that it might all be for nothing. We then begin to diminish our own efforts, compare ourselves to others who seem to have more challenges to overcome yet can still perform, or seem to do less but still achieve more.

In this anthology of Asian voices and experiences woven into stories that beg to be heard, dear reader, you will find that privilege does not always equal to success, that these seemingly safe havens hide corruption and the abuse of power in dark histories and bloody hallways, and the way haunting is done not only by ghosts but also by the living. And perhaps by the end of these tales, you might find yourself looking at the hallways of your past schools, not so much with nostalgia, but with eyes that can spot the fingerprints left on the walls, the crimson footprints on the tiles, and the bruises behind unwavering smiles and the mask of seemingly wise guides.

EDITOR'S FOREWORD

MAY SELESTE

Every school has its own ghost story, right? Of how someone saw a figure in the gym hall after dark, or whispers in the locker room of that one student from that one class all those years ago that mysteriously "snapped." For someone like me, the kid with a great interest in the macabre, I came across my fair share of creepy tales and rumors. Because as you see, dear reader, most of my life, and I expect most of yours, too, has been school. An endless cycle of study, exams, graduate. Study, exams, graduate. Rinse and repeat until you've reached the next level—climbing higher and higher until there's nothing left but a vast plane of nothing, and everything at the same time. Even as I write this, I sit in the solace of the old post-graduate library—surrounded by a soft shifting as someone tenderly leafs through the pages of a book older than everybody in the room combined, and the faint scent of coffee and panic in the midst of "final project" season. Despite the stress, this is home. From the after-school tutoring centers that were really just a single room in the back of a building, to the historical institutions that have stood for generations before mine. That had seen many faces before mine.

That had seen many, *many* lives before mine.

So when the conversation with fellow gothic authors arose about haunted locations—what else could I say? Mansions, churches...schools. Where the halls are lined with hope and glory, dreams, and friendship—where aspiration is met with a gold star and sweet validation. Yet when the lights turn out, and the whispers get loud enough for you to hear them—*really* hear them—you hear the stories of fear and desperation that spans generations, people driven to the brink of madness, of prayers aimed at whichever entity deigns to listen. When the gold stars and validation start to rot and taste like blood. And from there, *Haunted Hallways* was born.

When word was sent out for authors to contribute, there were two main considerations—amplifying Asian voices, and whether they could truly capture the sinister essence of the unique ways academia could possibly haunt you. For the former, if one is put in a position to uplift marginalized voices—should we not take the opportunity to do so? And with the rich history and variety of spirits and ghouls—most of which are rare to find in global media—these stories warrant being heard in a joint effort to both diversify the voices we read, but to also enrich the genre and bring forward what we define as "horror" or "gothic" into contemporary times, and how we choose to define it going forward.

For the latter point, we decided to set the stories in one location—the "Mallory Thorne School of Excellence"—to truly consolidate the fact that so many tales and so many experiences can be uniquely encountered all under one roof. That almost everyone has a story they left behind in the hallowed halls of their youth. For some, this followed themes of war, colonisation, and generational trauma. For others, it was about the secrets living in the walls, sinister whispers from the past, and shattered reflections. And when the time comes for you to leave, and you look back and see the shadow of the person you once were still standing in the hallway, books in hand and still in the same uniform—what other choice do you have, then, to turn your backs on each other as you go into the world, and they relive the stories you left behind?

So what exactly is the "Mallory Thorne School of Excellence?" It's constructed to be a boarding school in a fictional English countryside, spanning from the Victorian era[1]. Being British myself, the inspiration came from the many architectural structures littered throughout the country[2]. We believed that this would be the best location, as it allowed for us to envision the setting as a truly ominous and secluded environment that one would imagine when thinking of the word "gothic." The school is said to be started by the fictional Thorne family with the title of "Head Teacher" being passed through the bloodline as time progresses, and with the original "Lady Mallory Thorne" forever immortalised in the school crest. In writing the stories contained in this collection, the authors were given basic guidelines of location, school structure, and a brief history. For the rest, they were given free rein to let their imaginations run through the dimly lit stone halls of the academy. Whispering their tales inspired by mythology, psychology, identity, life. And perhaps in one of these stories, you'll find that shadow of your old self that you had left all those years ago, reaching out their hand, ready to pull you back in—even momentarily—to face the haunted tales of those cold, quiet hallways.

---

1   Despite the vast history of the school, the earliest records that could be recovered were from the 60s. Everything that came before went missing under mysterious circumstances. Allegedly.

2   Namely King's Cross St. Pancras station, the Kings College and St. Pauls Cathedral libraries, and, of course, the Bodleian at Oxford, which I visited on a school trip once and could never forget.

THE MAGIC THEY NEVER TAUGHT US

AUDRIS CANDRA

Schools never taught us magic. Especially not when it was important.

When Gita vomited clumps of the longest, shiniest black hair I'd ever seen, the teachers waved it off as her seeking attention. Like a desperate cat. When Muthi disappeared for a week and was found on the locked rooftop, alone and screaming until her voice shattered, the staff wrote it off as a case of hysteria.

Schools never taught us how to survive. Least of all this one.

I still had scars on my tongue from when I'd thrown up nails. The steel had raked my throat, and rust had tainted my meals for weeks. At least back home, the local ustad and pastor would have tried to exorcise me. It might have worked. It might not. It was the effort that counted.

Just like our effort.

Gita pushed the crude doll onto the table, the three of us surrounding it. The coconut made for a perfectly round head, and the body was two bamboo chopsticks tied into a cross. Frayed burlap sack covered most of it, painting the illusion of a strawman. Once I tied a short pencil to its arm, the doll wasn't a doll anymore.

The oil lamp shone gold on Muthi's brown skin as she pulled back. "I don't know, this all seems like a bad idea. I'm not...I'm not comfortable doing anything involving magic."

"You can just watch us, and if anything bad happens, you can recite Al-Fatihah or Ayat Kursi. Or don't. We're doing this, with or without you," Gita said. "I'll give you some time to think."

The elders would warn me not to play this game—to do this ritual. But I can't remember why. I can't even picture my—our friend's face. I only know that we haven't seen ▌ for a week, and neither the teachers nor the faculty members would even acknowledge that ▌ ever existed. Her name wasn't in the records. I don't know if I should blame the teachers—they fancied themselves our second parents, but they could only move within the rules of the school. Maybe I should blame the school itself, as this old institution only cared about producing the best students.

I remember one thing, though. Deep in the night, we both woke from the same dream. That somehow, I'd been cursed for being so far from home. That I must consume flesh or else I'd perish. I waved it off as a stress-induced dream from the coming exam.

▌ dragged me to the kitchen and brought the cleaver down on her own pinky. I screamed, and she pushed the little thing into my mouth. Shoved it down my throat.

We never had nightmares again.

"I guess...I'd rather be here with you," Muthi said. "This is for ▌."

Gita pulled out a blank paper. "What's the worst that can happen anyway?"

"I don't know. Possession?" Muthi glanced around. "I guess I could make makeshift holy water should anything happen."

Gita rolled her eyes. "Oh, please. That's the mildest western movie shit. That's the stuff white people are afraid of: losing control. But us? We never had control to begin with."

I pinched the spot between my brows. Whenever I grasped around for her name, all I found were the laws of thermodynamics and the various complicated chemical formulas. What had school done to me that I couldn't even recall the friend who had mutilated herself to save me?

"Do you know the story of a Muslim and a Christian in Indonesia's guerilla war against the Dutch?" Gita glanced at Muthi.

I shrugged. I probably knew this story, once.

Now, I could recite the Geneva convention word by word, but I couldn't repeat what my mother told me before she dropped me off into this hellhole.

"'The war was tough for us, right?' the Muslim said to the Christian, or the Christian to the Muslim, whatever, doesn't matter who said what. What matters is that one said to the other, 'Hey, we got two gods between us, and the Dutch only got one. What do we have to be scared of?' And they charged and we got our independence in the end."

Yeah, we did. But did those two fighters survive?

Who knows.

"We've got three deities among us." Gita's cross glinted as she swayed. "What do we have to fear against one spirit?"

"I've got multiple." I grinned and pointed at my multi-colored Buddhist bracelet. Not out of confidence, but to soothe myself.

"At least three, then." Gita grinned back. "As long as we can send the spirit back, we've got nothing to worry about."

I drew in a sharp breath. "Let's get this over with."

Gita picked up the doll. "We'll just go with the short version.

You know the mantra, right?"

I nodded and reached out to the doll.

"Jailangkung jelangsat,

di sini ada pesta.

Pesta kecil-kecilan."

Jailangkung jelangsat, there's a party here. A small party. Well, not quite, we don't have offerings of flowers and incense. Just ourselves.

"Jailangkung jelangsat,

datang tak dijemput,

pulang tak diantar."

Jailangkung jelangsat, you come without anyone picking you up. And you return home without anyone escorting. A lonely existence, being called only to answer questions.

"Jelangkung jelangsat, where is our friend?"

The coconut head shook. The pencil trembled, and so did my hands. It scratched against the paper, ready to write the answer.

The door slammed open. My heart stopped.

A figure walked in; long hair draped over her face. Familiar in her quick gait. I leapt and ran to embrace her, but she pushed me away.

"What are you doing! You're supposed to be sleeping in your rooms! The dorm matron will have my head if she finds out about this." Lisa, our RA, pulled me by my wrist.

I opened my mouth to protest, but she was already dragging me down the hallway. Muthi, relief clear on her face, followed us. Gita folded her arms, cursing under her breath all the way.

"From now on, I'm going to keep my eyes close on you."

She might as well have glued herself onto my skin. Whenever the teacher told us to group up for a project, Lisa inserted herself with us. Convenient, because usually we needed a group of four to five. Distressing, because she always followed us back to the dorm after class and checked in on us a few minutes before lights out. She'd never fill the hole in our group. Not that she'd know that there had been a hole in the first place. When I asked her what she thought of our missing friend, her face was blank. "Who?"

A lump formed in my throat, just like my friend's little finger once had.

Gita didn't take kindly to the new addition. She spent most of her time before bed cursing and venting. All I could do was bury my head into my pillow. Lisa's persistence made me wonder if she would grab my ankle in the middle of the night.

Muthi was harder to read. Her room was far from ours, and she avoided us like the plague in the week after Lisa found us. Withdrawn, quiet, even when we stumbled upon each other in the bathroom.

Water rushed in the sink. Muthi stared at the flowing water, unblinking.

Lisa took a step forward, unsure. "Muthi, are you alright?"

There's one question people would always ask back in my hometown. Evil spirits and demons hated that one and only thing, and it was the best indication one had of a demon's presence if they weren't a mystic. Carefully, I pushed my voice to come out as a cool, neutral, even sound. "Muthi, when was the last time you did your solat prayers?"

Muthi broke into a wide, crooked grin.

I'd never been able to sense spirits, much less see or hear them. But I could recognize evil.

Dark shadows pulled the lines of Muthi's face. Screaming, she dug her nails into her cheek and raked six bright lines. Horrified, I jumped to restrain her, but she knocked me away and started laughing. Lisa could only shake in place, and I couldn't blame her for that.

The laughter rose and rose until a cough interrupted her. She hacked and retched, and a stream of gurgles replaced her voice.

Blood poured out of her mouth, splashing against the ceramic tile and painting splatters on her white shirt.

A red round thing leapt out of her mouth.

Her heart, still beating, now in the middle of her pool of blood.

Muthi smiled before crumpling to the floor. Dead.

Lisa croaked, eyes wild with panic. "We—we have to call someone."

"And what, Lisa?" I shouted "The teachers don't give a crap about us, and the principal only cares about how this might affect the reputation and the prestige of this cursed school. You think that they'll help us? We don't even have a counselor!"

Lisa sobbed even louder. I probably shouldn't have been yelling at her, but I was on the verge of pulling my hair out. "We have to find Gita and her doll. We didn't send the Jelangkung back!" I grabbed her by the arm, scrunching hard enough I was sure I bruised her. "Because of you! Because you interrupted the ritual! And now we're going to die!"

She shook her head. Tears streamed down her red cheeks. "I—I didn't—"

"It doesn't matter if you meant to or not. We need to find Gita. Now!"

We tore through the dark hallways, our shoes rapping against the dark hardwood floor. Lisa was sobbing all the way, and me, grinding my teeth to dust. By fate or by curse, none of the staff members stopped us for running in the halls. Nobody came to us either when Lisa screamed again as soon as I opened the door.

Gita stared back at us with two dark hollows for eyes. Her whole head had dried out, with strands of short coconut hair and a tough brown shell for skin. She reached out, arms stiff as bamboo poles. "Help," she croaked.

"Oh my god," I gasped. "I—it's not too late. We need the Jelangkung doll to send the spirit back. Where did you put it?"

"I...threw it...burned it..."

Muthi was right. We should've never done this. How was I supposed to fix this now?

Gita's joints creaked when she moved, crooked and uncanny. Her shadow elongated, and watching it, my heart dropped. The Jelangkung was here, and it was taking its due. There was nothing we could do, no prayers we could say to stop it from taking shape. The Jelangkung, once a spirit, now had Gita's flesh and Muthi's heart. With this power, it started to take corporeal form, kneading itself out of darkness. Gangly limbs, bulky torso, a swath of shadows dripping from the edges like a melting blanket of black wax.

A long appendage reached out to Gita, who stood frozen in place. It caressed and stroked what had once been her head and her shiny black hair. The malevolent spirit tilted its elongated head. It didn't have eyes to look down on us, nor mouth to grin its victory—not yet.

Our friend was not here to save me. I had to save myself, no matter how grotesque the method. I ran toward Gita, finding that her skin was more bamboo than flesh. Still I hugged her stiff body. "Jelangkung, jelangkung," I sobbed and struggled, "please go home."

The poem to send it properly back to where it came from was lost from me. My brain was too soaked in panic and fear, my knees losing all control, and soon my bladder too.

I turned toward Lisa—she needed to recite the poem for this to work.

"Lisa—"

Too late. Lisa was on her knees now, with none of her fingers and blackened stumps for arms. No, they weren't just nothing. They were unraveling into numbers and alphabets, into calculus formulas and trigonometric equations. In the end, as meddling as she was, we were the same. We were nothing more than the knowledge and theories crammed into our heads.

My throat rattled. I wanted to laugh, at the absurdity of this, at the foolishness of this all. Even calling for help wouldn't do anything.

Something scratched against the walls of my throat. My shin split into a million pieces. I didn't dare look down. One moment I felt like blood was pouring out, the next I couldn't even feel the skin of my legs.

A sharp sound escaped my lips, something between a sob, a snort, and a shriek. I would cry, too, if not for its futility. Even Lisa's tears were turning into sharp musical notes.

If I were to die now, at least, I wanted an explanation. I wanted to scream. Why was this happening to us? What happened to █ in the first place?

But a weak "Why?" was all I could manage.

A horrendous, loud cackle echoed like a gong. The creature unhinged its jaw, revealing blackened gums and rows and rows of sharp golden fangs. Its voice was a cacophony of wails masked by an inhuman clarity. "Four is the number of death, and in this school, that rule is more real than anywhere else. Did they not warn you?"

My thighs shattered, now paper white as my bones broke and my skin turned to stone. Pain burned through my spine, and everything clicked into place. There were four of us, before my dearest friend disappeared. And then we were four again, when Lisa barged in on us.

All of █'s sacrifice was now in vain.

But then again, this wouldn't have happened if our school taught us magic. If they had told us the dangers that lurked within these walls, if they had let us know how to fight and stand for ourselves. Instead, all I could think of was the international water laws and the history of World War II.

And here, as my bones calcified and broke and calcified again, I could only feel a sharp prick on my face as I cursed this forsaken school till the last of my breath.

TWIN DAGGERS

MIRHA BUTT

1968, England

"*We must be mad, literally mad, as a nation to be permitting the annual inflow of some fifty-thousand dependents, who are for the most part the material of the future growth of the immigrant descended population. It is like watching a nation busily engaged in heaping up its own funeral pyre...As I look ahead, I am filled with foreboding. Like the Roman, I seem to see 'the River Tiber foaming with much blood—'*"

Faridah Malik clicked the OFF dial on the cable TV, closing the convex glass cover over the snuff-coloured cabinet. It was an expensive invention—a fifteen-inch Silvertone, the Sears and Roebuck brand—but the Mallory Thorne School bought it cheaply due to the ugly scratch on the wooden boxed enclosure.

"Enoch Powell's 'Rivers of Blood' speech," she said, turning around. "You recited it to my sister in the moments before you attacked her. *'The discrimination and the deprivation, the sense of alarm and resentment, lies not with the immigrant population but with those among whom they have come.'* Do you remember, Alfred?"

She'd found the reel from her history teacher's collection; Mr Moore had built a curriculum portraying her kind as deceitful, dishonest, and exceedingly depraved. She was the only brown person in her class.

Instead of bringing stationary to Moore's class, Faridah had grown accustomed to bringing a steel knife. Yet, no amount of steel would bleed the depravity out of them.

"What did you tell my sister?" She paused, played with her dagger, and pretended to think. "*All I know is that to see, and not to speak, would be the great betrayal.* Your greatest betrayal isn't that to your country, Alfred, it's that to your personhood, your humanity." She cut a careful incision in the tip of her finger, let her blood soil the cream-colored carpet. "See? My blood is red, same as yours. I live, I bleed…I am human, too."

Alfred Blodwell's father had been an Inspector General in the ranks of India's Imperial Police, a position reserved for the British, before being replaced by the Indian Police Service following partition. The upbringing of a policeman's son had had adverse effects on Alfred who, living in quarters behind various police stations and being escorted to and from school by a sepoy during riots, had developed the superiority of kings and emperors.

He thought himself a dignitary, but he was merely too privileged for his own good, having attended a public school for the gentlemanly elite of Victorian politics, armed forces, and colonial government, on his return from India.

"*Paki,* you called her," Faridah wore a standard uniform of black trousers, a white shirt, and a blood-red vest, same as him. "You know, Alfred, my mother always said that we would hear the same words as we passed. If the last words you utter are the *Shaha-*

da—the Islamic oath—you may be guaranteed Paradise. We would all hear the same words the moment we passed...I didn't think that word would be *Paki*."

"See, Alfred, when Ammi was working at the family newsagent shop in East London, she was cornered by skinheads, beaten with wooden bats and killed, that ugly word the last thing she ever heard."

Faridah peered through one of the floor-to-ceiling, arched windows that were wet with condensation. A low, cold moon hovered tenuously in the twilight, providing a light so dim that it was barely light at all.

"You're very quiet, Alfred," she said. She laughed, suddenly, eyes brimming with tears of mirth.

Alfred was pale, slumped in his ladderback chair, blood gushing from his neck in time with the beating of his heart, his pulse slower, weaker.

It hadn't been Faridah's intention to kill him, not at first. But blood will have blood; in that sense, her violence was inevitable.

So she took that steel knife of hers, and she hacked into his neck, pulling out his carotid. Blood had gushed from his neck with sickening determination, in a steady but dying rhythm, painting the classroom a violent shade of crimson.

He hadn't called her the same word that had been her sister and mother's curse. *Bitch*, he'd choked. She'd crouched beside him, smiled. "Behind every bitch, Alfred Blodwell, is a man that made her that way."

She left, swiftly.

We must be mad, she thought, *literally mad, as a nation to be permitting the growing inhumanity of some hundred-thousand racists, who are for the most part the material of the future growth of the small-minded, bigot population. It is like watching a nation busily engaged in heaping up its own funeral pyre.*

Powell wasn't the only one who could play a good game of semantics.

Faridah's family had immigrated from India, before the empire on which the sun never sets steadily receded to the darkness.

They had been the lucky ones. The ones privileged enough to escape before bloodshed dyed the earth red, and cries of grief hollowed the ground as it split apart forever. Despite concerns that a woman's only true armor was marriage, Faridah had felt that the education of women was a sacred obligation.

But a white palette does not like to see a speck of colour.

For so long, Faridah Malik had been her twin sister's mirror-image. Until the mirror cracked. Like their relationship, it was better to leave the mirror broken than to wound herself trying to mend it.

As children, Faridah and Nazar spoke, moved, and acted in tandem. They had a psychic affinity with one another, finishing each other's sentences, divining what the other was thinking. Now, she stared into a broken mirror at her corrupt reflection, a thousand pieces that would never reflect the same.

Nazar saw things—dead things, mostly. The sort of twisted things that gave you night horrors. Death enthused her, but Faridah didn't think her own death provoked similar enthusiasm.

It had been the final period of the day, students ignoring the ghostly howls beneath floorboards, which their teachers swore was nothing but the sonance of a faulty sewerage system.

Yet no one could ignore the powerful, splintering scream that shook the walls, materializing like a rabid beast that preyed on fear. Nazar's body was in twisted, shattered shreds at the bottom of the imperial staircase of ornate baroque architecture, the pool she lay in brown on the rough stone, clotting as if it could still save the girl who lay cold within it.

Soon, whispers in the hallways were describing Faridah in a similar way to her deceased sister. She was solemn, strange, but grief ate men whole. They came into the world together, but they would leave apart, and yet the most pitiful thing was Nazar's affinity to the death of others.

It wasn't so much a murderous tendency, but a curiosity as to how something so rare as life can be so fleeting. How our bodies adapt in such particular ways but never enough to become indestructible.

Her death was like an archer being impaled by their own arrow.

The school bell rang: a long, loud peal. Normally, this would signal the end of the school day, but it was late at night, and the bell was mounted to a belfry, requiring an individual to use the bell pull to operate it. Its echo was riotous rather than melodic.

It was a warning. *No action is without consequence,* as her mother would say.

Faridah stopped at the top of the stairs, took in a large inhalation as she grasped the carved oak banister with a sweat-soaked palm.

Just for a moment, her sister, Nazar, was lying at the bottom of the steps, gagging on blood as it congealed around her mouth, her slowing heart beating blood out of her snapped neck.

She whispered a prayer beneath her breath as she cantered down the steps, then peered out onto an empty hallway, a cavernous expanse of walls and stained glass, broken up by elaborate tracery.

Thomas Girton was waiting for his friend, Alfred, by the bottom of the stairs, just as the weak boy had told Faridah he would be. When he looked up and saw her there, he stood a little straighter. His dried-blood-red vest looked black in the dusk, his blond, tousled hair at a slant beneath his cap.

"Are you bald beneath that headscarf?" He was grinning, too much of a fool to question what she was doing away from her dorm so late at night.

"Leave me alone, Thomas," she muttered, certain that her insistence would only heighten his refusal.

"Did you not hear us the last time? You should go back to your country before I deport you myself—"

"And where would you deport someone British-born? The hospital? Perhaps I'd be deported back into my mother's womb to be reborn as anything you can stand, though that seems unlikely."

Thomas Girton was an angry man, and no beast is more savage than a man who thinks his anger is reasonable. So, when the first fist was thrown, Faridah made bloody well sure it was hers.

When her knife edge came down, the connection of steel and skin was quick and agonizing. Thomas had no time to react before Faridah tore his flesh, as if trying to carve his heart from his chest.

"When my sister was killed, they didn't open an investigation," Faridah recounted, as if telling an old story. "They said she was part of a 'suicide epidemic,' called it a tragic act of self-murder and left it at that,"

It was as Faridah's mother would say, *jungle mein mor naacha kisne dekha*. A peacock dances in a jungle but who saw it? If I sleep at dusk and awake the next day, did the sun even rise? *If nobody saw it, did it even happen?*

But Faridah saw it. She saw it all.

Thomas staggered backward, each breath coming in short bursts. His chin trembled as he dropped to his back, blood leaking through his fingers as they clasped the grisly flesh.

"No one will wonder how you died, either," When Faridah placed the bloody dagger and hand-written suicide note into his open hand, closing his fingers over it, he was too debilitated to resist. "You'll finally understand what it feels like. To be the unseen, the unfortunate wretches."

And, for a moment, Thomas Girton and Alfred Blodwell were the most unfortunate wretches of them all. But the moment would pass, and men like Thomas and Alfred would live on, wreaking havoc, taking lives, destroying souls. Faridah could hardly kill them all.

There was a full-length mirror resting against the wall to her right, patina upon its brass frame, black freckles adorning the glass.

In the mirror, she saw a famous face, one marked by sweet adoration and gentle praise, the finer, prettier, more beloved twin emerging in its platinum face. *Is this what Nazar saw before she died?* Faridah thought.

Only perfect mirrors can make perfect reflections of one another. If one mirror is broken, the other might appear so, but the truth is that the corruption of one corrupted the appearance of the other.

As one soul begins to shatter, their twin soul wears similar cracks.

She walked on, hyper-aware of the footsteps that were a miniscule quarter of a beat behind her own. The color quickly drained from her face.

"Do you remember when Ammi would read the Qur'an to us? There was one story," She didn't dare turn around as she spoke. "Habil was righteous and innocent, and his brother, Qabil, was full of arrogance, pride, and jealousy. He slew Habil, but in doing so, he ruined himself. The God-fearing would never murder for the sake of envy—"

The air was suddenly rent by the sound of breaking glass. She brought a hand over her mouth to stifle a scream as she returned to the mirror, where fragments sharp enough to cut on contact littered the porcelain floor tiles.

Yet, somehow, the mirror was still perfectly intact.

She raised a hand, and her reflection did the same—a tenth of a second later. Before her brain could register the sound of breaking glass, a million new knives fell over her exposed skin, painting her crimson. An explosion of pain burst through her as she staggered backward, glass crunching beneath her black loafers.

Her reflection climbed out of the mirror, a thick shard of glass so tight in her grip that bright red took on a brownish hue as it gushed from her palm.

"You're—you're supposed to be *dead*," she gasped, walking backward until she hit the slender, stone colonnette behind her and froze in place.

Nazar looked exactly like her, with brown hair, dark, down-turned eyes, and a hooked nose. Faridah steadied her breath and tried to calm her panic.

"I escaped the mortuary, barely alive, found the help I needed. I know what you did, Nazar," said Nazar. *Not Nazar.*

She could keep her façade, play the part well enough to continue, or she could give up and revel in her identity: the lesser twin, a picture of pure grief as she sought after the revenge her sister never could.

"I didn't kill you," she said—Nazar, once more.

"No, but you left me for dead," Faridah was shivering, glass still clenched in her palm. "Why, Nazar? Why didn't you help me? Why did you steal my life?"

Self-delusion was a human's greatest power. Sometimes, Nazar thought that it was the only thing that kept most people sane. A desire to reject what is true, construct what is false.

Love, hope, happiness. All were abstract fantasies that gave life meaning. Without delusion, what are we? Insipid, hollow individuals who wandered the earth without a path, and never stopped at a destination, or wondered why.

But when she was Faridah, she mattered and, just for a moment, people listened.

Her parents had called her Nazar. The evil eye, the envy of the envious. The belief that some can bring pain, illness, or even death to those around them. The superstition said that objects that are gazed at with jealous eyes will break or shatter. *Not every face that smiles at you is your friend,* their mother had told them.

It was always Faridah she worried about. Her famous child.

Whilst Nazar was quick to condemn the injustices that meant almost every disappearance thus far had been a student of color, exploring every death as if it were her own, Faridah had always preferred to assimilate. Her sister's comfortable, unassuming place in rich, white society was a door Nazar had walked through in a bid to get what she wanted: *retribution*.

She mattered. But the moment passed quickly, and oblivion swallowed her whole once more.

"I just...I just wanted them to listen," she said.

Nazar was the eye of her own storm; she would never have Faridah's life, nor could she escape her own. Only fools were too afraid to live as they'd been put on Earth, but she was a fool, and she was a coward.

Her sister's smile was pained. "You wanted vengeance, but before you seek it, *behn*, dig three graves. Two for them, and one for yourself."

"At least I'll be blessed with a proper burial," Nazar felt tears welling up in her eyes. "That's what you wanted, wasn't it? To return to the soil. Instead, they dissolved your skin and bones to ashes—"

"Nazar, the best revenge is to live *well*—"

"How can I live well?" Nazar cried, and Faridah stood, affronted. "How can I live well after death breathed down your throat? How can I live at all when they punish us for just that? How can I ever find peace?"

"You've always been so...so enamored by death, Nazar, so attached to the idea that we're all expendable. How is this any different?"

"Because death is just. It's uncolored, objective. Anyone could contract cancer, or get an infection, or find themselves in a motor vehicle incident. In the end, all are equal."

They were identical, technically, but Faridah looked worlds apart from her, her hijab jet-black and pressed tightly to her scalp, wearing a skirt that reached her ankles as opposed to trousers. "You'd call Thomas's death just?"

Thomas Girton was bleeding out onto the old, lacquered oak. But the blood was ice-cold, and it was black, congealing, and thick as molasses. It was a living force, reaching for Nazar's ankle as it dragged along the floor.

And it was fast, faster, until she was running down cold, stone corridors, each footfall chaotically spaced from the last. Frigid air bit into her lungs as she gained momentum with each push of her legs, her body cold with dread.

It engulfed her foot, and she cried as she fell to her hands and knees. Terror washed over her, raising the fine hairs on the back of her neck, her pulse beating loudly in her ears. When she turned, the monster had vanished, and an empty pool of scarlet blood was spreading before her eyes, with bloody footprints leading back to the stairs she had left her sister to perish at.

"Faridah?" She looked around. The school hallways were dark, marble floors and wooden walls of ribbed vaults and pointed arches, large stained-glass windows and ornate decoration, with glossy doors and brass, baroque handles. "Faridah!"

"Behind you."

She turned. Faridah smiled; Nazar smiled back. She looked like a heart that beat in time with its double.

"You scared me," Nazar said, shivering as cold sweat soaked her skin. It was never cold in India. Here, you could never be entirely warm, not inside. It was as if everyone's souls had been frozen to ice, leaving them with an inability to feel.

"I know." Her smile fell. "Nazar, you need to ask yourself... does murder suddenly become just when it's a repercussion, as opposed to the initial act?"

Their father had continued his travels but abandoned his daughter at the Mallory Thorne School following his wife's death; he couldn't justify the costs of bringing them along. Even with all his British blood money, all the Indians that starved so that he could eat, or died so that he could live, it still wasn't enough.

Greed was a lesson their father had learnt well: lick a white man's shoe, and you'll soon be wearing a similarly expensive pair.

Faridah was gaunt, almost ghostly, her skin pressed thin to the bone. "I never escaped the mortuary, Nazar. I never survived my wounds," she said. Nazar's small, crimson lips parted into an "O." "You know, as a child I feared ghosts. Now, I realize that the ones who live are far scarier."

Ghosts. A shard of ice struck Nazar's heart as candlelight flickered overhead, bathing her in dull, orange light.

This isn't real, none of this is real. The only escape she could find was to close her eyes, the darkness of shut eyes providing her a temporary comfort. For a moment, she could pretend that she was in India, and the air was warm and smelt of exhaust fumes, incense, and heady spices.

And the traditional riad their mother had been raised in smelt of camphor and coconut oil. Outside was a clash of color and a cacophony of sound. At home, no one mocked your accent, or called your food foul-smelling, or asked if you were bald beneath your hijab. You were not an *other*. You belonged.

She opened her eyes. It was dark, the air foreboding and still. Without the bustle of chatter and steady stream of order, the hallways felt bizarre.

A great tremor overtook Faridah, but her gaze was always steady; she never let it fall. For a sinister moment, she looked completely, utterly *real*. She looked living. Nazar knew it was an illusion, her mind playing tricks, telling her that someone soulless had life, that someone hollow had blood.

"Ask yourself, Nazar," she whispered, "why, of all the people that wronged you, or left you, why am I the one you see?" She unconcealed a stiletto knife, and it glinted as it caught the orange light overhead. Nazar could've sworn she'd given Thomas Girton the knife. "Why am I the one who punishes you?"

"I...I don't know."

"Yes, you do," A mad glint lingered in Faridah's eyes, the color of rich, rain-soaked earth. "You wear guilt like shackles on your wrists. It is your greatest companion; you do not even see how it robs you of your humanity."

Nazar's brain stuttered for a moment, and every part of her froze as her thoughts caught up. Her life was still in fragments, like a body caught in a crossfire, but for a moment, she could piece each limb, each organ, nail, and strand of hair together.

After a wash of cold, she caught Faridah's eye. Then, her face lit up. "I remember," she whispered.

"Of course you remember. Ghosts don't forget. Without a heart beating blood and lungs pumping air, the only thing keeping us here, half-alive, is memories of what we were."

Faridah had been dead long before she had been pushed down the stairs: and Nazar really had taken her place. So why was Nazar here, dead, all her grief and regret and failings materializing at once, fighting to be kept alive?

She thought she was alive like any other, a vessel of flesh with bloodied organs and intricate veins. She thought she was human. But she was here, half-alive, a vessel made of guilt, regret, resentment. She was an imperfect thing, made entirely of her own sins, but she was not alive. Not really.

Spots of red were bleeding through Faridah's shirt, where their father had stabbed her.

"The soulless come for the soulful," Faridah whispered. That's what her Ammi often told them; she never warned them that their father would be the soulless one. "Honor killing, he called it."

"Where is the honor in murder?"

"I said *no*, I begged them. Abbu said that I had brought dishonour upon the family regardless," said Faridah. The shadow that veiled Nazar's skin was cold and grey, a sorrow that chilled what was once warm inside. "He said that my death would be the only way to restore his reputation. *May dust and soil protect you now*, Abbu told me. *In your grave, you will be safe,*"

The day he found out that Faridah had been brutally raped by two skinheads from the school, he had told Nazar: *She is beyond saving, child.*

"*Shame,* Abbu said. *Think of the shame.* It's fear of judgment that drives men to murder. When I was killed, I thought I would slip into the past without a trace, but you took my place, kept me alive even if it meant killing yourself. Thomas and Alfred may not have murdered me, but they destroyed me in every other way."

When their father had killed Faridah, Nazar had been there, hiding, watching. She knew something was wrong when he said he wanted to visit, but *wrong* has many definitions. When he left, he said "see you," with no "soon." The end of that sentence should've been "see you *in Hell.*" Only then would they have their bittersweet reunion.

His sleek, black automobile had drifted down the long road that separated the school from society, the wind howling, steady downpour sounding like running feet as it pummelled Nazar's skin.

A newspaper had tumbled around the asphalt, and she had stooped to pick it up, just catching the headline before the ink dissolved into the paper. **INVESTIGATION CLOSES FOR INDIAN BOY, 19, FOUND DEAD AT LOCAL SCHOOL.**

She came to a very brisk conclusion, then. The authorities would never wonder how Faridah had been murdered, or why. They would never investigate the sickening happenings that occurred behind closed doors, or the fatal lust of the school's most trusted students.

So, if a widely adored student like Faridah could sink into oblivion, a nobody like Nazar could do so with ease.

She dragged Faridah's body to the bottom of that imperial staircase, along with her named books and resources. The next day, news spread that Nazar Malik had jumped from the stairs in an act of self-murder. *Tragic,* the papers had called it, but it was not on the front page, and the police hadn't even opened the case before it was closed. She was part of a "*suicide epidemic of colored students,*" the papers had said.

Taking Faridah's place had been Nazar's way of enacting revenge with ease, of engaging with the school community through the eyes of someone who it accepted. She realized very soon that they would welcome you with open arms, sit with you at lunch, but they would never see you as anything beyond the other.

She would never belong to the "*us*," no matter how many sandwiches she shared, or dresses she complimented, or jokes she laughed at. Because those sandwiches would always be more tasteful than the food from her culture, the dresses more charming, the jokes at her own expense.

It was dawn now and, inside, frost grew over the windows, and each breath rose as white-puffed clouds. Standing at the bottom of the stairs again, a long, broken mirror was faced down on the tiles, and glass detritus crunched beneath Nazar's feet.

In the empty hallway, large, silver candelabras held lambent flames, an arc of gold in the darkness that brought a natural hallowed glow of flickering yellow to the walls. She'd always known that her father would take Faridah's life, caring more about his reputation than his offspring. *Blood will have blood*, as her mother would say.

"Do you know how the story of Qabil and Habil ended?" Faridah's fragile voice floated on a cold breeze, bereft of life, the air stagnant with the smell of blood. She was here, somewhere, and soon, Nazar would join her. If she tried hard enough, she could see her still, her uniform bloodied and bemired, her nose dripping crimson down her neck, and wild, bloodshot eyes unable to focus on a particular thing. "After Habil's murder, Qabil, in his shame, begins to curse himself, full of guilt and deep sorrow."

"And he became of the regretful," Nazar whispered, a cold tear running down her cheek. A black, inky crow perched at one of many windows, its sleek wings flapping against the glass. Nazar had read in a book, once, that humans were not the only ones who held funerals and mourned their dead. Crows did, too.

A black-garbed group of watchful figures, congregating nearby the lifeless corpse. Referred to as the particularly apt "murder," crows were vigilant over their deceased. God sent a crow to bury the corpse of Qabil's brother, as he had been unable to. Nazar wondered who would bury her. Would her parents bury her, dressed in white? Would her body be dissolved to ash despite her wishes to return to the earth? Like her ancestors in India who starved in the famine, would she be abandoned in a mass grave by the side of a crowded Delhi highway, left to rot in a small, walled cemetery?

The crow left in a swooping arc for the newly defrosted grass, its black plumage soaking up the early morning sunshine. What did death look like to crows, up in the sky, as they passed the angels, one leaving, one coming?

Death came, quickly, quicker than it had before.

She could still see, though not through her own eyes. She saw things as an onlooker would, detached yet somehow there, faded into obscurity.

Her teacher, Mr Moore, came to the top of the stairs, stared down. Immediately, he was aghast; the only comparison fitting was that he'd "seen a ghost." Still, he was cooler than most, emotionally removed.

You took a knife to Moore's class, spoke to Alfred, Faridah's voice, again, *but you never killed him, did you? Or Thomas—*

Nazar realised then that a voice constructed entirely by your own mind was particularly easy to silence—if necessity arose. Faridah could not force her to address any worldly truth she'd already fashioned to be false. Self-delusion was a powerful thing.

Moore spoke in a dull, baritone voice. "Everyone, return to class."

"What happened, sir?" Alfred cried in the distance; Thomas stood next to him. And Nazar knew that they cared about as much as one would if it were an obituary in small print on the fifth page of a newspaper after the crosswords and celebrity gossip.

"It seems likely that she couldn't handle the grief of her sister's untimely passing," said Moore. "When twins get separated, their spirits fly away to look for the other."

"We need to call for the policemen via radio, *quickly*," one student exclaimed, her black skin as rich and deep as English oak in spring rains. *Did she realise that she was next?* Nazar thought.

Her name was Mary, and she was strong and intelligent, having descended from merchant seamen living in port cities in London's East End. Like Faridah and Nazar, she'd always had something to prove; existing wasn't enough when even your existence offended others. Nazar wished she could warn her. *"They will never be your friend,"* she would say. "She may have been attacked—!"

"I saw her jump," Thomas said, quickly. "It was suicide, sir."

They took her to the mortuary. Her body never returned to the earth; instead, it was burnt to ashes on a cold, lonely night where even the crows dared not leave their homes.

"That's not what happened," said Faridah, "is it?"

"You're here, again," said Nazar. "Why are you here?"

"The living fraternize with the living, the dead…they have only themselves. But," she smiled, "some connections can never be severed. You and I are twin souls, embers from the same flame."

When you were undead, the only thing that could kill you was boredom. The fire they had thrown Nazar's body into ignited the night, outshining the stars and choking the air with heat and light. They had left her there, her skin melting into her bones and rising in a dirty plume of smoke.

Ghosts didn't feel the cold, which was advantageous when you lived in England.

"I wanted to be buried," Nazar whispered, golden embers illuminating her eyes. "You took a knife to Moore's classroom, spoke to Alfred afterward."

"Yes, I remember."

"What happened?"

"I attacked him, I killed him."

"Try again."

Nazar swallowed. "I wanted to kill him."

"But you didn't kill him, or Thomas."

"I didn't," Nazar was shivering; ghosts didn't feel the cold. "Or Thomas."

"And, at the top of those stairs, you began to delude yourself." Faridah had seen it all, her sister's fits of madness. Guilt, and fear, had depraved her, maddened her. She had broken a mirror, cut herself on its shards, held a dagger to her own throat.

But she returned—to the top of the stairs, looking down.

"And then I jumped," said Nazar.

"No."

"I fell."

"You didn't."

"I..." Nazar swallowed, hard, as the flame began to spit and choke. Above, the lucid moon was heaven's eyes, shining in the black, cold night like a watchful mother. "I was pushed."

"You were pushed."

The truth was that Alfred Blodwell had taken after his father, Thomas Girton after a similar bloodline. Their skin was armor to conceal their blackened hearts, so no one would label them murderers, or rapists, nor would they label Faridah and Nazar victims.

Nazar, like Faridah, had wanted her body to be bathed, then enshrouded in white linen and buried with her head facing toward Mecca. They cremated Nazar's body in an open-air pyre because then it could not be unburied, and no one could wonder *why*, or *what* happened.

Thomas and Alfred would continue to be students, and Faridah and Nazar would remain the unseen.

"I was too loud," Nazar said. "A nuisance. They can't stand nuisances."

"Then they ought to kneel." Faridah crossed her arms. "If they knelt, kissed the earth, and prayed, then they might find humility."

They watched in silence as one of the Mallory Thorne School's most gifted students crept from her dormitory, furtively, and stopped by a body she assumed to be Faridah's in the dead of night, her thick, umber tresses braided in neat rows along her scalp.

"Mary," Nazar said, watching as the girl fell to the dirt in a dishevelled heap, her body wracked with an onslaught of uncontrollable tears. "She is the only one who wished you goodbye."

Faridah's heart panged, and her shoulders slumped under the weight of Death's hands, as her secret love kissed the earth that she'd always hoped she'd be buried beneath, the bonfire spitting ashes at her, mimicking the way her peers would spit at her as she crossed the corridors at school.

Just as light remains light, even within the darkness, their love had remained love, even when illicit and untouched. She'd disregarded every desire, ignoring the things her heart told her. Her father had told her that it was a test from God, and she thought she'd passed.

"The only crow at the grave," Nazar whispered, as Mary covered her face with shaking hands. Gut-wrenching sobs tore through Faridah's chest.

Crows, kites, scorpions, rats, rabid dogs. Supposedly, the Final Prophet claimed these were the only creatures for which there was no blame on the one who killed them. Faridah was starting to believe that it was not five creatures and they—the outnumbered, the wretches, the lost and forgotten—were the sixth. There would be no blame on the ones who killed them, either.

Mary stayed at her burning for a long while, the heat of Nazar's corpse drying up her tears. Perhaps she would be next; perhaps things would change, and Faridah's love would be saved from the cruelty of powerful men, dangerous men.

"We did nothing wrong, Faridah," Nazar said. "We were wronged...but we did nothing wrong. One day, they will beg for the mercy they refused to give."

Ghosts didn't feel the cold.

But a cold night gave Faridah and Nazar a reason to draw closer to one another, to feel the natural warmth they were born to give but could never give in death.

THE SUMMONING

ARCHITA MITTRA

content/trigger warnings: bullying

The sing-song voices of the schoolgirls prickled against Radha's skin. *Totla, totla, totla,* they chanted, rapping their knuckles on the desks. She tried to ignore them, turning the yellowed pages of *Wuthering Heights*, perched surreptitiously between her knees. The words on the page seemed to stutter—she wasn't sure if she was wandering the fictional wilderness or trapped inside a small, hot classroom as their chorus got louder. The girls encircled her. A rusted nail dug into Radha's left leg, but she remained affixed to the wooden chair. Their chants reached a crescendo, then dissolved into jeers and laughter.

The girls were still not satiated. Tanvi, the ponytailed leader, pulled Radha's pigtails. "*Totla!*" she said, viciously gleeful. "Is that your nickname at home?"

The class worshipped Tanvi. Tanvi, who was repeating a year, who snuck in bottles of port wine into the dormitories, who looked at Radha on the first day of the new term like a hawk eyeing its prey. Radha's mouth felt like a cavern swallowing dark water. She dared not open it lest something spilled out. But the stormy winds carried Tanvi's voice to the lonely moor, now joined by Kamala, her sniggering best friend.

"What's wrong? Did someone Sellotape your mouth?"

"Maybe she's become deaf now."

"Why won't you talk to us? We think your voice is very beautiful."

The class tittered with more taunts. Radha gritted her teeth to remain silent. She reread a tedious description of the heath, but she could no longer smell the gorse. She wished that Mrs. Chatterjee would hurry up for history class—they were halfway through the French Revolution. Tanvi, perched on Radha's desk, reached for the book. It was a battered copy from the library, dog-eared, filled with faded pencil marks and a little chewed around the edges. If Radha lost it, she would have to pay a hefty fine.

"St-sto-stop it!" she cried out, jolted. She hated the desperation in her voice.

This was the moment the class was waiting for. The girls erupted in violent jubilation; Tanvi clapped the loudest. "Did you hear that? Our maharani talks!"

"Why don't you re-re-read aloud from that book?"

"Yes! All of us are so eager to hear a *Totla*."

The class knew no mercy, and Radha could not turn invisible like a ghost. She closed the book and locked eyes with Tanvi. "Well, I m-might be a st-stu-stutterer, but at le-least I'm not a failure like you."

The class gasped. For a moment, Radha was convinced that Tanvi would slap her, but the other girl looked too astonished. Radha was surprised herself. A ringing silence filled the room. She imagined their anger swirling in the fetid air, like dust motes glittering in the sunlight, armed with invisible barbs.

Eventually, Tanvi summoned her voice. "How dare you say such a thing!" she snapped, fighting back a sob.

Marina, the pug-faced peacemaker, quipped in, "Radha, you shouldn't say such things. You don't know what things are like for her at home. You don't know why she's repeating a year." There were murmurs of assent. The class's selective empathy had always baffled her, but now it made her feel worse. Kamala demanded that Radha apologize. She was saved from replying by the timely arrival of Mrs. Chatterjee. The girls scrambled to return to their seats and took out their textbooks. Radha sighed in grateful relief. Out of the corner of her eye, she spotted a girl, sitting a few benches away, looking at her with an odd mixture of pity and curiosity. Radha could not recall her name.

Mrs. Chatterjee droned on about the prisoners storming Bastille. Radha found the correct page in her novel and meandered through the moor for the rest of the period. Later that night, she dreamed about burning the school down.

The school library was Radha's favorite place in the whole world. The ornate almirahs were crowded with illustrated Bibles, *Encyclopedia Britannicas*, and leather-bound tomes of the classics. Except for a few older students, the cavernous room was usually empty. Tanvi and her cronies could not follow Radha here, and even if they did, they could not talk except in hushed whispers. In this gentle silence, surrounded by the smell of polished wood and paper, Radha felt unusually powerful. The books talked to her, and she was happy to listen to their stories.

After *Wuthering Heights*, Radha moved onto *Pride and Prejudice*. A hundred pages in, she yawned. The bell rang, signaling the end of lunch break. Radha did not feel like going back for math class.

"It's a rather lovely book."

Radha turned to the sound of that voice. It was one of her classmates, standing in the bright spot of sunlight that streamed in through the mullioned windows. Radha didn't know her name, but she knew that this girl sat between Marina and Safia. She was the one who'd been staring at Radha during history yesterday. Her dark hair, left open, glimmered with a bronze sheen.

Radha suddenly felt cold. She opened her mouth and then closed it stupidly. The girl smiled. "You can also try *Jane Eyre.*"

"D-done."

"*Frankenstein?*"

"Tw-twice."

"*Dracula?*"

Certain consonants strained Radha's vocal chords more than others, but it was a constantly rotating list. She struggled to mouth the word "boring" and so in her mind, she switched to a word that began with a vowel. "Exciting," she uttered, displeased for picking out the wrong word.

"Wait, you're joking right? I kept falling asleep through that one."

Radha felt relieved. "I actually l-liked *Carmilla* more," she said shyly.

The girl beamed. "Me too! Do you also like Ann Radcliffe?"

And all of a sudden, on a gray October afternoon, the thirteen-year-old Radha—who preferred the company of books to people—found herself absorbed in conversation. The alphabets still fumbled in her mouth, but the other girl either didn't notice, or didn't seem to mind. Radha felt lighter than ever, sitting next to her in that dimly-lit alcove. In low voices, they discussed the *Castle of Otranto* and a number of penny dreadfuls and swooned over *The Prisoner of Zenda.* At one point, Radha brought out a book of Emily Dickinson's poetry and together they squealed in delight, inviting a warning look from the librarian. By the time the librarian kicked them out, it was dusk, and Radha had never felt prouder of herself for skipping classes.

"What's your n-name?" she asked at last, as they walked down the shadowy corridor to the dormitories. They passed by the many statues and oil portraits of the school's founders, watching them menacingly in the lamplight. In the half-dark, Radha could barely make out the girl's features, but her voice soft and so unlike Tanvi's grating tone, shone like a torch.

"Myna," the girl replied. She said it like she was offering her a present.

Radha's bones felt light enough to fly. "Like the b-bird?"

The girl nodded.

"Myna," Radha repeated carefully. It filled her with pride that she didn't stumble on the syllables this time.

The list of things that Radha hated about boarding school began with the watery-green soup that tasted like sipping a puddle of slime, served each day at breakfast without fail. Mutton and fish rarely made an appearance, and when they did, Radha was too low in the pecking order to get any. Every time the ceilings leaked, she cursed her top bunk, beneath which Tanvi snored peacefully. The towers of homework got taller each day. Radha stumbled her way through the classical dance lessons and P.E. classes, flailing her limbs like a drowning person. Only her friendship with Myna made school sufferable.

They usually sat on the last bench, reading a library book from Radha's lap. She was careful that their knees did not touch. Sometimes, she drew dirty doodles of Tanvi along the margins, which made Myna giggle a little too loudly.

When textbooks went missing from Radha's bag, Myna pretended that they were on a treasure hunt. That was how Radha discovered the green room behind the stage, filled with scenic backdrops, dusty gowns, and other props. When Radha suggested that they dress up and dance on the stage when no one else was around,

Myna turned up her nose, saying she had stage fright. Radha understood that sentiment and didn't press further. Later, they found the keys to the terrace. They hid behind the moss-stained water tanks, and Radha stretched out her arms to pluck jamuns from the tree, occasionally tossing them at the heads of unsuspecting students strolling in the playground below.

But it was the dusty, unused classroom on the top floor of the science building where Radha felt as though she were in another world. When notes scrawled with expletives in Bengali and Hindi, signed by Tanvi and Kamala, mysteriously appeared in Radha's pencil pouch, Myna taught her to make beautiful origami out of them. They placed those paper cranes and tulips along the windowsill that looked out from the empty classroom onto the world below, silent spectators to their conversations.

Toward the end of October, the music teacher gently told Radha that her singing was too off-key, and she should leave the Christmas troupe to try something else. In search of a silent role, she joined the rehearsals for *The Little Mermaid*, then *Red Riding Hood,* and finally *Sleeping Beauty*. But no matter how convincingly Radha pretended to sleep, the drama teacher declared that she just wasn't good enough. Her skin was so brown that neither the magic of makeup nor the flickering stage lights could turn her into a princess, a role that necessitated fair skin, although the teachers would never say that aloud. In the end, she was shunted to being one of the stepsisters to Tanvi's Cinderella.

When she broke the news to Myna, the girl shook her head. "We need to steal her glass slippers."

"No, we can't do that!" In truth, Radha was more afraid of the consequences if they got caught.

"Tanvi is always stealing your things. We'll do the same and set her on a wild goose chase around the school. She'll end up dirtying her gown, and you will look so much more beautiful."

The purple juice of the jamun dripped down Radha's cheeks

and stained her shirt. "I don't think that would be right. We all have to play a role."

Myna looked frustrated. Radha felt a little frightened, as though Myna would lose her patience and scream at her, like her mother often did at home. But Myna had a better plan. She continued, "Maybe we can steal her gown later, and you can wear it here. We can have a midnight picnic!"

The thought of dancing under the starlit terrace with no one but Myna sounded like a dream come true. It reminded her of the upcoming Autumn Ball, an annual formal dance that usually coincided with the timings of Diwali festivities and Halloween preparations, where the hallways were decked up with fairy lights, candles, and diyas, and the students dressed up as they pleased. But what made the event even more special was that girls and boys from the nearby boarding schools were also invited. Tanvi was always showing off her friendships with Raj and Sameer, whom she met at a hockey championship, and there was a rumor that Kamala was only following her around so that she would get the boy that Tanvi eventually discarded. Radha wanted to ask Myna to come with her, but she wasn't sure how to say it. Myna was probably a superior dancer and better off with Marina or Safia. Being turned down by her only friend was too high a price to pay for asking.

Traipsing down the rickety spiral staircase, they began to excitedly flesh out the Cinderella-gown-stealing plan, which continued all through physics class. Even if Radha had no one to go the ball with, she could still look forward to the midnight dance. It made her grin like an idiot.

Miss Rao, their stern teacher, noticed and pointed it out to the whole class. "Why are you smiling? What's so funny?"

Radha jerked still. "N-nothing, Ma'am."

Miss Rao wasn't the sort to let things go so easily. "Come on," she said. "I'm sure the joke is interesting enough to share with the whole class."

A few sniggers sounded through the room. Radha was petrified.

"Stand up when I'm talking to you."

Radha got up from her seat, legs trembling. Beside her, Myna had gone strangely silent.

"Tell me the definition of pressure."

Radha looked down at her closed textbook. Pressure was force per unit area, but "P" was a difficult sound to pronounce; so was "F." She tried rearranging the sentence in her head, but she knew the moment she opened her mouth, the syllables would jumble up, the class would burst into titters, and Miss Rao would think she'd given the wrong answer. She decided that the best course of action was to remain silent.

"This is what happens when you don't pay attention in class."

Someone whispered to her, "The answer's written on the blackboard."

Radha looked up. "P=F/A" was indeed inscribed boldly in chalk, but she already knew that. The dam of tears welling up inside her was threatening to burst forth. She wished she could explain that she didn't have a problem with memorizing definitions, but with speaking. She thought of writing down the answer on a piece of paper and passing it down, but she was afraid that Miss Rao would consider that to be rude. So, she kept mum.

"Look at her! Absolutely paralyzed."

The class guffawed. A textbook hit her. Radha bent to pick it up.

Miss Rao's voice cut through the din. "Did I ask you to sit down?"

Beside her, Myna sighed angrily. "I-I wasn't," Radha said quickly.

"Get out of my class."

Hot tears trailed down her cheeks. Myna reached out to hold her hand, but Radha moved away quickly, burning in shame. She felt jealous that Myna was unscathed when it had been both of them smiling and whispering in the last row. But stepping into the corridor and standing under the shadow of a gargoyle was a relief. Radha only wished she had a book of Emily Dickinson's poetry with her. Perhaps she could compose a villanelle inspired by the griffin in her head and later write it down and show Myna.

As if on cue, the mahogany doors opened, and Myna joined her.

"How d-did you g-get out?"

Myna flashed a mischievous smile. "I pretended to talk to myself until Miss Rao noticed and threw me out. That woman is under some serious *pressure.*"

Radha laughed. Myna sat down on the cold marble floor. Radha looked around in case any of the other teachers were patrolling the corridor.

Myna added, "I didn't want to leave you alone."

The knot in Radha's chest loosened. She asked Myna if she would like to accompany her to the Autumn Ball.

Radha didn't have pretty dresses, and neither did she visit the town when the girls occasionally went shopping. She got very little pocket money, anyway. But the old trunk she brought from home contained a beautiful blue lehenga, constellated with bronze curlicues of vines, flowers, and birds. Radha always thought that she was too ugly to wear it. Even on the rare occasions when she was all alone in the dorm nursing menstrual cramps while the girls chased each other in the playground, she couldn't bring herself to wear it. She was too afraid that she wouldn't be able to fold it back again, and her back still carried the scars from when her mother would hit her back with a khunti for not folding the laundry right. She also wasn't sure if her dark skin would look nice with the sapphire blue. Tanvi, who had the fairest skin amongst them, often played a game where they rested their arms against each other, and the fairest arm was declared the winner. If Radha and Myna played it, Myna would certainly win. She looked pale as a ghost and could give Tanvi a run for her money. But Radha wouldn't mind losing to Myna.

Radha waited until the dormitory was empty and the sound of laughter and fireworks emanated from outside before gingerly putting on the dress for the first time and looking at her sad reflection in the mirror. She put on some makeup—kajal, face powder, and lipstick—stolen from her mother's dresser last summer and probably expired. She tried to smile but her face twisted into a grimace. Unsure of what to do with her hair, she left it open and headed down the stairs.

Myna wasn't waiting for her.

The long banquet tables had been cleared from the dining hall, where the students danced hand-in-hand as a jazz band played on a makeshift podium. The crowd was studded with jeweled anarkalis, saris, ghagras, pavadais, lehengas, gowns, and low-cut dresses. The teachers, too, were dressed up in somber colors, chaperoning the young folk. Radha roamed through the waltzing crowd in a daze. Familiar faces sniggered at her or cast pitying looks. Everyone was dancing with someone else, and Radha felt that her feet were trying to drag her underwater. She kept looking around but she couldn't spot Myna in the merry crowd. A few people even wore masks, constellated with sequins, and Radha wondered if Myna was among them, if this was one of her games, and Radha had to seek her out. Radha wished she too carried a mask.

But after almost two hours of wandering, Radha's feet were finally ready to give up. Her kajal had probably melted, stinging her eyes. She walked to the bathroom to wash her face and heard murmurs from one of the stalls. Warily she tiptoed toward the sound, and then through the gap in the door, she saw Kamala in a fiery-red choli, pressed against Tanvi, kissing her swan-like neck. Tanvi's eyes were closed, her face carved with ecstasy, her silvery blouse unbuttoned. Desire shot through Radha's veins. She took a step back, ready to leave them to their own devices when Tanvi moved.

Her dewy eyes opened and latched onto Radha's.

"You wish you were me, don't you?" Tanvi said, a triumphant grin on her face.

Kamala turned, horrified, but Tanvi pulled her close again. She cupped her cheeks and kissed her, her eyes still fixed on Radha.

Radha fled.

She pushed through the stragglers and ran up the stairs to the dorm. This whole evening had been a disaster. She should have taken advantage of the dorm's emptiness and stayed in to read a book. She could have called Myna to her dorm room or gone to hers. There was indeed a book of Toru Dutt's poetry waiting for her that she'd checked out yesterday from the library. She would get lost in the descriptions of the Casuarina tree. She would forget what she saw in the bathroom. She wouldn't imagine Myna, dressed in Tanvi's clothes, pulling her mouth close. Myna, who didn't even show up to the dance.

"Oi, watch where you're going!"

In her haste, Radha had bumped into Marina. She dropped her bag and a plastic bottle of port wine tumbled out.

"I'm s-s-so-sorry!" Radha exclaimed.

Marina looked afraid. The bottle was sauntering to the edge of the stairs, the bannisters wound with twinkling lights. Radha stopped it from tumbling down all the way with her leg. She picked it up and gave it to Marina.

"You can keep it. Just don't tell the teachers about it," she squeaked.

Radha had no wish to keep alcohol with her. For all she knew, Tanvi was trying to plant the bottle on her and later complain to a teacher. But Tanvi was in the bathroom making out with Kamala. The image seared itself into Radha's memory and filled her with longing. "No, it's y-yours."

Marina took the bottle and considered her. "Actually, my friends and I are having a little party in the chemistry lab. Why don't you join us?"

"No, it's f-f-fine. I'm…I'm actually waiting for a fr-friend."

Radha was prepared for the laugh, but Marina looked at her curiously. "You can ask him to come too."

"It's not a boy," she corrected. Perhaps Marina had misunderstood, or she was insulting her lack of a dancing partner. Radha was already dreading coming to class tomorrow.

"Who is it?"

"It's Myna. I-I think she f-fell sick today, but I'll go to her d-dorm and ask her about it at d-dinner." It suddenly occurred to her that she did not know which dorm Myna stayed at.

"Myna who?"

"Myna, our c-classmate. She used to sit between you and S-S-Safia before she—"

"No one sits between me and Safia."

"Yeah, not anymore, b-b-ecause she s-sits with me now."

"You sit alone in the last row."

"No, I don't."

A motherly look came upon Marina. "Listen, I know sometimes that Tanvi's jokes get too much, but you don't have to play along. I mean, you can always sit between me and Safia if you're feeling lonely."

"I'm not lonely," Radha declared.

"Is that why you keep talking and smiling to yourself in class?"

Radha stared at her. The joke had gone too far. "Seriouslyareyoujustgoingtop-p-retendthatM-m-ynaisn'treal?

But Marina's voice was soft and full of concern. "Slow down. I understand you better when you speak slowly."

Radha took a deep breath. "I s-sit with Myna."

"What's her surname?"

"I don't know."

Marina took a step closer, and Radha instinctively moved backward. "Surely, you must know her surname. If she's real and sits next to you, doesn't she give attendance?"

Radha had never paid that much attention to attendance and such things. She had books to read. "Are you ac-accusing me of l-lying?"

Marina touched her arm. It was a gentle touch, but the other girl flinched. "Radha," she said softly, "I think you're talking to a ghost."

Radha brushed that arm away and fled.

"I've heard tales from our seniors," Marina called after her. "It wouldn't be the first time! You can talk to us!"

Radha did not want to talk to anyone ever again.

The school was always full of stories about ghosts. The prefects always spooked them with the tale of the White Lady who was pushed down the bannisters by the school bullies, and made to look like a suicide. Then there was that rumor about the two women who died of suffocation in each other's arms after the music teacher caught them kissing in the toilet and locked them up as punishment. That was why the last bathroom stall was usually avoided. Later, the story went, their friends dug out their coffins from the church graveyard and buried them in the playground, which was why a particular rusty swing often swung without a breeze and occasionally threw off unsuspecting girls to the muddy ground. Once, when the girls couldn't sleep due to a thunderstorm, Safia had regaled them all with the story of a girl who got accidentally locked up in the library—they had found just her bones next term, surrounded by half-chewed books.

Radha wondered if Myna was really a ghost, or worse, a person she made up just to cope with her loneliness. Myna who always gave her a large share of her own food during mealtimes, knowing how Tanvi sometimes told the girls to take large chunks of rice and eggs, even if it was just to throw them later in the bin, just so that

Radha would have less to eat. Myna who had given her an extra set of keys so that Radha could sneak into the library or the kitchens at odd hours of the night. Myna, who always knew in which corner of the school Radha's missing books were hidden.

Radha ran to the library, citing a desperate need to research the lives of English monarchs to the annoyed librarian. She headed to the section filled with old newspapers and started flicking through, flooded with a sense of unease. Her eyes jumped from one accident to the other but nothing about a school-related death.

"Are you looking for something?"

Radha got so startled by the librarian's voice that she dropped the heavy pile of newspapers on the floor. Dust rose like smoke between them. "I... d-did any girl a-actually d-die in this school?" she blurted.

The librarian looked at her the same way Marina did. "You look like you have seen a ghost."

Before Radha could reply, the middle-aged woman continued, "But yes, as a matter of fact, twenty years ago, a girl did die. It was a tragic accident." She turned her gaze to the open window, sporadically lit up by fireworks. Her voice dropped as she went on, "The drama club was staging a production of *Othello*. Someone had replaced the prop knife with an actual butcher's knife. When Desdemona came on stage and acted out her lines, the audience swooned. That girl was a terrific actor, and so when Othello stabbed her to death, they thought it was part of the act until it was too late."

Radha thought that the original play ended with the man smothering her, but she understood why a knife was more dramatic. She recalled how Myna's eyes suddenly came alive in the green room but she was so against going on the stage. Radha cursed herself for not seeing it sooner. The librarian rummaged through the dusty shelves, found the newspaper article, and showed it to her.

Radha skimmed over the text. She spotted the name Myna Adhikari at the bottom, and a shiver ran down her spine.

The last stragglers of the ball had left by the time Radha emerged from the library. Her feet dragged her down the stairs. Her head hurt. Her stomach made growling sounds, but all she wished was to see Myna again, convince herself that she was real and not an imaginary friend. The school felt strangely empty. She had already missed dinner, and she needed to go to the bathroom. She vaguely wondered if Marina and her friends were still drinking illicitly in the chemistry lab. It suddenly struck her how the school, so unwelcoming to certain people, had still managed to become a home, even to Radha, who never felt at home either in her house in north Calcutta or at school, neither in her mind nor in her female body. She was only content in those magical moments spent conversing with Myna or when she escaped into a book. Home wasn't a place, she realized, but a person or a thing.

As she stepped into the bathroom, she wondered if she really wanted to kiss Myna the way Tanvi kissed Kamala or if she just wanted to see her again. She wondered if love could exist without a body. She wondered, if she killed herself, would she become a ghost? At least she would see Myna again.

Lost in her thoughts, she didn't notice the wet floors. She slipped. She felt a tear in her lehenga. There was the sound of water gushing out. Had a pipe burst?

Then, something, or someone, was pulling, no, dragging her hair. Radha screamed.

The shadowy figure revealed herself as Tanvi. Kamala's lipstick-smeared face also appeared next to her. "Promise us you won't tell anyone what you saw," Kamala mouthed.

Tanvi seemed more relaxed. "You think anyone will believe her?" she said with a careless laugh.

"I don't think we're safe."

Radha wanted to say that she didn't care. Tanvi replied, "She's a *totla*. She will start stammering before she can even speak the truth." Kamala didn't laugh. There was a sense of urgency in her tone. "She may write to the headmistress, and we'll be thrown out!" Tanvi remained flippant. "How about we sew her mouth shut?" "St-st-stop. L-let me go," Radha whimpered. Every bone in her body hurt. She felt her arms being pulled harshly. They dragged her to the last stall, the one that the girls always left unoccupied. Tanvi knelt beside her. "Promise us," she whispered.

Radha nodded weakly. She couldn't summon the strength to speak.

"Say it!" Kamala shrieked.

Tanvi shushed her. From a tiny ventilation window, moonlight filtered in. Both the girls looked so silvery, like ghosts. But no words came out of Radha's mouth. It would have been so much easier if she'd been born deaf. It would have been so much easier if she were dead.

"Fine. We'll teach you a lesson," Tanvi decided. They pushed her in and latched the door from outside.

When their footsteps faded, Radha screamed. But the world was silent. She screamed again and again. Surely some girl would wake up at night to use the bathroom. Surely Marina would puke after drinking so much. Surely a janitor or usher would hear the shouts and set her free. A dark thought entered her mind—perhaps they could hear her but simply didn't care. Perhaps this was a punishment for daring to come to the dance without a partner. Or a penalty for using the library after hours.

Shivering, with her skin all clammy, her thoughts returned to Myna, how when they read books together it was always Radha who turned the pages. She couldn't recall if their arms or knees ever touched. The thought had always made her nervous. What she felt for Myna was too precious and strange to put into words. If she read enough books, surely, she'd find the right words. But now there wasn't enough time. She tasted blood. She didn't even have the strength to sit up. The bathroom stall, scrawled with expletives, stared back at her, unmoving, locking her inside this hellish nightmare she couldn't wake up from.

There was no way to tell how much time had passed—nothing except for the soft, silent flicker of moonlight. If she was still alive when daylight broke, she'd miss the morning assembly and breakfast. She prayed that someone would let her out during break. Of course, she wouldn't tell anyone what she saw or what happened. Girls kept secrets like that. It was an unstated thing. It struck her that Tanvi did not see her as a girl. In the cold, weighed down by her heavy dress that clung to her uncomfortably, she wondered if she even was a girl. Her body had always felt so strange and inconvenient, like an ugly vessel she had to lug around. She remembered the story of Atlas carrying Earth on his back and suppressed a hysterical giggle. Her thoughts drifted to Myna again—if Myna was a ghost, was she also a girl? It was easier to be a ghost than a girl, Radha was sure.

The door unlatched. In the silvery-dark, Myna appeared almost translucent.

"You looked beautiful," Myna said.

Radha stretched out her hand. Myna looked at her sadly. She held onto the commode and slowly sat up, though every bone in her body ached.

"I'm sorry," Myna said, bending down beside her.

Radha's anger and sadness all dissipated. They were so close. She saw the curve of Myna's lips and bent closer. She wondered if it would be like touching cold air. Myna tilted her head.

Radha swallowed, her nerves getting the better of her. "You're d-dead, aren't you?"

Myna looked crestfallen. "Yes, and Tanvi wants you dead too."

"Why am I the only one who can see you?"

Myna smiled and repeated the question back to her. "Why am I the only one who can see you?"

They exchanged a look. Radha said quietly, "When you're here, I can f-feel you ar-around me, ar-are you..."

"I'm not really here."

The sadness and longing in her voice broke Radha's heart. She asked, "Then how did you open the latch?"

"Sometimes, if I really focus, I can push things around."

"Why d-didn't you c-come today?"

"How would you have looked dancing with the air?"

"You c-c-could've told me."

Myna looked down, sheepish. "When you asked me, you looked so hopeful, I couldn't bear to tell you. I was waiting for you on the terrace. I thought you'd come up for some air. And I...I don't like crowds. Being in the classroom is stifling; that's also why I come out to join you. When there are too many voices around, I feel like I'm dissolving. I feel the call to the other side more strongly."

"Wh-what's there on the-the other side?"

"It's a secret." Myna laughed.

"Tell me your st-story."

Myna shrugged, but seeing the look on Radha's face, she went on. "It's nothing. I just had a flair for the dramatic, and some girls got jealous." She told Radha that the drama teacher thought she was too good and considered switching places with the Othello actor. Everyone thought Myna was deliberately usurping the other girl's role by performing Desdemona as well as she did. "But I really wanted to be Desdemona so I could wear a pretty gown," she continued bitterly. "On opening night, the girl playing Othello decided to take matters into her own hands. Today, twenty years ago, is the day I died."

Radha stretched out her arms and Myna filled the space between them. Radha felt thin, cold air enveloping her, and it made her feel warm.

"I don't want Tanvi to kill you, but I'm afraid she might," Myna said, at last.

"I would-dn't mind," Radha blurted out.

Myna didn't look too shocked. She smiled at her sadly. "You wouldn't like it much." Then after a moment's pause, a familiar mischievous grin flickered on her face. "But I know what you might like—revenge."

Radha nodded. "I'd like to frighten her, really frighten her."

"I have a plan."

The next day. Radha relished the look of surprise on Tanvi's face when she saw the girl energetically slurping the soup. In the first period itself, Kamala got thrown out of class for not having her physics book. Without Kamala to prompt her, Tanvi stumbled in her answers.

At lunch, Tanvi cornered Radha. "Where's the book?"

When Radha didn't respond but placidly continued reading a book of poetry, Tanvi changed her tone. "I'll really kill you if you don't tell me."

Radha handed her a letter. Tanvi opened it, read it, and crumpled it. The bell rang.

When the clock chimed midnight, they were waiting for Tanvi in the auditorium. With Myna guiding her hand, Radha had drawn a pentagram on the stage with salt. Candles were lit on all five corners. Radha had heard stories about tantric rituals and exorcisms being performed at Kali temples back home, but she didn't really believe in such things. Yet that didn't matter, for she believed in Myna.

Tanvi cautiously stepped in and walked down the aisle. "Radha?" she called. She noticed the flickering lights and walked up onto the empty stage. At the center of the pentagram lay the physics

book. The wind moaned through the trees outside. "What a sick joke," Tanvi said, stepping into the circle. She lifted the book and then let out a shriek, as though she had touched red-hot iron. "It burned me," she cried out, dropping the book. "What the fuck have you done, bitch?" She ran to the edge, but she couldn't get out. It was as though a wall of invisible glass had descended upon her. "Let me out," she screamed, her hands flailing at the emptiness.

The cobwebbed chandelier turned on. Tanvi screamed, startled by the lights. "Stop it! It's not funny anymore." The bolt loosened. The chandelier swayed dangerously. Tanvi's shrieks for help fell upon an empty stage. "Radha, please stop it. I'm sorry," she begged.

"I t-think that's enough," Radha said, emerging from her hiding place backstage.

"C'mon, the fun has just started," replied Myna, materializing on top of the chandelier, her face glistening with glee. "We need to complete the ritual."

"Who is that? Who are you talking to?" Tanvi shouted, helpless, trapped under an invisible bell jar. Behind her, the book burst into flames, and through that, a black hole appeared. Myna pointed Radha to it. Tanvi followed Radha's gaze and yelped.

"What the fuck is that?"

Even Radha was confused. "Myna, w-whhat is that?"

Myna didn't answer. She soared around the circle, like a caged bird set free. Finally, Tanvi saw her and screamed, "Marina was right! All this time you were really talking to a ghost!"

Myna flashed a smile at Tanvi. "That's the other side."

"What are you tr-trying to d-do?" Radha asked, her voice betraying a thin note of fear. "I s-saaid it's en-nough."

Myna turned to face her. Her eyes glittered with a strange light, and suddenly Radha felt that she couldn't recognize her. "Is it really? Do you know for how long I watched you in the dormitories, crying yourself to sleep? Holding a pillow to your heart because nobody would ever touch you? All because a couple of silly girls made fun of you?"

Radha stared at her, aghast. Myna went on, "She isn't going back. I'm taking over her body."

A spectral hand appeared from the chasm. "Help me," Tanvi shouted, but the soundproof auditorium was too far away for anyone to hear.

"We c-can't k-k-kill her!" Radha screamed back.

"I thought you hated her."

"That's not the same as wanting someone dead!"

Myna stopped. "Isn't it?"

Radha took a deep breath. "I know that's what happened to you, but we can't just sacrifice Tanvi!"

Myna's face was glazed with spectral tears. "Even if it means I can live again?" The spectral hand was scurrying toward Tanvi. "That's why I did this!" Myna cried. "My body's gone but my soul is still here. I can breathe again in Tanvi's body. I can run in the playground like the other girls. I'll taste chocolate and wine again. I'll hold you like no one else did. Don't you want that—if not for me, for yourself?"

Radha stared at her best friend, incredulous. "You…you'll be in Tanvi's body?"

"I know you find her body beautiful."

"Please, I'm sorry for everything," Tanvi wailed. The spectral hand gripped Tanvi's leg. She stamped at it, and it let go, but the chasm got larger. "Please, Radha, I'm sorry for everything."

"Myna, you n-need to st-stop this," Radha cried.

"I can't," Myna replied.

Radha looked around, trying to find an escape. She surmised that the creature wanted a soul. The pentagram would prevent it from escaping, but it was also trapping Tanvi. She'd have to break the magic circle—but that was too great a risk. For a moment, Radha looked up longingly at Myna and wondered what the other side would be like. She thought she could see a way. "T-Tanvi," she whispered.

As if reading her mind, Myna's ghostly hands shoved Radha's shoulders. "Stop it, what do you think you're doing?"

The force of that spectral throw set Radha tumbling off-balance. But she had shouldered harsher blows and bruises during P.E. She got back up and placed one foot inside the pentagram. "We need to push that cr-creature b-ba-ack," she cried to Tanvi.

Myna screeched at them. "I did this for you! I did this to save you!"

Radha looked up at the ghost. "No, you did it for yourself!"

"A life for a life!" Myna cried. "That's how a bargain works!"

Tanvi reached out and caught Radha's arm. Myna was so close to them, beseeching Radha, "You wanted me. You wished that I was real. You almost kissed me."

Tears streamed down Radha's cheeks. "I'm not g-going to ki-kill for you!"

Myna's expression faltered. "You're nothing, *totla.*"

Radha didn't flinch; instead, she concentrated on pulling Tanvi out with all her might. "I'm n-nothing like you," she screamed.

She fell backward, with Tanvi on top of her. Her feet displaced the salt lines, breaking the circle. A livid Myna swooped down to them, but just then the spectral arm reached out, grasping for Myna's shimmering form, and the lights went out, plunging them into darkness. Tanvi found Radha's hand and tightly clutched it. Radha heard the feral scuttling of claws getting closer and closer. Without another word, they ran hand-in-hand, out of the auditorium, into the chilly grounds. As Radha bolted the doors shut, they heard the chandelier crash and shatter.

"Do you think it will hold it?" Tanvi gasped.

"I think the cr-creature will go back, now that it's had its f-fill," Radha said, but she wasn't sure. And the only person who might have had the answer was gone.

Tanvi looked at her with terror, as though Radha could destroy her life in an instant. But Radha had no time to relish the feeling of being powerful, as something pounded loudly on the doors.

They ran through the moonlit playground, holding hands till they reached the dorms when Radha could not hear the scuttling anymore. As she crawled into bed, with a sobbing, shaking Tanvi below her, Myna's beseeching face swam up. Radha fought back her tears as it slowly dawned on her that love and hate were two sides of the same coin, each a ghost haunting the other. A girl and her hated reflection in the mirror. She realized that the other side wouldn't be any different, and she wept softly for the ghost of the girl she could have been.

REMAIN NAMELESS

KATALINA WATT

Meli heard the story from Teresita, leaning against her locker the morning Headmaster Reverend Thorne had found the girl's body. Meli rolled up her skirt, watching Teresita's cleavage straining against the buttons of her school blouse. At least Meli was taller, gangling limbs and all.

"Found her tangled in the willows at the lake," Teresita said, winding gum around her finger. "Thanks for the curfew, bitch."

"What happened?"

Teresita shrugged. "Couldn't cut it, I guess. Rather her than me."

Meli adjusted her pile of books. "No note? Don't they know who she was yet?"

"They never know anything."

The ghost of the girl watched Meli and Teresita discussing her death. The willow branch crept around her neck, embracing her. The life had been squeezed out of her. Water in her throat, mulch in her nose. Now she was no longer a girl; she was a kaperosa. She silently screamed her name, but they didn't hear her.

"Are you going to see him again?" Meli asked, applying the wand of cherry lip gloss. The bottle was nearly empty already. She'd have to steal more of Teresita's cigarettes to trade.

Teresita cupped her hand against her mouth. "This weekend."

Meli squealed. "What are you gonna wear?"

"I need you to alter my dress." Teresita smoothed her hair, an impulsive habit Meli knew like a warning.

"You have such a good figure, I can definitely work the neckline."

Teresita practically purred.

"He's gonna love it," Meli agreed.

The blood wouldn't stop. Meli sucked her finger, hot rust filling her mouth. It was a good thing the dress was red, otherwise she would have ruined it. Their Sunday dresses were shapeless crimson drapes of wool.

"I'll be too hot," Teresita lamented, flopping down onto Meli's bed.

Meli shrugged. "I can't exactly cut it."

Teresita threw a pillow at the wall. "We're all gonna die virgins wearing those sacks."

Meli cracked a smile. "Look here," she said, pulling Teresita up and holding the dress to her. It was long, almost touching the floor, but Meli had pinned soft pleats so the fabric didn't swamp. She'd nipped in the waist and adjusted the sleeves so it would fall off Teresita's shoulders. When her friend tried it on, she was pleased by the strong suggestion of cleavage.

"He won't be able to resist."

"Did you see Willow's body?" Rosa asked. The others had started calling the kaperosa Willow, on account of where she was found.

"No, but Tess did."

Rosa's eyes widened, looking around the chapel. The girls filed in for afternoon mass and the teachers gave up trying to quiet them.

"She's not here," Meli said.

Rosa gave a knowing look. "At least one of us is getting some. Poor girl though, what year was she in?"

Meli bit her lip. "Fourth year, I think. She looked young, according to Tess."

"God, the babies are too soft these days. Do you remember The Strikes?"

Meli shuddered, her buttocks reddening at the memory of the wooden paddle, the horrid slap of wood on flesh.

Rosa put her mouth to Meli's ear. "I overheard Tess's confession one time—she said she *liked* it."

"You're making that up."

"It's true. You're just offended because she told me and not you."

Meli reddened, trying to think up some cutting response, but the organ sprang into life. They barrelled into the first hymn and Meli pulsed with anger, channelling her rage into an unwavering alto. If she couldn't rip Rosa apart with words, she could at least deafen her reedy descant.

Reverend Samson Thorne was counting heads. Meli watched the Headmaster's lips moving. Their eyes met. Meli pressed her forehead down into her clenched knuckles, choking back the smell of candle wax. She turned to the crucifix, but Thorne blocked her view.

"Teresita?" he asked, folding his arms.

"Studying for chemistry," Meli bleated.

Thorne nodded.

Teresita had smirked as she'd fed Meli the lie to regurgitate. "My grades have slipped. He'll approve of me being proactive. Besides, you're his favorite pet. He'll eat up your every word."

Teresita was studying chemistry—of a kind. She'd hopped the crumbling old walls at the edge of the grounds, trying not to muddy her shoes by the willow banks. Her boyfriend was waiting with his motorbike. He'd brought a picnic, and they sprawled on the soft grass watching the clouds. Finally. They'd messed around before, but only over-the-clothes stuff.

"I never get to have fun anymore," Teresita sighed, stroking his dark curls.

He pouted. "It's that stupid curfew, right? So unjust."

"You have no idea how hard we work," Teresita agreed, taking a swig of beer. "We just want to blow off steam, have a little fun."

"We could have a bit of fun," he said, running his hands up her leg.

Teresita knew pleasure. She had taken it from herself, fingers into soft hot dough in the sleeping hours when Meli's breathing was deep and rhythmic on the other side of the dorm. She dreamt of boys slipping inside her, wrapping her arms and legs around her boyfriend. Of bodies rather than brains for once. She wanted to be pretty, and she wanted to be wanted. She knew sin and it was delicious.

Meli whispered feverishly, repeating prayers and incantations until they ceased all meaning and became desperate sounds. She thought about Teresita. They would be having sex, no doubt about it. She might be on her knees in the dirt. She would tell Meli all about it, whether she asked for the details or not. Teresita was like that, and partly because Meli thought she felt sorry for her.

"You never show an interest in boys," she'd said, something sharp beneath her tone.

"I'm not interested in boys," Meli deliberately let her gaze linger on Thorne.

"No?!" Teresita gasped teasingly. "You are *full* of surprises, Meli."

"I just want to be treated right. And you know boys our age don't know how to do that."

That was before Teresita got her boyfriend. She thought about Rosa's barbs. Meli blushed now in the pew as Thorne swept past her. His cologne was woodsmoke and whisky. God, how often she had looked at their chapel Renaissance icon of Jesus. He was holding his cross aloft, like it weighed nothing, the strength of his muscles and that flimsy white cloth around his waist. She had secret night thoughts, imagining she was the cross and Thorne was Jesus.

Teresita adjusted her dress and checked her face in the compact.

"Excuse me, miss," the young man emerged from the woods. She jumped out of her skin, expecting herself to be alone. Her boyfriend was taking a piss. "Where's Mallory Thorne School of Excellence?" He checked his paper and blinked in the afternoon glow.

He was cute. Teresita smiled and watched him blush, taking in the motorbike, the picnic remnants on the grass. Then she noticed his car, the caduceus: two snakes coiled round a staff. A medicine mark.

"Mallory Thorne?"

"That's right. I know it's around here. Got a bit lost just outside town. Not sure I followed the right road."

"Yeah, some of these roads lead nowhere," Teresita said, and he noticed the ice chips brittle in her voice.

"You a student there?" he asked, pushing back his glasses. It was her turn to shift uncomfortably.

"Maybe."

He laughed. "Do they know you're out here?"

"What's it to you?" she crossed her arms, looking back into the trees. "My boyfriend's here so you better watch it."

He held his hands up in surrender. "Just looking for the school. No trouble."

"You don't want to go there."

"Why's that?"

"The school *is* trouble."

His upper lip quirked in a bemused smile.

"That girl you're collecting, do you know what happened to her?"

"Finding out is sort of my job."

Teresita let out a frustrated grunt. "She killed herself. It's toxic up there."

He softened. "I'm sorry about your friend, but I've got a job to do." He turned back to his car, defeated.

Teresita reached out to grab his arm. "You're not listening. It won't be long till you're fetching another body."

Their eyes met. Whistling and branches snapping. Teresita's boyfriend emerged from the trees and became alert, sussing the situation.

"Who's this?" he asked, stiffening.

"Looking for directions to Mallory Thorne," the medic asked, brandishing his paper.

"Up the hill," Teresita's boyfriend pointed. "Follow the dirt track to that massive fuck-off castle. Can't miss it."

The medic smiled tightly and stalked back to his car.

"What a creep," Teresita's boyfriend said. "Good thing I came back when I did."

Teresita gave a brittle laugh, looking back up the hill at Mallory Thorne. It threatened to tumble into the lake which surrounded it.

"I can't believe you set me up, you bitch!" Teresita slammed into Meli, knocking her to the ground. "Why did you dob me in? After everything I've done for you?"

What was Tess talking about? Dizzy as she was, Meli wasn't sure. Tess was her only friend, but an average one at best.

"I didn't tell!" Meli insisted, scrambling to her feet.

"You liar. Thorne pulled me into his office after breakfast. He knows I broke curfew. Why didn't you cover for me?"

"I did," Meli yelled, bewildered. "I told him you were studying for your chemistry finals. He didn't follow up."

"Then how the hell did he know?"

A bunch of girls had gathered around them, and Meli felt their curious eyes. Some watched with a detached interest, in the same way they might observe a biological specimen in class.

"I don't know, Tess. Maybe he joined the dots? You're not that subtle, you know."

"You fucking told him. You can lie to me, but you can't lie to God, Meli."

She stalked off and Meli looked on, stunned. She had never heard such earnestness in Teresita's voice when invoking the Lord's name.

Meli walked back alone, trying to rub the mud from her black skirt. She didn't tell, she would swear it on Christ himself. Could it have been Rosa? She was seething after mass. Meli dreamed up little revenges: gum on the back of her skirt. Hiding her tampons. Wiping her lip gloss wand around the toilet bowl. It was easy for her to lose track of time, of where she was going. The grounds at Mallory Thorne weren't expansive, but the tracks in the hillside meandered. Huge trees acted as a canopy, sunlight and birdsong barely piercing through. You could only tell where you were in the gothic sprawl of the school itself, which reached high above the forest and overlooked the dinky toy town in the distance.

Meli gasped as her feet sank into the mud at the edge of the willow bank. She squelched her way around slowly, and then she saw the shoe. One little Mary Jane, t-bar strap open. Standard regulation.

There was a girl in the water. Not a girl, a kaperosa. She stared at Meli from the lake. Then a cold wind rushed into her lungs and Meli fell to her knees. A hand reached out of the lake and brown fingers curled around Meli's wrist. The ghost of the girl who died.

"Willow," Meli mouthed, as the hand dragged her under.

Willow waits under her namesake tree, where they used to meet. She has always been unnerved by twilight, the way you can't quite see and the shapes look strange. Her mother tells her Mallory Thorne will knock the childish ways out of her. She knots her crimson dress in her fingers, twirling the material around obsessively.

Meli stands in Willow's memory, watching her but inhabiting her at the same time. It's like she can feel everything Willow felt, can share her thoughts. Meli watches, both silent and confused, a specter dragged into the past by the kaperosa. What does she want her to see?

Willow settles as the stars begin to come out. The ink of the night sky is strangely calming in its deep abyss. The chapel brightens. They must be lighting the candles for mass. Hopefully he'll come soon, or she'll be missed at service. Although the only person who she could get in trouble with is him.

He covers her eyes with his hands and she almost yells, but then he speaks.

"I didn't mean to frighten you." His voice is honey.

Willow turns and kisses him. He turns her back around, pushes her skirt up and gets on with it. She looks at the willow tree, swaying rhythmically as he grunts. He finishes quickly, with a labored sigh, and slaps her ass as a signal to get sorted. Once she's decent, she touches him, trying to tell him she wants to be held. But she's too shy to be bold.

"We can't keep seeing each other."

The world falls out from beneath her.

"What do you mean?"

He strokes her cheek. "It's not fair on you. You're in your prime."

She flushes. "But I love you."

His mouth quirks, and she feels bile rise in her throat. Is he laughing at her?

The birdsong stretches painfully into the silence. After a moment, she meekly asks: "Don't you love me?"

"How can I love you? Willow, you're a child." His voice is something else, something she's never heard before. It's vicious steel and woodsmoke and leather. She's suddenly aware that he is a man. It seems stupid she's never realized before how much bigger he is than her. When he first touched her, he was so careful.

"Am I not—good?" she asks quietly, feeling the prick of tears. She's too old for tears and tantrums, her mother said.

He snorts. "This is over. You need to grow up."

She can't bear it when he turns to leave. "I'll tell!"

He throws a look over his shoulder, and she knows she has lost him. She's a soft baby, and he's done playing with her.

"I know I'm not the first. How many years have you been doing this to us?"

That gets his attention. He cracks his neck and rolls up his sleeves and comes back to her. She tries to look defiant, but it's difficult when he comes close and squares up to her. Still, she thinks it's a game.

"Willow, think carefully. You have a promising future ahead of you."

"You don't think I will? You'd lose your job. The school would get shut down. You might even go to prison. You know what they do to nonces—"

His hands are around her throat faster than she can speak. His eyes are lit like wildfire from within as he moves, enraged. She scrabbles at the bank with her feet; her fingers are scratching at his skin, but she can't get at his face—he's too tall. He's pushing her under the water now, wrapping the willow branches around her neck. He's so strong, and the mulch is in her throat. She wonders why she's struggling. She could just let go. The pain is heavenly.

Meli screamed, choking on lake water and weeds. She found the dirt, breaking fingernails and gouging flesh to get out of the bog. She heaved herself onto the bank, desperate animal sounds escaping her body.

He silenced you Willow, Meli thinks. *He used you and kept your mouth shut forever.*

Her labored breaths turned to wracking sobs, and she retched up her breakfast, sinking back down onto the spoiled grass.

"What the fuck happened to you?"

Teresita stood at the other side of the lake, hugging herself and watching. Meli's vision spun, and she could barely make out the other girl. She didn't look like herself. She looked strange, stripped, hollow.

Thorne slid the silver scissors across the desk and indicated to the en suite bathroom attached to his office. He draped a towel around Teresita's shoulders, pushing the hair back from her neck. She felt his hot acrid breath on her skin.

Hot tears began to pour down her cheeks, and she burned all over. She picked up the scissors, her hands shaking violently. His touch was cool as he steadied her. "You'll want straight lines, Teresita."

He sat back at his desk and nursed his tea as her knees shook and she began to cut. He didn't close the door and she didn't dare. She started slowly at the bottom, cutting off dried dead ends. He slammed the table, and the scissors flashed up in the light, nicking her on the neck.

"Shorn," he insisted, low and sharp.

She moved the scissors up, higher and higher, watching his face in the mirror. He blinked once and she cut, locks like autumn leaves around her feet. He watched her the entire time. The chair creaked, and then his hands were on the uneven stubble of her scalp. She felt the cold fingertips on her throat as he turned her to face him.

"You'll think twice before flouting my rules again." He looked at her steadily, then added: "The curfew is there for your safety. You're safe on the grounds, in the school."

A sob escaped Teresita's throat, and her shoulders heaved.

"It's only hair, Teresita. It will grow back."

Meli's hair was damp, plastered to her forehead, but at least she was clean and dry now. They sat on Teresita's bed, Meli wrapped in a blanket over her nightclothes and Teresita worrying her shorn scalp, fingers rubbing back and forth across the stubble of hair and irritated skin.

She turned to Meli. "I know you didn't tell Thorne. There was this guy—the coroner who came for the body. He saw me in the woods. I think he got me into trouble with Thorne."

"Did Thorne do this to you?" Meli asked, quietly.

Teresita nodded.

"Shit, I'm sorry," Meli said, touching Teresita's shoulder.

"You saw the girl?" Teresita asked, her voice a rotten husk.

Meli nodded. "Willow, or whatever her real name was. The

fourth year."

Teresita stared. "Let me get this right—you saw her and then she pulled you into the lake. And then she...showed you what happened?"

"It was her memory, her past. She took me there somehow—I could see and hear everything. I was in her head; I could hear her thoughts—feel what she felt. It sounds ridiculous, I hear that." Meli let out an exasperated breath.

"You sound absolutely unhinged, but I believe you."

"I don't understand it. But I felt it," Meli said. "It was disgusting."

"Did she feel—bad?" Teresita asked, searching for the right word.

"Like malevolent?" Meli asked. She considered, looking down at her wrist. There was no shadow of a mark, only the memory of touch. "I felt...overwhelming sadness."

"I believe he could do something bad to a girl," Teresita said. "I've never seen him how he was today. It was different. He was almost—dangerous."

Meli looked out of the window. There was no one down by the lake, just the dark remains of where she herself had lain on the banks. "I think Willow wanted to be heard. For someone to know what happened to her. That she didn't kill herself."

"What good is the truth?" Teresita asked. "She's still dead."

Meli couldn't stand to think of the coming winter and those girls who didn't have anywhere to go over the holidays. They would be cloistered with him throughout Christmas, choking down mince pies and drowning in mulled wine he pushed on them.

———

"I'm so glad you agreed to meet me," Meli said, unsure whether to hug Teresita.

"Why wouldn't I?" Teresita smiled as she took the armchair opposite.

"I wasn't sure you'd want to remember," Meli admitted.

Teresita's face shuttered for a moment and they both listened to the whirr of the coffee machine. Meli glanced through the window. Tongues of orange danced in the sky as the evening drew closer. It was autumn, an inauspicious time in her mind. But it was when Teresita was free, and she had been genuinely surprised when she'd agreed to meet. It had been years—both of them had grown into their bodies, more comfortable. Teresita had laughter lines by her eyes; she fiddled with a sparkling ring on the fourth finger of her left hand. Meli was desperate to ask, but she felt the chasm of the years between them. Despite everything, it was good to see her old friend after all this time.

"Your message was too intriguing to resist," Teresita said.

Meli traced her finger around the cup's rim. "It took years to work up to it."

Teresita unzipped her smart black handbag and opened her notebook, pen poised. "Pulling everything together, or working up the courage to reach out?"

"Both," Meli admitted.

Teresita leaned forward. "Are you sure you want to do this? I want to make sure you know exactly what you're asking."

Meli sighed. "I've been thinking about this every day since we left."

It was the closest way she could tell Teresita. Her aversion to water. A shiver when she drove past a church. Her browser's alerts for any crumb to do with the school or Thorne.

Teresita's pen hovered. "You think about her often, don't you?"

"Always," Meli said, without pause.

Teresita smoothed her hair back behind her ear. Meli noticed she seemed to wear it short these days, but she smiled fondly at that old mannerism still. "Have you got the material you wanted me to look at?"

Meli fumbled for the folder in her bag. She felt Teresita's eyes on her and wondered what she saw. She handed it over reluctantly. Teresita saw the hesitation. "This isn't a guarantee of anything, Meli. I don't want you to get your hopes up. I'll need some time to follow up on your research."

"But you were there too, Tess."

Teresita pursed her mouth and then sighed. "We need to be careful with our sources. I have to keep my history with this story under wraps for now. The newspaper won't like it if they think it's a personal vendetta. They may consider it a conflict of interest—my professional reputation is on the line."

"Isn't it personal?" Meli asked, quietly.

Teresita shook her head, trying to find the words. Meli wondered if she carried regret like a stone in her pocket.

"I'm a journalist, Meli, not a miracle worker. This isn't vigilante justice—"

Meli's phone began to buzz, vibrating the table with a jarring sound. Bea's name flashed up, and with it Meli's lock screen photo of their wedding. Meli apologized, flipping the phone over.

"Let me take a look at this. I'll be in touch." Teresita tucked the folder into her neat handbag and stood. "It was really good to see you, Meli. I'm so happy for you—she looks nice."

Meli hugged her then. "Bea, my wife." They separated, and Meli tapped the ring on Teresita's finger. "I hope you're happy too."

Teresita smiled and then sighed. "I can't guarantee that anything will come of this. I can't undo what happened—even if this gets picked up and makes waves, he might not face justice. God, he might not even be alive anymore. I have to track him down, and I'm not a judge—I can't put him behind bars. So much time has passed, any physical evidence is gone. All I can do is try, as a journalist. It's the least I can do. I just want to manage your expectations."

"There's some files in there on Willow—some school records, her grades, her mother's old address—"

Teresita looked at Meli, eyebrows furrowed.

"The girl Thorne murdered. Her name really was Willow."

Teresita looked at Meli. "For Willow. And for the others," she said, patting her bag. "It's not a promise, but it's something."

RENEWAL NOTICE

TEHNUKA

Mira jumped up from the bus stop bench. "Monday? Are you sure?" That made the second time this term she'd forgotten a deadline.

"What did you think I was working on all week? What were *you* working on?" Lily shook her head. "I guess you aren't coming, then. If you want my notes, they're on my desk."

Mira stared down at her hiking boots. "Thanks." She was the one who offered notes, not the other way around.

"Don't worry, I'll be fine on my own."

Lily would always be fine out walking on her own. It was only that Mira so wanted the distraction of a day out on the moor, not trapped in her own head.

After five years perfecting her cursive, Lily had developed handwriting so ornate as to be indecipherable. Mira flicked through her notes, guessing from the little she could read that they'd been assigned different topics. Taking her notebook and satchel, she clomped down stone-flagged corridors in the boots she'd forgotten to change. No one was about this early to care.

Two forgotten assignments in a term wasn't a pattern. She'd just been distracted—worrying about the things her parents didn't, or couldn't, mention in letters, but that she read about in rare newspaper articles or using her weekly internet allowance to search online. Of course, none of that helped her get word of their relatives. And apparently she should have been researching a natural science assignment instead.

The dorm corridor opened into the hallway. Ahead were the dull brass letters: Hopkins Library. Amma would say, "Chee, can't they clean the sign?" and go after it with baking soda and an old toothbrush. Mira didn't mind it appearing so rundown. Money saved on maintenance might go to scholarships like hers.

A voice rang across the atrium as she pushed the glass doors open. "How did you get in?"

"I..." Mira hesitated in the doorway. The speaker was behind the issues desk, dressed in her usual suit and tie. Mira saw her frequently—Ms. Johnson was one of the full-time librarians.

"Who are you? How did you get in?"

"Mira. I'm a student."

The librarian pushed aside her chair from behind the issues desk and stood, short blond hair giving a small bounce. "Where's your uniform?"

"It's Saturday, and I'm in Fifth Year. I just came to work on an assignment..."

"Oh, goodness, so sorry Nalini! Of course it's you, I remember from Poetry Club, I just didn't recognize you in mufti. Sorry." She checked the clock hanging above the desk. "No one's in so early on the weekends, and it startled me. I thought you must be from outside the school." Ms. Johnson sat back down with a wide smile. "Just let me know if you need help!"

Nalini, a new Second Year, looked nothing like Mira. But it was wisest to accept the apology and disappear among the shelves as soon as possible. Ms. Johnson was friendly enough on a good day. The card catalog never made sense, so Mira wandered between tall wooden shelves lit by dim bulbs, squinting at titles, hoping to spot anything relevant. Other libraries had sensor lights. And bigger windows. Still, Mallory Thorne's had enough books to supply a hundred schools, if only there'd been a digital system to help find them.

Bright blue cloth binding and gold lettering caught her eye. *The Water Cycle*. A few decades too old to be much use for her essay, but a good starting point. She'd pick a few up-to-date ones too. The hard part wasn't finding references—it was finding the focus to read and write.

She added several plastic-covered textbooks and took her pile to a partitioned desk under the narrow windows at the far, quiet end of the library. Ms. Johnson was right—no one else was around. She shoved her satchel under her chair and opened her notebook, then *The Water Cycle*, cover clacking against the wooden desktop.

Focus. She leafed through, stopping at the index.

The letters grew faint, dissolving into the page until they faded entirely, like ink diluted in water. Nothing remained but old, yellowing, paper.

Mira scrunched her eyes and looked again.

Now, the blank surface shimmered. She groaned aloud, but this was not her and Lily's dorm to make noise in. She flipped the cover closed.

The gold embossed letters rearranged, straight lines looping into very familiar characters. As far as she knew, though—and she'd searched through the library, when she first started at Mallory Thorne—the only Tamil writing in the school was in the letters her parents sent, and an occasional line in her notes when she couldn't think of the English.

The title of *The Water Cycle* now read *Uthavi*. Help.

Mira slid the stack of books into the middle of the desk, displacing *Uthavi*, and rested her head on them. She shouldn't have read those news articles last night—reports of bombings and deaths and graphic photos she couldn't unsee, even with eyes closed. Knowing she couldn't help. Knowing she was supposed to pretend it wasn't going on, embrace helplessness, focus on her studies; that her parents, though they wrote every fortnight, didn't mention it because they didn't want her to worry.

Well, she was worried anyway. How could she agonize so much over a meaningless school assignment when other people's worlds were ending?

After five deep breaths, she straightened and reached for the next book—an introductory text she'd used for an assignment earlier in the year. Diagrams and subheadings and little boxes of highlighted information might get something into her head that paragraphs of small print wouldn't. She opened it to a random page, a glimpse of trees, a river, and clouds, a textbox colored pink—

This time, the text swirled, circling into the middle and vanishing, the diagram swept along with it. The page was left white and glossy.

It remained blank for only a moment.

Then, letters re-emerged from the center, tracing the same spiraling route back.

Uthavi

And the words kept pouring out to fill the page.

Uthavi uthavi uthavi

Uthavi read the cover, when Mira slammed it.

Uthavi read the spines of the books underneath, as the stack tumbled across the desk.

Uthavi read her own handwriting in her notebook.

She didn't stay to watch it spread. She didn't even pause to pick up her satchel. Eyes down, away from the shelves, feet too heavy to run in stupid hiking boots, she shouldered through the doors and was gone before Ms. Johnson looked up from the returns box.

She lifted her face from the damp pillow when Lily unlocked the door.

"Oh! You're in. Finished the essay?"

"How was the hike?"

"Great, really nice in the woods." Lily dropped her pack and unlaced her trail shoes. "It's too hot on the moor, but the bogs were so dried out I didn't get my feet wet. Ugh, I need a shower. How about you?"

If only she'd gone, too! At least there would have been something good that day. Mira buried her face back in the pillow, conveniently blocking the sweaty sock smell. "The essay's a disaster. I've lost my mind." If she kept her tone light—but her nose was still stuffed and her voice shaky, and—

"You okay?"

"Yeah. Book dust." Mira sniffed and rolled onto her back so Lily could hear her. "They should clean those library shelves. I bet some of them haven't been touched since it was built."

"Ookay," said Lily in a tone that indicated she knew Mira had been crying, but if she wouldn't admit it, they wouldn't discuss it. "Did you find anything useful?"

Lily had been Mira's roommate since they started at Mallory Thorne. The one who'd taken her to buy hiking boots and lent her a good rucksack so they could escape the confines of the school together for approved walks. The one she followed into woods and bogs and up hills. The one who had seen her cry, once or twice, because it was unavoidable when you shared the closest thing you had to a private space. And the one she'd fought with, because that, too, was hard to avoid—and because Lily was the only one she trusted enough to fight with. But she wouldn't understand this time, would she?

"No. I had a weird thing with the books and...I don't know. I left my stuff in the library."

Mira tried to smile but her lips kept bending the wrong way.

"Want me to stay, or do you want your peace and quiet back?"

"No, you need your shower. And please get rid of those socks!"

Lily stripped off her socks and held them between two fingers, away from her body. She hesitated. "Are you sure? About not staying, I mean, not the socks."

She could ask. She *should* ask. *Can you come to the library with me?* Easy.

Mira studied alone. She'd got her grades and scholarships on her own. She and Lily weren't the type of friends to always do homework together and accompany each other to the toilets. Lily wasn't offering to chaperone her to confront the scary books; she wanted confirmation Mira was okay so she could wash her hair in peace.

They were the sort of friends who discussed school and exams, complained that Mallory Thorne needed a better recycling initiative, commiserated about Mira being mistaken for Nalini, gossiped about what Andrew had said to the calculus teacher. They didn't talk about truly personal things. When Mira tried to open her mouth to explain, the weight of it felt so much her throat seemed to drop toward her stomach, and all she said was, "Totally sure. About not staying, and definitely about the socks."

"Point taken," Lily said, unhooking her towel. "I'm going to the library after dinner, though. I need a new book. In case you want to come." The door thunked shut behind her.

Reading for leisure. When had Mira last done that? Not this term. She sat up, reached for the closet door, and tugged a shirt and uniform trousers onto her bed, leaving her blazer hanging. After the essay, she'd stop scouring newspapers and use the time for something relaxing. Today's hike should have been that, but with little chance of another sunny twenty-degree day for weeks, she could at least ask Lily for a novel recommendation.

The dining hall was sunset gold when they arrived for an early dinner. Hot food wasn't ready, so they piled their bowls with pasta salad.

"I should've taken something nicer for lunch than muesli bars," Lily said, leading the way to a still-sunny patch at one of the long tables, hooking a chair out with her foot before setting down her bowl and glass of water.

"Bet they tasted better hiking than they did in our room." Mira took the next seat and passed her a fork.

"You must've been working hard to eat those. You'll finish easily now; it's only a couple of thousand words."

"Doubt it." The pasta was overcooked and salty. Mira leaned back in her chair, her gaze catching on the blood-red flowers in the stained glass panel at the top of the window.

Lily mumbled a question through a full mouth.

"I haven't written a word," Mira added.

The electric lights flickered on, dim and yellowish in their brass chandeliers. "Ah, has the dreaded procrastination finally struck you? Happens to the rest of us constantly."

"Procrastination, you say?" Andrew, red-faced, swung into a seat opposite them. He lined his tray up with the edge of the table. "I get it. I've been lying in the sun all day instead of doing homework too."

"Should've stayed in. Or worn sunscreen," Lily said, scraping her fork around an already-empty bowl.

"No one expects to get burnt this early in the year. And hey, I made the most of the weather. Join the dark side, Mira, procrastination is good for the spirit!" He rolled up his sleeves and picked up his knife and fork.

Andrew had the luxury of joining "the dark side." His parents would pay his university tuition. Unless Mira managed a scholarship, she'd return home in two years when her visa expired, if there was a home left to return to.

She didn't need to respond, because Lily noticed Andrew's plate. "There's pizza?"

"If they haven't run out." He looked around at the rapidly-filling tables. A group of First Years, arriving for their set mealtime, raised a clamor a few seats down. "There were a few toppings. Check the blackboard, down the bottom." He began cutting into the large slab of pizza.

Mira and Lily both stood to squint at the chalkboard above the serving hatch where hot food was offered during casual meals. The pale scrawls seemed to waver.

Uthavavum

"Mira! Coming?"

"Can't you see it?! The chalk!"

Lily turned to the board, then back to Mira. "It's always hard to read. Let's go up. You can make up your mind while I get the one with olives before it runs out."

"No, I mean—the letters…"

"The first line says 'noodles,' Mira. It always does. And then it's—"

"It says 'You're to help.' It says 'uthavavum.' Who am I meant to help? It doesn't make sense!"

Lily turned her around, away from the board. "Sit down and… here." She pushed her glass of water over. "Have you strained your eyes? Or are you really seeing things? Because either way…you can get help. They'll get you an appointment in town if the school nurse doesn't know."

Mira drained the glass and wiped condensation from her fingers. "I don't think I've drunk anything since yesterday."

"Uh, maybe that's why you're hallucinating?" Lily looked from her to the queue at the front.

"Go get your pizza before they run out," Mira said. Weekend food was always more varied, but pizza was a rarity.

"I'll try to get you some!" said Lily, refilling her water from a nearby jug before she left. "Rehydrate. Then we'll go to the library so you can stop stressing over that stupid essay."

"How was the walk, anyway?" Andrew asked, putting his cutlery down. "Weren't you crossing Thorne Woods and out to the moors? Must've been scorching; how'd you survive without water?"

"I didn't go. I stayed to work on that essay, just...I couldn't focus. But yeah, Lily said the bogs were all dried up."

"You could've gone and written an observational piece about how the dry weather and heatwave killed the peat!"

Mira remembered passing over a headline about the winter drought when she was seeking news from home. "What's your essay on?"

"Contemporary extinctions. I forgot to come up with research questions, but it worked without them; I just used interesting facts. Did you know a frog died out in East Anglia just recently? Turns out it still existed on the continent, but I'd already written that bit, so..." He shrugged.

Nothing fazed Andrew.

Ms. Johnson was rummaging behind the issues desk when they returned to the library.

"Hi Ms. Johnson, have you got anything new?" Lily asked.

"If you mean novels, a box arrived today. I haven't opened it yet, but if you come back in a few minutes, I'll have them out." Ms. Johnson thumped the cardboard box on the counter.

"Oh, thanks! We'll fetch Mira's stuff that she forgot here earlier, and then I'll come choose some."

Ms. Johnson glanced at Mira, seeming not to notice that she

wasn't Nalini, then returned her attention to Lily. "You can choose *one*. I'm not processing all the new books tonight. The library will still be here tomorrow, and I'm sure you won't need another before then."

Lily grinned and followed the others down the main walkway separating the shelves.

"I left it here," Mira said, stopping on the right. The desk she'd occupied in the morning was behind several rows of shelves, near the wall, but she was sure the shelves had been facing one another, not outward into the wide aisle. A ninety-degree rotation seemed in keeping with her present state of mind.

Then Lily said, "That's weird. When did they move the shelves?"

"So, they've moved?"

"That's a big effort. They're pretty solid." Andrew knocked on the wood paneling. "Surprised you didn't notice them doing it, Lily, being here every night. Must've had your nose in a book."

"I'm not here *every* night! And I would've noticed if they emptied the shelves to rearrange."

Mira stopped at one of the narrow gaps between the shelves, peering into the darkness. The lights were switched off there.

"This layout is awful," Lily continued. "You don't use the library enough to understand, but you need to see the labels on the ends of the shelves to know what section you're in, right Mira?"

"There aren't any numbers on the shelves now." She might as well say it. "And...I thought they were perpendicular to the walls this morning, so they must have changed today."

"Ms. Johnson didn't mention rearranging," said Lily. "How did they do it so quickly? Are the desks still back there?"

Andrew poked his head between shelves. "Can't see. They won't want us in there before they're finished—that's why the lights are off. Ugh, it's musty." He turned, nose wrinkled. "No wonder they were rearranging. They should get dehumidifiers in."

"My stuff could be in lost and found. Or Ms. Johnson sent it to

Nalini's dorm by now. Ugh." She had friends with her. They'd find her books that she'd take back to the dorm. She could spread everything out on her duvet and work cross-legged on her bed, while Lily devoured her latest novel. Company would help her focus.

Back at the issues desk, Lily started browsing the newly unpacked books while they waited for the librarian to reappear. "She might let me borrow two, if I ask nicely. It can't take that long to process another."

Andrew leaned against the counter. "You planning to stay up all night reading?"

"Yep, right here, waiting for Ms. Johnson to check this book out," said Lily, already half a page in.

Mira paced the atrium. The lost-and-found crate was kept behind the issues desk. She could duck behind it, find her bag and notebook...but just her luck if the librarian came back right then. Misplacing her books was no excuse for late submission. Nothing short of serious physical illness would be, and then they'd expect her to hand in the notes she didn't have for marking.

And it was only a stupid assignment, when other people's worlds were ending—but doing the stupid assignments was all that would let her stay in this one.

"She's not in the office," said Andrew, appearing in the doorway behind the issues desk. He didn't seem concerned about the rules. "Anyway, the lost-and-found isn't back here. Let's go. You can come back tomorrow."

"I don't mind waiting, Mira." Lily turned a page. How quickly she forgot the world! "Find the light switches and check properly. You'll be up all night stressing otherwise."

"You just don't want to leave without your book," said Andrew, going back toward the office door. "No one will know if you take it, she won't have done the—you know, the alarming thing."

"The magnetic strip? No. But... I couldn't. Why can't we get self-checkout? Even the village library has it. Should you really—"

Andrew re-emerged with a torch in his hand, flicking the switch repeatedly so it flashed along the countertop. "Coming, Mira?" She hesitated, staring at the on-off of the beam.

Amma would say to go to bed, deal with problems in the morning. She would say not to risk trouble with teachers. She would say to study hard and do well in school.

For that, Mira needed those books. Andrew was here, offering help. And Andrew was the one who'd rummaged through the office—she wasn't doing anything wrong, was she?

"I'll come find you if Ms. Johnson shows up," said Lily. Mira caught a glimpse of the book cover as she settled back against the counter. *Thanjam*, it said, over some swords-and-sorcery cover. Sanctuary. Not a word she ever used, although it showed up in books sometimes. What a word to hallucinate.

She followed Andrew back down the aisle, stomach churning again. What good were the books anyway? If he and Lily couldn't keep the words from changing—and she should have realized that at dinner—how would she study? How could she tell her parents she was on the verge of failing, that she couldn't focus, that she was leaving school, that instead of university and a job and visas for the family, she was bringing their hopes home to be blown into dust?

"Here?" Andrew squeezed into a crack between the shelves, taking the light with him.

"My green satchel's under the desk, if they haven't moved it, and the books are on top." She followed him into the first aisle, then through another gap into the next. "Wow, it does smell damp."

"Is something *dripping*?" He paused and shone the light along the shelves, which extended into the darkness on either side.

Yes, that patter—like a light drizzle. It couldn't be a roof leak; there hadn't been rain for weeks. It was cool, too, almost cold. When she took a step toward the gap in the next line of shelving, the oak flooring squished underfoot.

"There must've been a leak. I'm surprised Ms. Johnson—"

Mira didn't hear what he said next, because the whispering began. A single word, first. Then hoarse, overlapping voices speaking over one another:

Uthavi

Thanjam

Abayam

Adaikkalam

"What *is* it?" Andrew shone the torch at the roof, back down the aisles, at the books. If he heard it too, why did they speak in Tamil?

"They're saying 'help' and 'asylum,' things like that."

Were they ghosts from the war?

Andrew edged closer. "Maybe let's head back?" he called over the whispers.

Why would they come here? Why cross seas and continents to ask Mira for sanctuary, to help the dead, when she couldn't even help herself?

Or were they voices of those alive and trapped somewhere?

"Since it's not actually a hallucination, I'm going to see what it's about," she replied, talking straight into his ear. "Coming?"

He bent slightly to speak into her ear. "I liked it better when it *was* your hallucination. Let's find Ms. Johnson, or a teacher. This is…" He gestured wildly with the torch, presumably at the disembodied voices surrounding them, growing louder.

"Yeah, don't you want to know what this is?" She touched the nearest shelf. It was damp, rather than dusty, but seemed like the same shelving the library had always had. The voices, though— they were real, and new. It was real. The letters had truly changed for her, demanding help. The others just hadn't noticed. She wasn't losing her mind.

Andrew looked at the gap they'd come through, which seemed further than three steps away, and gave a vigorous head shake.

Whoever was pleading for help, she couldn't leave them—not when they'd been asking all day.

"Give me the torch, then?" she shouted.

Andrew pressed it into her palm. "Hold it for me while I get out." The distance back now was as far across as the width of the library. She lit a path along a moss-textured floor, and he strode across, fists clenched, then sidled between the nearest row of shelves. She could just see the tiny sliver of the final gap beyond. The whispering softened—he must have got out. She turned toward the next row. Had the whispers come from the books?

Those texts were in English, though, or Latin, or French…

She continued between the next set of shelves. The floor softened further, her school shoes squelching. Should've brought a jacket—her shirt was too flimsy for this evening chill. "Hello? Vanakkam?"

The whispers stopped.

"Will you tell me what you want?"

Silence.

A fog grew as she progressed. Fine water droplets scattered her torch-beam by the time she reached that morning's desk. She wiped the muddy base of her satchel on her pants—the damp had already seeped from the air into her uniform.

Her notebook was on top of the pile.

The pencil rolled off as she lifted it down, revealing the next, familiar book, with the title clear: *The Water Cycle*.

In Tamil, the words for "to listen" and "to ask" were identical: kedka. They weren't communicating with her now, but what if she asked the right questions? She nudged the chair out. Its legs rocked on uneven ground, then steadied as she sat. She propped the torch against the partition to illuminate her notebook.

Who are you? she scribbled at the top of a page. *Where are you?*

Nothing.

Neengal yaar?

This time, her letters fractured, reformed. *Ayalavar,* came the answer, tiny, neat. Neighbors. Those nearby.

She continued in Tamil. *Why are you writing to me?*

We need your help. Your world is...

The text she'd written at the top rearranged, as if they needed existing pencil-marks to communicate.

...drowning ours. Your world is drowning us. You understand us.

Mira steadied her grip on the pencil and took a deep breath of musty air. Should have brought warmer clothes. Should take the books and go. But they were asking for her help.

How?

Don't know.

What do you want?

Viduthalai. Pazhi.

Freedom. Revenge.

She shifted the library books into her satchel. Her fingers kept sticking to the covers. Common sense said to leave—this wet, dingy version of the library and these unknown neighbors' desire for revenge weren't safe.

But who, if their world was being destroyed, wouldn't want freedom? Or even revenge? She should understand—it was mere luck she carried schoolbooks rather than a machine gun.

"Freedom means...?" No answer.

Over the full satchel on her lap, she wrote, *Freedom means?*

Let us come.

Weren't they already here?

A squelch behind her, and she sprang up, feet sinking.

"Mira? Oh, you're here." Lily stood by the shelves, fuzzy in the mist and ankle-deep in the viscous substance replacing the floor. "You okay? What is this?"

The chair wouldn't move, and Mira had to climb over it to get out from the desk. "I don't know. Can we go?"

"Obviously, yes, please!"

Lily's arms were folded, hands tight on her elbows. She lifted alternate feet, frowning at her shoes. Mira slung the heavy satchel over a shoulder and plodded through the sludge, notebook in one hand, torch in the other. Lily caught her arm. "Is this payback for all the bogs I dragged you through?"

"Nah, I would've made us wear boots if I knew. How'd you find me?" Mira slipped between the shelves, Lily close behind.

"I heard you muttering. Seriously, are you seeing this? It's almost raining! Inside! And you're...sitting taking notes?"

How could she explain? "Remember I said the writing changed? Like on the dining hall blackboard? Well, it does, when I look at it."

"And that's to do with the library flooding?"

"I think so?" The writers—the mysterious neighbors—were letting them leave. The distance between aisles had lost the earlier distortion, from when Andrew had left... "Where's Andrew?"

"He came out positively yelling for Ms. Johnson. Then said something about voices and went to find an adult. He was a mess. We will be, too. Did you need your books that badly?" Lily sounded perplexed, not annoyed. And there was the dull yellow light between bookcases. Mira waited to answer until they reached the warmth of the library.

Greenish slime coated their shoes and trousers. Lily's shirt clung to her, and Mira could feel hers doing the same. Steam rose off her bag.

"I was asking questions. They're telling me to help, in Tamil. I think...I think they're, I don't know, spirits from the war or something."

Lily grimaced, wiping gunk from her ankles with the side of her hand. "You don't think it's odd they asked you, specifically, not someone closer? Or an adult? Like they came to a boarding school in England to find you?"

She was trying to help, Mira reminded herself. "No, I do think it's odd, unless they're doing it everywhere."

"You know weirdness has happened here before, right? We've heard the rumors. Maybe you hit a...weirdness patch and your stress attracted them. Gosh, Andrew should be back."

They'd said Mira understood them, though. And she wasn't the only one stressed—half the Seventh Years subsisted on chocolate and study guides, and rarely appeared in the dining hall. She tucked the torch under her elbow and wrung several drops of water from her shirt.

Lily copied her. "It's like the rain we haven't had this year all ended up in there."

They'd said the same. *Your world is drowning ours.*

"What if it has? That's what happens here, right? Short-term climate patterns give places different weather—isn't that the Southern Oscillation you wrote about in your notes?"

"Something like that. So what, their world's out of balance because of our climate? And where *is* everyone?"

The clock above the issues desk showed 9:30, meaning they'd been here over two hours—far longer than it had felt—past the library's closing time. Mira snatched a pen from the issues desk. The ink smudged on moisture-curled notebook pages.

Neengal manitharkalaa? Are you human?

Aavi

Spirits—or steam. Spirits of the dead? Or another being? Or water vapor, overcrowded in an increasingly humid atmosphere?

Lily left no time to clarify. "That's bizarre, but Sedgwick? Or teachers' common room?"

"Ms. Sedgwick." Their soft-spoken dorm master always asked Mira if she'd heard from her family. Leaving her satchel in the seemingly-empty library—Lily not even glancing at her abandoned novel—they returned to their wing. They also left a trail of goo on the flagstones that Lily, uncharacteristically, didn't seem to notice, though Mira expected angry shouts any moment.

Ms. Sedgwick was responsible for the Fifth to Seventh Years, but gave them space in the evenings, with occasional visits to common rooms or strolls down the corridors to check all was well. Her door was ajar as usual, an invitation to students wanting to see her. Lily knocked, calling in a questioning, anxious tone Mira hadn't heard before.

"Come in!"

Ms. Sedgwick sat on her tatty sofa in electric blue pajamas, holding a steaming mug and a magazine. "Hello, girls. How's your family, Mira? Oh, goodness! What's happened?" She put everything down. "Are you hurt?"

"We're fine, but there's a swamp in the library, and we can't find Ms. Johnson, and I don't know where Andrew's gone either—maybe he followed me back in when I went to get Mira?"

"These—" Mira began, but Ms. Sedgwick was halfway out the door, putting on her fluffy blue slippers, even though Lily hadn't made any sense.

"Supernatural nonsense, and right at lights out! Are you okay to come, girls? Or do you need a rest and a shower? I won't mind you staying up, obviously."

"No, we'll come," said Lily. Mira tried to flatten her hair, which frizzed in the humidity, and waited for Ms. Johnson to lock the door.

"There are these spirits," she tried to explain.

"They've turned the shelves around," added Lily, and told how Andrew had shown her the entrance before going for help, how Ms. Johnson had disappeared, and shouldn't the library be closing for the night now?

But when they reached the library, Ms. Johnson stood at the desk folding a cardboard carton. "Ms. Sedgwick! Mira, is this your bag on the counter? Lily, I thought you were going to borrow a book?"

"As you can see, Ms. Johnson, we came in a hurry." Ms. Sedgwick gestured at her pajamas. "Lily tells me there were...occurrences?"

The librarian laughed. "Yes, perhaps a portal? Or so I hope—otherwise that's worrying for the library. I'll have to put in a maintenance request. I went to shelve some returns, but everything was rearranged, and the lights weren't working. I got entirely lost."

Lost any sense of time too, apparently. Mira edged forward for her notebook while the others talked. The last line, written in pen, was smudged; just one word replaced it.

Mira

"Stay with Ms. Johnson if you like, Mira," said Ms. Sedgwick kindly. "We're going to have a look back there. Andrew or other students might have wandered into—whatever it was."

A spirit realm, Mira wanted to tell her. Or a steam realm. But if they wanted everyone to know, they'd have written in English. If Lily and Ms. Sedgwick didn't care, maybe it wasn't important to anyone else.

"Don't go wandering off like Andrew," Lily added as they went. Ms. Johnson gave her a wink and began sticking labels on the new books.

How do I free you?

The ink blotted, responding as she wrote. *It's already done*

Blue spilt out from the page, misting around her.

She stumbled back. It followed.

Had she brought them out, in her sodden clothes and hair? In that stack of books? All the moisture that had escaped from between the shelves, was that *them*?

"Ms. Johnson!"

The librarian looked up. "Don't worry Mira, they won't hurt you."

She seemed to be right. The ink swirls dissipated high above.

But Ms. Johnson never remembered her name.

"Ms. Johnson, are you...okay?" She kept her distance, standing a couple of meters back.

"Why yes, thanks for asking, Mira. It was cold and dank in wherever that was, wasn't it? Though you seem to have got the worst of it. You're soaked, poor thing! I had to clean so much slime off my shoes—that's why I was gone so long—and it's set off my sinuses, but I'm fine."

She might be fine. She didn't seem to be Ms. Johnson though. Sinuses invaded by spirits perhaps. Just like Mira's hair and trousers and shirt.

But if they'd messed with Mira's mind, they wouldn't be writing to her. And they'd said she understood them.

She approached cautiously and opened her satchel. *The Water Cycle* glittered at her. "I'm sorry about these books. I was going to borrow them for an essay, but they got wet."

"That's not your fault, dear," said Ms. Johnson, which was wrong. It was Mira's fault they'd been able to find a way into the library at all. "But these are only a touch warped. Tell you what, I'll make a note they're damaged, so you won't be in trouble if another librarian handles the returns."

Her satchel was dry, too.

Where had they gone?

Ms. Johnson stacked the books back into Mira's satchel, placing the notebook on top. "Don't you worry about that essay tonight, though."

Footsteps, and there was Andrew with Ms. Sedgwick and Lily.

"No ghost world, just Andrew," said Lily cheerfully.

"It was there a minute ago! I was stuck inside." Andrew had acquired slime on his shoes too. "I couldn't find Ms. Johnson, and when I went back to Lily, she'd gone. I couldn't remember which shelves we were at." He shuddered. "Where I went in, I kept seeing tiny green flashes. There was a humming noise. I was bloody terrified. I ran in circles looking for you, but it wasn't the library anymore."

"You could've gone for actual help instead of—" began Lily, but Ms. Sedgwick said, "That's enough. Lily, Mira, you may use the showers, but quickly, please—it's well past bedtime. Andrew, I'll come for a word with your dorm master. Goodnight, girls."

Were they acting different? Was Ms. Johnson the *revenge*, or was that yet to come?

"If I'd expected this, I wouldn't have showered after my hike," said Lily. "Are they going to tell us what happened? There's a lot of water damage; they'll have to explain that to everyone." Water damage, yes—but there didn't seem to be much actual 'water' from the other world left that she could see. She imagined the neighbors spinning up into the arid summer heat, finding pipes, creek beds, and peat bogs to inhabit, filling in the spaces where they would be welcomed, or at least unnoticed.

She and Lily kicked off their shoes outside their door. Her socks felt crackly now, like she'd left them to stiffen on the floor after one of Lily's hikes instead of putting them in the wash.

"I actually think I might know." Mira took a fresh towel and her pajamas from the closet. "But it's a long explanation."

"I won't get to sleep until you tell me! Is it to do with them writing to you?"

"Yeah. There's some stuff back home to do with the war I should tell you about first, so you'll understand."

"You know you can tell me whatever, right?" Lily didn't sound congested—she just sounded like Lily. If she was acting more open than usual, well...after today, Mira was feeling more open, too. As for Ms. Johnson's sinuses, that could remain Ms. Johnson's problem.

Mira let her hair get wet, though Amma would say going to bed with wet hair would give her a cold. Steam swirled, filling her shower cubicle. Were the neighbors inside? Would they always be with her now?

It might not be such a bad thing, if it meant she'd given sanctuary to those who needed it.

OF MICE AND PIGEONS

MOACHIBA JAMIR

Old Amongba could still remember the first time he stepped inside the halls of the Old Chapel in Mallory Thorne. Its arched entrance towered above his five-foot-three frame. He imagined the chapel's walls had once been a pristine white, but had now turned beige with pockets of yellow daubing the facade. Inside, benches were arranged in rows like huge caterpillars in motion, until the front, where the hall opened into a carpeted podium. The choir boys were already seated to its left. Behind the podium, a large open Bible and a crimson cross oversaw the congregation below, mostly young students, but he also noticed some older people, presumably the teachers and staff of Mallory Thorne. One peculiar thing that struck Old Amongba was the puffy odor—probably due to the dampness from the open drainage flowing beside the chapel. Although he had grown accustomed to it over time, the smell had reminded him of that time he'd upturned his dying aunt's bed to find black mold scattering unchecked—underneath was where the stench had been brewing, ebbing and flowing, spreading quietly like fungal leprosy.

He had already decided, then, that he would not be joining the Old Chapel after all.

As he was coming upon this conclusion, the gradual quietening inside was so subtle that Old Amongba didn't notice it immediately. But sitting there in the last bench of the Old Chapel, he soon realized everything had gone completely quiet. No bells to announce the start of the service, only a quietening.

The chaplain walked up to the podium and faced the congregation, crimson cross and open Bible behind him. A gentle spotlight illuminated him from behind and from the front. He stretched his arms wide, and his tailor-made sleeves gleamed from the spotlight like iridescent wings. He welcomed his congregation, breaking the silence. He smiled.

Later, at home, Old Amongba would realize that he had been paying too much attention to the chaplain, whom he would later come to know as Chaplain Julius Thomas Thorne. The whole student congregation, in fact, was engrossed, lapping up every word that spilled from the chaplain's mouth. At that moment, though, he was not entirely alarmed.

Every day after this first encounter, Old Amongba would decide to start off in search of work in another place. Yet, it seemed as if all roads converged toward the Old Chapel in Mallory Thorne, and so, every Sunday, he would find himself facing that imposing structure once again.

A month later, while he was listening to the chaplain's voice emanating from the two giant speakers up front, Old Amongba felt the bench repelling him. Push-push, up off his seat. And as he stood there in the middle of the information session behind the general congregation, it dawned on him that he had just volunteered to be the nightwatchman of this Old Chapel, to be demolished soon.

After the service ended, everything happened rather quickly

inside Chaplain Thorne's office. The chaplain thanked him for his "much needed sacrificial service for the Lord." He would have to start as soon as the chapel was demolished to make way for the new one and he'd have to come every night. The chaplain shook the man's hands.

That evening, as the soon-to-be nightwatchman squatted in his thatched one room-kitchen, giving himself time to think about the events of the day, he realized—not completely accepting its implications, not fully burying his doubts deep-deep down—he hadn't been invited to sit down in the chaplain's office.

It wasn't entirely a new experience for Old Amongba. Even when his unequal legs bothered him enough to shift his weight every few seconds whenever he stood still, he was never offered a seat. But even so, he had assumed the chaplain's office would be different.

Maybe Chaplain Thorne was excited and he forgot, Old Amongba thought, as he stared at his plain rice and chutney. He swatted the air in front of him, whether to shoo away the fly that had snuck in through the holes of his thatched house or his creeping doubts, he did not know.

Old Amongba's unequal steps brought him down into the open space that would eventually become the main hall for the New Chapel. For now, it is Old and filled with the remnants of a sleeping construction site, imprisoned by skeletal scaffoldings above and around him. He'd been coming here every night for the past five years now, but always found the place a little different than how he had left it the night before. The pigeons and chapel mice were perhaps the only constants in this shifting darkness. They came out single file, like peas being squeezed out of a pod.

As always it was the male pigeon that came out first, strutting about with his wings stretched wide, his feathers glistening in the moonlight, a reflection of a reflection.

The male pigeon: *I told you he couldn't stay away. Didn't I tell you? I told you.*

The chapel mice: (singing) *Yes. Yes. Yes, you did!*

The thirty or so chapelmice sang in unison. Old Amongba felt they couldn't communicate individually even if they wanted to. As they sang, they tried their best to mimic the sounds of the choir boys, but they just couldn't figure out how to split their parts into altos and tenors and basses.

The female pigeon: *Stop pestering him won't you? I hope you had a great day, sweetie.*

As far as Old Amongba could remember, the female pigeon's feathers were always fraying and greying along the tips, almost dying but never quite dead. *You wait and see,* she'd say, *I'll sprout new feathers one of these days and fly right up outta here.* Her voice was like a mother's homemade soup, boiled and sweetened with care, served with tenderness.

The nightwatchman: (sighing) *Not too good, to be perfectly honest, I'm always so tired and grumpy. Nobody wants to talk to me.*

The male pigeon: (laughing) *ohOHo! Anyway, listen to me. Heard your aunt's sick? I say, use it to your advantage. Ask for some money. You've been working here for what? One thousand something days now, and you still don't get paid? Volunteering, they call it HohoH!*

The chapel mice: (singing) *What fine advice! Such fine advice!*

A voice, perhaps of an as-yet-uninitiated mouse, squeaked a note longer than the rest. This made the rest of the chapel mice laugh accommodatingly.

The female pigeon: *Well, there are good days and bad, just hang in there, all right, sweetie? You're doing great!*

The nightwatchman: *I appreciate that. I really do.*

The male pigeon: *Stop being a dumbass, you old fart. And ask for some money.*

The chapel mice: (singing) *Very tru—*

The nightwatchman: *If I hear another word from you two, I swear!*

The male pigeon: ...

The chapel mice: ...

The female pigeon: (with concern) *Sweetie, are your legs still giving you trouble while walking these days?*

The nightwatchman: *Yeah, but it isn't unbearable.*

Later, he would hear the familiar chatter of the Mallory Thorne students sneaking inside their dorms from their night out partying wherever. The echoes of a new day. The mice and pigeons would meld into the dwindling darkness, and the nightwatchman would flop down toward that ever-elusive sleep that would hopefully come during the day.

The chaplain's office, which had temporarily been relocated to a nearby building, was a little bigger than the night-watchman's rented thatch house. Once the New Chapel was completed, he would move into an even larger one, to accept appointments from the many high-profile members of his congregation. The chaplain's desk covered a large part of the room, behind which he sat in his padded chair, looking at some documents, as if unaware of the nightwatchman standing in front of him. A wooden cross loomed behind the chaplain, under the wings of which hung two framed pictures: of himself to the right and his family portrait to the left.

"Ahmhmm," the chaplain cleared his throat, finally looking up. Despite his age, his face was a fair one, wrinkleless.

"How's the work coming along?"

"Good, Chaplain Thorne."

As he stood there, the nightwatchman looked around, only now noticing how large the office actually was. Right in front of the chaplain's desk—four padded chairs. Earlier he had noticed five more plastic chairs glued to the wall, which were now behind him, as he stood there in front of the chaplain's desk, beside the four padded chairs, chair-less.

"Anything new to report? Disturbances at night?"

"I'm not disturbed."

"Good. You know this already but, uh, report directly to me if any problems come up, yeah? Hope you don't get lonely there at night?" He smiled. "But then again, pigeons and mice are good company, no?"

The nightwatchman's eyes darted around like a bee bumbling behind just cleaned glass.

"Hahah, only kidding of course, only kidding." The chaplain let out a satisfied sigh. "Okay, then."

Over the five years he had volunteered here, the nightwatchman had come to understand the chaplain's *Okay, then* as his cue to leave. But he lingered that day, shifting his weight, left-leg, right-leg, left-leg... Standing still always hurt a little bit more than walking.

"Is there something else?" The chaplain looked down to face his documents again, as if looking up was an exercise he was too tired to complete.

"Y-yes chaplain, I was thinking—could I be able to take a short leave...next week? My aunt. She's not feeling too well..."

The chaplain looked up then, at the nightwatchman, whose face was starting to get as jittery as his legs.

"And you're telling me this now?"

"Sorry, Chaplain."

"How do you expect me to find a replacement within three days?"

"..."

"No. Look, I'm sure you have some family looking after her. Okay then?"

"H-how about, if I find you a replacement myself? For the time I'm gone? I promise I'll come back soon. Please—"

"I'd have to interview them first. And I have so much work already. Besides, I can't just hire anybody off the streets. This is church business, after all. I'm sure you understand."

"Yes b—"

The chaplain had a smile on his face. And as much as the nightwatchman wanted to tell the chaplain to *fuck off I'm gonna do whatever I want*, he couldn't make his vocal cords vibrate to the rhythm of that profanity. It was like he was a primary school student all over again, cowering in the presence of an overly strict principal. And so he looked down. Nod nod nod.

"Good. Oh, and nightwatchman, please inform me in advance if any such problems arise in the future, yeah? Okay, then." The chaplain smiled.

The sounds of midnight pulsed inside the dome of the unfinished New Chapel. Crickets creaked and bats sliced the air with their mocking cries, making the youngest children of Mallory Thorne cower underneath their warm blankets. Inside, the nightwatchman thought about the long night ahead.

The orange bulbs in front of him flickered like a babbling brook while the male pigeon once again entered center stage, flashing his recently preened feathers. He fluttered about, naked but for a rosary round his neck.

The male pigeon: *You know you want to take my advice.*

The chapel mice: (singing) *You want to! You want to!*

As they sang this, the chapel mice moved their bodies in sync, like overly excited children following the steps of their Sunday school teacher in front of them.

The female pigeon: (with concern) *You look troubled, sweetie, what's wrong?*

The nightwatchman: *I've decided to stop volunteering here.*

The male pigeon: *OhoHo! Stop volunteering, he says. Like hell you will.*

The chapel mice: (singing) *Like hell, like hell.*

The female pigeon: *Have you really thought this through, sweetie?* *It's your choice of course, but I wouldn't want you to regret it. Not when it's too late. I also want my feathers to sprout again, but not at the wrong time, you know?*

The nightwatchman: *Thank you. But I really have thought about it, for five years. This isn't the right place for me. Besides, my aunt needs me right now. And I can't stand another minute of this staying awake at night business.*

The male pigeon: *Nonsense, you can't just leave! Take my advice, I've been telling you. Ask for some money from the chaplain. A clever fellow, that chap—ahemhmm...but yes, money, money, ask for it.*

The chapel mice: (nervously, voices no longer together) *Yes, yes, ask for it, ask for it.*

The female pigeon: *I hope it works out for you, sweetie.*

The female pigeon's metamorphosis, when it finally happened, felt like the fulfillment of a long foretold prophecy. Her old feathers fell off like leaves in senescence, only to be replaced by green-violet plumes blooming out from within her pigeon skin. For someone who had been perpetually roosting in the scaffoldings the last five years, she looked quite natural in flight as she hovered above them all.

The nightwatchman: (smiles) *Thank you, for everything.* [Exit]

The male pigeon: (voice cracking gradually) *Yo! What the fuck are you saying? You can't just leave! Hey, get back here right now! Don't you walk away from me—*

The chapel mice: (shouting) *No! Please don't leave we can't survi—*

Chaplain Julius Thomas Thorne was sitting on his veranda drinking freshly ground coffee when he heard the *knock-knock-knock*. It was the most perfect series of knocks he had ever heard in his life. He took his time to rise from his chair, but the knocks started sounding louder with each staccato, more urgent, hurry up.

knocK-KnocK-KNOCK.

"Coming," he said, getting a little irritated by the self-importance of it all. Who was in such a hurry at five in the morning?

Whoever he had expected, the chaplain was not prepared to find the nightwatchman standing there, with his unequal legs perfectly poised on the slowly elevating steps of his front door, giving off the impression that he never did slump to the right whenever he stood on level ground.

"Oh! What is it, nightwatchman?"

"I need to speak with you."

"Couldn't this wait until later, in the office?"

"No, it can't. Can I come in?"

"I uh—yes, sure."

The nightwatchman had only ever stood outside the chaplain's house. It was an eerie experience to be inside it. He almost forgot the determination he had brought with him as he took in the sheer whiteness of it all. Marbles, tiles, whatever you called it, seemed to fill every corner of the kitchen.

The chaplain cleared his throat, "Ahmhmm."

"Uhh," the nightwatchman began, gathering himself. "I came to tell you that I've decided to stop volunteering."

Old Amongba pulled out a chair then, from under the chaplain's dining table. Its legs screeched from being dragged across the marble floor. He sat down in front of the standing chaplain and looked up at his face.

He had expected it to show surprise. Even anger would've been acceptable, but this was something else entirely. Panic, on the chaplain's face, looked absolutely out of place.

"Wh-what nonsense is this?"

"I'm quitting."

"But—didn't I tell you to inform me beforehand, before you decide to make decisions like these? Seriously! What's gotten into you lately?"

"I've already made my decision."

He had been ignoring it for a while, but the longer he sat on the chaplain's dining table chair, the more his legs were starting to ache. He tried shifting his weight, left butt-cheek, right butt-cheek, but it just didn't feel quite right. Moving his feet around didn't seem to help either. Unable to bear it any longer, he got up and stood there again in front of the chaplain, with his unequal legs tilting him a bit to the right.

"No."

"W-what?"

The chaplain's face changed from its unusual panic to its usual smile. Calm. Everything in its rightful place.

"No. You will not leave. You made a commitment before me and before God to serve this chapel till it is completed. I don't know how you can allow yourself to go through with this. Doesn't it fall heavy on your conscience?"

"It's not like tha—"

"The word of the Lord tells us it is better not to vow than to vow and not fulfill it. Why did you make that commitment if you weren't ready to commit?"

"I-umm—well, my aunt's not feeling too well—"

"So that's what you want?"

"Huh?"

"All right, I'll have a meeting with the Board members today and discuss about giving you some money. Fifteen thousand should be sufficient I hope?"

When he'd come in that morning, Old Amongba was definitely sure about wanting to stop volunteering. He had knocked on the chaplain's door with that determination steeped inside his knuckles. He looked down at his calloused hands then, hardened from working in the fields of Longkhüm. He remembered how he had made the decision to come to Mallory Thorne because he wanted to get away from his rut and make a better life for himself in the city, perhaps find himself a wife and start a family of his own. But he never really got to talk with anybody else other than the chaplain, and some days, it felt like he and the chaplain were the only two human beings in the world.

"O-okay," he said, extending his craggy hand to meet the chaplain's fair one. Shake, shake. "Thank you, Chaplain Thorne."

"You're very welcome. Okay, then."

"Uhhmm," Old Amongba cleared his throat, suddenly feeling very out of place inside the chaplain's pristine kitchen. "I better get going, chaplain."

"Would you like some coffee before you go?"

"No, no, chaplain, please don't bother. I don't drink kah-py." He in fact had on occasion thought about trying coffee but never got around to indulging.

"Okay then," the chaplain said, as he ushered him to the door.

"Oh, and one more thing," the chaplain continued, as he stood inside his house, holding the door open for his employee. "I welcome everyone into our home you know, as the Lord wills. But there are certain ways of doing these things, yeah? My wife's a light sleeper, so morning visits are quite difficult to work around. I'm sure you understand."

He meant it to sound like light banter, everyday happenings shared between two civil neighbors. But his employee flinched under the cadence of his voice. And that smile. It wasn't that it was crooked, or sinister. It was genial, rather. Perfect. A little too perfect, as if any mistakes that happened to poke out would be trimmed the second it was spotted.

"Yes-s. Sorry,chaplain."

"No, no, please don't apologize." The chaplain smiled.

He plodded out of the chaplain's house, dragging forward his thoughts and legs, not entirely exhilarated about his work ahead.

I can always leave whenever I want. Whenever I want. Leave.
I can always leave.
Leave. Whenever I want.
Leave.

As these thoughts swirled and tossed themselves inside him, the early morning light continued to stretch its arms toward the vast grounds of Mallory Thorne and the semi-completed spires of the New Chapel. Slowly, his stunted steps carried him toward the shadows of the day. This was no time for a nightwatchman to be awake.

THE SAINTS OF STAINED GLASS

L CHAN

It was still. 3 a.m. still. That time when the only movement was the desperate rush of prey, or the sudden burst of the predator. It was 3 a.m. silent. That time when the only sound was the death of something small and furry. The silver moon above gave the old buildings of Mallory Thorne's sprawling grounds a flat, two-dimensional look.

There was a sound, coming from the small chapel at the back of the school grounds, its walls overrun with creeping vines, the stone pocked from wind and hail. There was a sound, and it was a voice clear and pure as a crystal bell. There was a sound, and it was a hymn, familiar and yet not.

There was movement, not the desperate rush of prey, perhaps more predatory. Between the frames of green there stood a series of stained-glass windows, each depicting the martyrdom of a saint, each bloodier than the last. Bodies were flayed, peeled, impaled, and eviscerated, all rendered in pieces of colored glass. As the moonlight hit the windows, the colors seemed to flow, the fragmented glass seemed to shift, and the figures danced along with them.

And then the song ceased, and the world was again still.

Jiahui sat down in the Conservatory practice room. The heating was off, and the cold from outside had seeped in, deep into the floorboards, their termite-ridden hardwood pocked with old knotholes and scarred from dragged furniture. Someone had left a window open, and she could see puffs of her breath in front of her. She was alone, a situation that she preferred and mostly found herself in. Mallory Thorne was not unwelcoming, not even for Third Year, international transfers. Her teachers had been accommodating, her classmates, kind. Jiahui was simply late to the dance. The thousand and first piece of the jigsaw, looking the same as the others but mysteriously with no way to fit in.

The silent practice room had an expectant air. It wore the quiet uncomfortably; its corners seemed too distant, its music stands too lonely. Jiahui called up the video she wanted. The latest single from POWER played. Though it had only been released a week ago, Jiahui already knew the words by heart, each choreographed step of Paensi, Olivia, Wyn, and Eun Har. It was, after all, her only escape. With the familiar things she brought from home rendered alien, and the things in Mallory Thorne being foreign to her, music was her only unchanging constant.

Jiahui panted, a puff of steam clouding the cold air and disappearing. It wasn't enough, not yet. POWER's newest single was due out in two weeks. There'd be a contest as usual; a swag bag each to the top ten fan videos submitted to their hashtag. All Jiahui needed was a partner. The choir was full—they were only taking First Years now. She considered contacting her friends from home, but they were eight hours ahead, getting on with their lives, while she just haunted them on social media, a girl out in the cold with her face pressed to the glass.

When she hit the lights, the room was bathed in moonlight. Shadows winked into existence along the floor, seemingly reaching out to her from the window. All edges became sharp and still, a flat tableau. And in that stillness, a voice, clear as a bell, echoed from across the courtyard. That was the sound Jiahui needed.

Mallory Thorne breathed at night, in the distant puffs of steam of her ancient boilers, piping hot water through the pipes and arteries of the building, which groaned and hissed in the cold. The moon glinted off a scattering of snowflakes. Jiahui recognized the tune; she'd attended a mission school back in Singapore, where a weekly service was compulsory for all the young students. She vaguely remembered that Mallory Thorne had a chapel from her orientation tour. Apparently, there were regular services and the school and the chapel had its own priest, but Jiahui did not know a single student that worshipped there.

The chapel was a creature of roughhewn stone bricks, almost silver in the snow and moonlight. Its bell tower was now dwarfed by the more modern buildings surrounding it. The singer within possessed a rich throaty alto, something comparable to Olivia's musical role in POWER. A voice that was just right if Jiahui needed a singing partner to film a video for the launch. All she needed to do was reach out to a stranger, at two in the morning, singing hymns familiar yet strange, in a church that hadn't seen use in all the time she'd been at the school. The soloist was a girl of Jiahui's age, flame-haired and fair-skinned, kneeling in front of the chapel altar in what seemed to be a regulation school uniform. As Jiahui pressed her face through the open doors, the reason for the juxtaposition of familiar and foreign became clear; while the tune was classic, the words were pure glossolalia, a mindless liturgy of nonsense syllables. Only when the door had opened enough did Jiahui see what was behind the altar, and it took her breath away. From chest height to the ceiling, the back wall of the chapel was dominated by stained glass windows, each a wonder in colored facets. It was only on closer examination that she found the depiction of the martyred saints to be far more detailed than she'd expected. The craftsmanship was exquisite. Their tortures were brutal and explicit; their bodies contorted in *extremis*. Through it all, they maintained beatific expressions: serene, almost expectant. The nighttime breeze squeezed through the gap and set the lights in the chapel swinging, casting shadows as they gyrated, making it seem like the figures were writhing in the glass.

Jiahui was unsure if it was the wind or her own weight against the door that caused that immense edifice, as firm and fragile as a childhood belief, to cease being a source of support and begin an accelerating inward swing. She stumbled, only catching herself with an outstretched palm that slapped the door with a report like a rifle shot. Against all expectations, the singing did not stop. The singer had turned to face Jiahui, her face twisted. The other girl's expression was hard to read only because Jiahui had never seen an expression of terror without screen or page as an intermediary.

"I'm sorry," said Jiahui. "The door was open."

The girl stopped singing, and the silence was very loud. "You can't be here," she said, not moving from her posture of supplication. Her voice, like her singing tone, was high and clear, the music lurking just beyond her speech.

"It's just that I heard you singing—it's beautiful. You should be in the choir or something." Jiahui was babbling now, her mouth jumping into gear before her mind could follow. The other girl grew more frantic.

"I need to finish the ceremony. They need to go back to sleep."

"Who? You know what, it's late. I should go." Jiahui made as though to leave, but her mind, already thrown off-balance by the strangeness of the situation, had already prioritized the worst possible actions. "I'm Jiahui, Fifth Year. Maybe I could look for you sometime in the week instead?" Of course, it was perfectly natural to introduce oneself to a stranger, in the hopes that they'd somehow acquiesce to star in a K-pop tribute video. Before the girl could answer, there was the tiniest of sounds, as tiny as a pebble preceding an avalanche.

They looked up.

A chip had fallen from one of the monstrous stained-glass windows. On her second look, the saints were even more disturbing— the crafter had taken liberties with flesh that no human body could survive. Bodies were contorted beyond breaking point, skin was flayed wholesale, viscera leaked through gaping holes. Jiahui found, with a shudder, that all their eyes were on her. When she took a step backward, they tracked her across the room. Jiahui would have screamed, but then the avalanche hit, and all the glass shattered. Beyond the broken and crumbling glass was only darkness. The night outside seemed to drink in all the light from the chapel, but the saints from the glass lingered in outline in the inky black, forms broken and incomplete, writhing bonelessly like things from deep in the sea. They rushed into the chapel, and then the lights went out.

Jiahui's family did not send her halfway across the world to miss class. Her roommate helpfully woke her; she'd only be tardy but not miss her first class. Other students sometimes missed the first or second classes. Not international students like Jiahui. She couldn't afford to be written up, not even if all the devils of Hell were upon her. Not even if she'd lain in bed, in a cold sweat, listening to the gentle snoring of her roommate, thinking of that last moment when the windows had stared down imperiously at her before they shattered.

Her window seat was uncharacteristically cold that morning, and she shivered under her regulation jacket. She did not take notes for the morning's classes; even the marginalia of POWER logos went without progress. It had been late; she had been tired. Perhaps the freezing temperature had addled her brain, the tiredness had caused her to see and hear things. The classroom windows were nearly opaque with the snowfall outside. She could barely see through the flurries to the dormitories, let alone the conservatory and sports facilities.

And the chapel.

That sublime voice, the nonsense hymns. The stained-glass windows that were grotesquely, impossibly, alive. She'd left the other girl behind in the dark when she fled. There was an email waiting for her in the morning announcing that the entirety of the chapel was out of bounds because of an accident attributed to high winds. Were they investigating? Was Jiahui in trouble? She hadn't touched the windows at all. And there was the other girl. Jiahui had never seen her before. Maybe she was from another grade. Jiahui shivered, not just from the cold, although the windows in the school provided scant protection from the flurries outside. Her sigh puffed from her lips and coalesced against the freezing glass, the condensation crystalizing into fractal branches, fingering out, meandering across the windowpane. Those tiny fingers of ice did not pursue a random walk across the glass; the lines split, converged, and traced something familiar to Jiahui. A face, twisted in a rictus that could have been ecstasy or agony, or both, sketched out in thin lines over glass, looked back at her. One of those from last night, and the dance of snowflakes behind it gave it a ghastly liveliness. Jiahui lifted her arm to erase the offending frost, except the corners of the thing's mouth turned up slightly at her approach, baring teeth in what could have been called a smile.

The clatter of her chair drowned out Mr. Silas's mathematics lesson. He insisted on scrawling his equations on a whiteboard, even though he provided the regulation PowerPoint handouts. The cacophony turned an integral equation into a quadratic graph. He cleared his throat loudly.

"Is something the matter, Ms. Li?"

Near ground zero, students had subtly inched away from Jiahui. If any of them could see the visage in the window, even now gnashing its teeth and raking the glass with its nails, they gave no sign. "Bathroom," Jiahui managed. "I need to go, now."

Mr. Silas sniffed. Jiahui was neither a lazy genius nor a disruptive joker, always in the top quarter of the class. Perhaps even this commotion could be overlooked. Even while meeting her teacher's gaze, her peripheral vision registered movement out of the corner of her eye, something high and keening on the edge of her hearing, like knives on glass. She leaned away from the window. The teacher nodded, and Jiahui fled, chased by the curious stares of her classmates.

Snow buffeted the windows along the corridor. Mallory Thorne believed in natural lighting. Jiahui stole a glance at the window, to the static screen fuzz of the raging snow and, in a bout of apophenia, thought she saw staring eyes, gaping mouths. But not faces. Like the frost, like the stained glass, these were broken somehow, all sharp corners and fragments. Her steps quickened. Again she heard the maddening tapping of something trying to get in, like fingernails on glass. Then she was at a trot, keeping her gaze resolutely forward, forward, forward. Until they came to rest on the regulation shoes and skirt of a girl down the hallway, the two items of clothing joined by shins so pale as to be nearly luminous.

It was the girl from the chapel. Staring down at her. In the daylight, the girl had a mass of red curls framing her freckle-dusted face, her uniform maybe a size too large, blazer hanging from bony shoulders. One of the windows between them was broken, shards of glass scattered on the ground. Except the shards weren't scattered at random, like the frost, they'd come to rest in an orientation that had lines and shapes Jiahui recognized. The mere fact of the fractured glass resting in the precise image of one of the tortured saints was not the only thing that was wrong, or even the worst thing. The worst thing was that the air above the glass on the ground was itself distorted, faceted like broken glass; a creature sketched out, not in flesh and skin, but in lines of twisted light. It raised its head, and Jiahui knew it was looking at her, and its face would be one of those tortured things in the glass from the night before.

Jiahui did not wait, she bolted. From behind her, she could hear the scrabble of something that very much sounded like nails on the hardwood floor. Whatever came through the stained glass, through the snow, through the window, and was now chasing after her might have had the form of a person, but it ran with a four-legged lope. She wouldn't make it back to the classroom; the thing was too close. The first door within reach was the toilet. She pulled a waste bin in front of the door, an ineffectual gesture but better than nothing. Backing away, she considered her options. The windows were open a crack for ventilation, giving the bathroom a hint of the chill from outside, but it was too small, even for her slight frame. The stalls would offer little protection. Her backward pacing had brought her hip in contact with the sink when the smallest of noises caught her attention. A tiny sharp sound. The window had been open. Just like the classroom, just like the one outside. Jiahui saw the network of cracks in the mirror, before something reached out, grabbed her by the hair and pulled her head into the glass.

Jiahui winced, but she could scarcely move with Nurse Fairweather's fingers on her chin. The nurse was a solid mass of muscle, her tight white uniform looking like it had been painted on. At times, Jiahui thought that she could hear the fabric creaking under the strain of containing the nurse's brawn. The medical office was sparsely decorated. There was a framed medal mounted on velvet, a series of pictures of Nurse Fairweather in combat fatigues, her face smoother and with less care in her eyes.

"All done," declared Fairweather, standing up and rubbing her temple, brushing her long blond fringe across her forehead, across the shaven sides of her head. "Now we need to have a little talk about why I'm gluing all these cuts together on your pretty little head, Miss Li."

Jiahui had already considered explaining that she had been pursued by things that lived in mirrors and glass, but found it simpler to say that she had slipped on a wet floor and caught her head on the mirror. Nurse Fairweather had ice blue eyes, and a thick accent that Jiahui now recognized as being from the north of England. The nurse snorted and typed something into a form, making a show of shutting down her computer and facing Jiahui again.

"We don't have a bullying problem here at Mallory Thorne, official or not. I intend to keep it that way. So, tell me again how this happened."

"I've already said, I slipped and fell," Jiahui insisted, never the best of liars but determined to see this through.

"By accident?" the nurse asked, her tone measured and disbelieving.

Jiahui nodded, slowly, trying to keep her expression steady. Nurse Fairweather's brow furrowed, and she sighed. "This school is one of the old places," she said, and there was a reverence in the way she said it, like it was a place of worship. Jiahui thought back to the chapel and shivered. "Funny things happen in old places. They don't obey the same rules we're used to."

"What things?" asked Jiahui.

Fairweather didn't answer. Standing up with a grunt, she touched the photograph of her younger self. "Used to be a medic.

Two tours. Funny thing is, that's exactly what the Thornes asked from the hiring agency. Combat experience."

Jiahui wanted to come clean to the nurse, but who could the friendless international student trust? She would do what she always did, which was to keep her head down and survive. Nothing made her special, nothing made her stand out. Even to whatever those things were.

"Not much of a talker, are you? Mallory Thorne is dangerous, but so's the world out there. If you can survive here, you can survive anywhere. One more word of advice: just because old places don't follow the rules of the world doesn't mean there aren't any rules. You just need to learn what they are."

Nurse Fairweather had known something—perhaps not the details, but she clearly suspected. At least the nurse had given her the rest of the day off from class. Jiahui would have to go through the video lectures on her own time. The pain in her scalp had faded to a dull throb. The dormitories were more modern than the classrooms, and the windows were double glazed and far away. She dared not look at them; even with her eyes on the ground, she found the light through the windows cast strange lines on the carpet.

Old places, the nurse had said. Mallory Thorne had its whispers of ghosts and worse, urban legends and tales the seniors made up to scare juniors. That was the way of the world, not things that hid in the snow and the glass and tried to pull her head through a mirror. Jiahui couldn't tell the nurse. Her roommate was barely there. They took to each other like a pair of unfamiliar cats in a confined space. Her family was eight hours' time shifted and half the world away. Jiahui was alone in the most populated spot of land in this part of the county. Except, it seemed, in her own room, where the girl from the chapel was staring at one of the posters on Jiahui's side of the room.

She turned to face Jiahui. A gasp squeaked from Jiahui's throat. Whatever had accosted her had gotten the other girl twofold. A small part of her brain, the part that recalled odd trivia during serious conversations and made puns at project meetings, helpfully highlighted the similarities between the plasters on the other girl's arms and the posters on the wall.

"Looking forward to the new album?" asked the girl.

Saturday. Saturday. Album launch, Jiahui thought. But more importantly—

"I don't think POWER's album is the issue now," Jiahui said. "How'd you get in here?"

The other girl dangled a keyring from a finger; Jiahui saw a dozen keys that looked like hers.

"Master key. Your next question is: why does a student have a set of keys? The answer is: I'm not a student."

Jiahui kicked off her shoes at the door and arranged them in a row with her other footwear. She glared at the visitor until the girl's shoes joined Jiahui's by the door. "You've still got a uniform," Jiahui observed.

"My Da is the groundskeeper here. I go to school in the village." After a short pause, she added, "When I can. Uniform helps me get about easier. I'm Charlotte, by the way, but everyone calls me Lotty."

Jiahui dumped her bag on the floor and sat on her bed. "I'm Jiahui," she said in return.

Lotty scooted over back to Jiahui's study chair and hitched her legs up to sit cross legged. "I'm impressed you've even got some of their work before they went viral." Jiahui raised an eyebrow. "You left the playlist on," said Lotty. POWER had a circuitous route to fame, casualties of one of South Korea's many grueling singing reality shows, each a dropout until one of their impromptu practice sessions went viral, taking the mismatched group with it.

"A fan?" ventured Jiahui.

"You could say that."

"Last night you were in the chapel. Something was there with you."

"Some *things*," corrected Lotty. "Look I'm in enough trouble as it is, with the saints getting loose and all. I can't catch them and babysit you at the same time."

"You don't look like you're doing too well yourself," said Jiahui, gesturing at the inexpertly applied plasters. "Did you call them saints?"

"Just something my Da calls them. He said once that they were the things that didn't fit, called them leftovers from creation." Lotty leaned forward, her tone conspiratorial. "Just part of the job, he said, sing the saints to sleep every night."

"The hymns? You've got a great voice."

"Something about the harmonies forces them out."

"And you're in my room telling me all this why?"

Lotty had the decency to look affronted, as though sneaking into the room of a student was the worst of her transgressions. Her tone grew urgent. "Da isn't in town. Business back home. This isn't the first time I've been left in charge, but this is the first time they've gotten out. The school is a dangerous place for everyone, but they tune into folk like them. People that don't fit in. People like…"

"Us," Jiahui finished.

"They'll be hunting, but they can't go much farther than the school grounds."

"Wait, did you say hunting?"

"Way my Da tells it, there isn't a reason for the saints, they just are. They're not really all here. Out of tune with the world, is how it was explained to me. But they want to be here."

Jiahui flinched, thinking of the thing that grabbed her through the mirror. "You mean they want to eat us?"

"I don't think we have words to describe what they'll do. Eating is probably an understatement. Anyway, I can't trap them back in the chapel if you're around. It's safer if you get out of here for a couple of days. Nurse Fairweather will write you up a note to excuse you from class; we'll say you went to town for a medical checkup and had to stay until the weekend."

"Fairweather's in on this, too?" Jiahui asked. "Just what on earth is going on in this school?"

"Come on J, every school has secrets. Normally it's just teachers having affairs and fights. It's just that this one's a little more dangerous." Lotty stood up, and as she smoothed down her skirt, she winced. Jiahui caught a glimpse of Nurse Fairweather's neat handiwork. Lotty seemed to have gotten the worst of it between the two of them. A day ago, Jiahui had been an unhappy international student in a school with gorgeous gothic architecture. Twenty-four hours and...well, same really, except demons were trying to come through windows and mirrors, because out of several hundred messed up kids in a school in the middle of nowhere, they'd chosen her to pick on.

Lotty had slunk over to the door in Jiahui's moment of introspection and was putting her shoes on. "Cover all the glass," she said. "Fairweather works late; just be ready to go." Lotty turned to leave the room, but not before Jiahui noticed the nearly imperceptible catch in her step as the other girl limped out. Jiahui turned the music up and waited.

Nurse Fairweather was at her door, five minutes past ten. She loomed in Jiahui's doorway, dressed in tight biking leathers that seemed to creak at the strain containing her bodybuilder's physique. A pair of motorcycle helmets dangled from one gloved hand. "Looks like you weren't honest with me earlier. Can't blame you, if Connor is involved. Oh, Charlotte's father. He called me earlier. He's on his way back here, but he won't be in till tomorrow night — that's if he can get the train. You all packed? Good, we'll talk along the way."

Jiahui locked the door behind her, leaving a note for her roommate. She kept her head down, not looking at the windows she walked by. "What favor did Lotty's dad ask you for?" The night chill seared the inside of Jiahui's nose as they left the dormitories. The sky was clear, and the afternoon's snow had settled, reflecting moonlight onto the walls of Mallory Thorne and leeching the color from the ancient buildings. The pair was alone; other students found it better to hole up sipping hot drinks than be out on a night like this.

"You know," said Fairweather, walking along the frozen pavement as though tramping across a warzone, "they hired me for three reasons. One, I can follow orders. Two, I can stick an IV line into someone under machine gun fire. And three, I can keep a secret. But the best way to keep a secret is not to know it at all."

"But you're telling a lie," probed Jiahui, struggling to keep up with the older woman.

"Just following orders, luv," said the nurse. The snow had melted down and frozen into a sheet of ice over the pavement, but Fairweather took her steps, confident as a snow leopard. Jiahui shuffled across the ice a little more like a penguin, taking small steps and shifting her weight carefully from foot to foot. The ice cracked with a snap. Jiahui kept on moving forward except there was another crack of the ice behind her, and then another. When she turned behind to look, the ice had fractured into shards in a shape that she recognized, something that looked a lot like a flayed figure, spread out on the ground like some sort of lizard. With another crack, the figure seemed to ride the propagating fissures in the thin ice, crawling toward her. She gave a squeak and instincts kicked in, but when her legs tensed to spring away from the approaching creature, the ice took her feet out from under her. The cold of the ground numbed her palms and legs where she hit it. Every time she scrabbled for purchase, the frosty ground snatched it from her. There was a moment where she strained to hear the ice breaking, but all she heard was Fairweather rushing toward her.

There was no need for the ice to crack any further, because the thing was already under her. It was then that something that felt sharp and smooth took her hand and pulled her down toward the ice. The next thing she felt was Nurse Fairweather pulling her up and propelling her along, off the path and through the thin snow so that she could find purchase. They said nothing until they were both in the parking lot; Jiahui bent over double and wheezing, Fairweather breathing evenly but heavily. She efficiently examined both Jiahui's wrists and proclaimed her fit for travel. Jiahui gaped. "Didn't you see that?" she asked.

"Luv, I've seen things in this school that I'm still wrapping my head about. Mallory Thorne attracts strange things, but it has a way of working them out. I think that's what the school does; that's why I'm still here." She handed Jiahui a helmet and led her to a well-kept motorcycle, black and shiny as an insect carapace, with an antique sidecar beside it. "I've seen people wrestle with all manner of monsters, both inside and outside. Let me tell you something, those on the inside are always the more dangerous of the two. If you can't get over those, then what hope have you of beating the other kind?" With that, Fairweather handed Jiahui a helmet and started the motorcycle, the machine responding with a purr that Jiahui felt in her belly.

She thought of the time she'd spent at Mallory Thorne, and the girl in the chapel that limped out of her room, covered in cuts and stitches, to solve a problem they had both created.

Again with the stillness and the cold stone of the chapel—the walls gave no shelter since the windows were gone, shattered on the ground in a frozen kaleidoscope. Lotty's breath hung in the air in rapid puffs as she tried to recover. Jiahui could see that the things, the saints, were there with Lotty. Not pursuing, as they had the times Jiahui had seen them, but waiting, held in check somehow. Jiahui could finally examine them in their stillness. Vaguely humanoid, like the tortured portraits of the saints, they were near invisible; looking at them was like looking at a piece of space that had been fractured and shattered, and they were composed of fragments of clear glass that bent the light wrong. As she watched, the group of them turned their heads to peer at her. Though she could discern no eyes, she nevertheless felt the weight of their gazes.

"What are you doing here?" asked Lotty, hobbling up. At the last moment, she stumbled, and Jiahui caught her.

"Fairweather spoke to me," said Jiahui.

"I thought I told her to get you into town," said Lotty.

"Oh, she nearly did. She was a little annoyed when I told her to turn around." The saints were rousing again, growing more animated. Whatever it was that Lotty had done was starting to wear off. "She told me your father asked you to go as well."

Lotty shrugged. "Couldn't leave the mess I made."

"The mess we made," Jiahui corrected. "Are you going to do something about those things?" The saints started to move, in their many-jointed ways, the light passing through their transparent bodies and casting sharp shadows on the ground. In their shadows lay their truth: the shadows in the floor weren't edged and shattered like their owners, but bestial, roiling, and fluid. Lotty looked up at Jiahui and rolled her eyes. "Not in a fit state for that. Where's Fairweather?"

"Outside. I told her to keep the bike hot, just in case."

"Running's good. That's what my Da asked me to do."

"But you're here. Maybe I can help."

"Up to date on all the ancient choruses of subjugation, are you?"

Jiahui snorted. Lotty seemed to be exactly the type who, when face to face with death, would make an inopportune comment. "Don't make me regret coming back for you, I don't have to run faster than them, I just have to run faster than you."

Lotty leaned heavily on Jiahui's shoulder. The other girl's voice was unwavering, but there was a shiver in her arm, and Jiahui didn't think it was from the cold. "I think it isn't the hymns that we need. Why didn't the saints come for me in my room? They've come for me everywhere else."

"Maybe it was a shoe thing?"

Jiahui pressed her lips together, biting back a reply she didn't have the time for. "It's not the hymns specifically. I think it's the music." The saints were getting more restless. "You said it yourself, it's the harmonies right?"

"If you don't have the hymns, then what can we do?" asked Lotty. "We are not going to try and fight demons with K-pop music, J."

"Why not? Olivia composes, and she's formally trained. Besides, what's better than the music of a bunch of misfits who made good? If you have a better idea, I'm all ears. I might be able to hear you from the parking lot." Jiahui knew it to be true, that it would work. Perhaps Lotty was a traditionalist, but there were only two scared girls against half a dozen writhing creatures on the floor. Except, writhing was too smooth a word; they weren't just segmented in unnatural ways, their geometries incompatible with three dimensional space as they kept folding and extruding themselves, ouroboros-like, from a dozen orifices, until Jiahui had to tear her gaze away. She'd not sung in front of an audience or even another person since she'd been at Mallory Thorne. The time came, and she couldn't find the words. Lotty started humming a melody, an introduction. Something simple and catchy. Something that went viral and launched a different four girls into superstardom. Jiahui joined in.

The saints grew agitated, their gyrations frantic. They surged toward the pair, making sounds off the edge of hearing, like fingernails on glass. Jiahui faltered, missing a beat, and the creatures grew even more agitated. But Lotty grabbed her hand, and they recovered together. There was a second when Jiahui thought that it wasn't going to be enough, that she'd been wrong that any music would work the magic on these misshapen things, that they were too late. But against all hope the broken, many-jointed things began to subside, sinking lower and lower into themselves, and from there into the ground, slowly losing dimensionality until they were as thin as shadows, and then not even that.

Jiahui stopped singing, and the silence rushed back to fill the void. It took her a while to remember to breathe again.

This was where Jiahui believed that the story should have ended, not with Lotty's father coming back and hugging the girl tightly before absolutely chewing her out. Not with them having to regularly sing the saints to sleep every night.

And even with all that practice, they didn't place in the contest for POWER's single.

INNOCENT SINNER

MAY SELESTE

If Dania Dalal could wish for one thing, it was summer. A beautiful, long summer that would warm her skin and shower her with flowers.

Instead, she was blessed with a seemingly endless autumn chill, surrounded by nothing but death. Death, and decay. It was all Dania could think about as she stood in front of the towering iron gates. Who could blame her? As far as she could see, there was nothing but rot. Whether it be in the lifeless, withering trees that surrounded her, or the wisps of brown grass beneath her feet. No wonder the taxi stopped half a mile away. She coughed, reaching out a finger to press on the cold buzzer.

Buzz. Static.

Dania shivered in her green coat, waiting to be let in. Her skin stretched painfully across her knuckles as she clutched her suitcase tighter.

Static.

There was a rustle in the trees. She looked over her shoulder and peered into the wilting woods, but the grey skies meant it was far too dark to see into it—even though it was barely quarter past two.

Static.

She bounced on one leg. What was taking so long? Dania reached out to push the buzzer again when a voice called from the intercom.

"Hello?"

She nearly stumbled to answer, leaning in close to the speaker. "Hello? Hi, it's Dania. Dania Dalal? I'm here for the teaching placement?"

A few moments went past. Then a few more. Did it cut off?

"Hell—"

"Come in," the voice said, followed by a high-pitched *beep* and the whir of rusty mechanics beside her.

The gates painfully screeched open, slowly revealing the grand architecture of the Mallory Thorne School of Excellence. A wind blew through her, inviting her in. Though it wasn't a warm, comfortable invitation, but more so the beckon of a mortician. She coughed again and popped a lozenge before stepping onto the cobblestone grounds.

Mallory Thorne hadn't been her first choice. Originally, she'd been gunning for one of the private schools in the heart of the city— but with so few positions, the competition for graduate teaching assistant placements was so cutthroat she was lucky to even get notified of her rejections. She had anticipated this to some extent, though, and held her old school in her hometown as an option. It wasn't like she'd have any competition there. Who else would go for some unknown school in an equally unknown town in a small, forgotten corner of the country? However, what she didn't anticipate was that her old school had since closed down, and that the strange academy she'd only heard about through playground rumors would send an opportunity straight to her inbox. Rumors she would've believed, if she didn't know better.

Dead leaves crunched under her boots as the sound of her heels echoed around the empty courtyard. She passed the large statue of Lady Mallory Thorne and pulled her jacket tighter, trying to ignore how her eyes seemed to follow her every move, or how the closer she got to the building, the more it felt like the architecture closed in behind her.

She finally reached the reception, where a bored-looking woman sat behind perforated glass. The muffled clamor of children resonated in the distance as Dania loudly shuffled toward her, setting her bags down with a *thud*.

"Hi, it's Dania—from earlier?"

"Right," the receptionist said. "The student."

"Gradua—" Dania caught herself. "Teaching assistant. I've just graduated."

The woman stared at her, dead-eyed. "Congratulations," she said, maintaining her tired tone. "Do you have your confirmation with you?"

"I...I *did*," Dania stuttered. The truth was, she'd had the email— she'd *memorized* it. But when she'd looked for it that morning it was gone. "I must have deleted it by accident. But I have my ID in case you need to double check—"

The receptionist shook her head. "No confirmation, no entry. School policy."

Dania felt her cheeks grow warm. She wanted to say something, but an all too familiar itch in her throat turned her words into a loud, uncontrollable hacking, which she barely managed to stop in time to see a tall woman in a flowy white blouse and dark red pencil skirt approach her.

"You must be Miss Dalal," the woman said, reaching out her hand. "I'm Headmistress Thorne. So lovely to finally have you here."

Thorne? "Hi! Thank you so much for having me." Dania smiled as the Headmistress's cold rings pressed into her palm. "So sorry I'm late. I didn't realize how long the walk was."

"Oh, don't worry about it. The class where you'll be assisting is still going. Though, I'm afraid we won't have time to drop your bags off in your room first if you want to introduce yourself," she said, peering behind at the messy pile of bags around Dania's suitcase. "Perhaps we can leave them here for now, and have Edith watch them in the meantime?" She gestured toward the receptionist, who sneered at Dania in response.

Dania shivered. "No! It's okay, I can carry them with me."

"Nonsense! We can't have you doing that!"

"No really, it's no trouble at all—I packed pretty light anyway."

Thorne raised a perfectly shaped eyebrow. "Are you sure?"

"Of course, of course!" Dania nodded a little too enthusiastically. "Besides, it's just to class and back. It's not like we're trekking the Sahara."

Dania would've preferred the Sahara.

She heaved as she dragged her suitcase up the stairs, barely managing to hide her embarrassingly labored breathing.

"Are you sure you're okay?" the Headmistress said, a few steps above her. Her deep voice echoed down the winding stone staircase.

Just where was this classroom?

Dania took a deep breath, feeling the sweat bead up on her forehead. "I'm fine! A little cardio would do me some good after a long drive." Her lungs felt like they were on fire, and she couldn't help but let out a small cough.

"You have quite the cough. If you're ill, we can continue another time, if it suits you?"

"No! No, it's fine. I was just born with funny lungs, so I cough a lot. It's ultimately harmless though. Other than that—" She heaved one more time as she took her bags over the last step and onto the landing. "—I'm fit as a fiddle."

"That's good to hear." Thorne smiled and continued down a

long hallway.

Dania leaned against her suitcase and let out a short breath before catching up with the Headmistress.

"This is the west wing. It has everything you need; an infirmary, cafeteria, staff room—so you won't need to leave, and I suggest you don't."

"Why not?" Dania asked.

"Well, we wouldn't want your presence disrupting the other students. Besides, new teachers tend to get quite *lost* in our structures."

Lost? Dania just nodded. She was only here for a while, anyway, so there was no point exploring the entire grounds. She took in her surroundings as they walked. Like the steps, nearly the entire wing seemed to be made of stone.

It must be the original architecture.

Thorne stopped outside a room before leading Dania in. Rows of students dressed in deep red uniforms watched her with a shared blankness as she entered. All but one. Sitting in the back was a girl glaring hard enough to burn a hole through her. A hand clapped onto her shoulder.

"Class, this is Miss Dalal, the new teaching assistant. She will be helping alongside Mr. Garcia for the rest of the year, so be on your best behavior, okay?"

The room chimed with a "Yes, Headmistress Thorne." All except the angry girl, whose glare still bore into her. Dania broke eye contact, afraid that she would disintegrate if she continued.

A man in a brown jumper reached out and shook her hand. "Miss Dalal, great to have you here. I'm Mr. Garcia."

Dania was about to respond when the room abruptly turned on its head. Her skull hit the floor, and the world was reduced to a muffled blur. It was only when she regained her vision that time caught up, and sound rushed back.

The class was hysterical. A student, the angry girl, was on top of her brandishing what looked to be a compass. A compass which, if it weren't for the teachers holding the student back, would've been swiftly lodged into her left eyeball.

Mr. Garcia restrained the girl as Dania scooted as far back as she could go. She didn't even know when they'd come in, but people dressed in white scrubs entered the room and escorted the student out as she kicked and screamed.

"It's all your fault!"

Headmistress Thorne knelt in front of Dania, while Mr. Garcia tried to calm down the class.

"My goodness, are you all right?" she said, helping her up. "You didn't get hurt, did you?"

Dania was barely able to register her questions. Her legs shook as she unconsciously leaned on Thorne.

"Miss Dalal? Dania?"

"Hm? No, no, I don't think she got me. I'm fine."

"Thank God. I'm so sorry about that, I don't know what got into her."

"It's…it's fine, I'm sure she had her reasons." Dania pressed her lips into a thin, awkward smile.

The fuss died down, and the Headmistress personally escorted her to her room, stating she could take the remainder of the day to "rest up." Dania settled down onto her bed, ears ringing in the silence of her new quarters.

Unfortunately, Stephanie has always been a little bit…unstable. But she's a really good pupil otherwise. Could you look the other way just this once?

Dania replayed Thorne's words in her head as she stared up at the ceiling.

"Stephanie," she said into the emptiness of her room. So that was her name. *Poor kid.* But still, it was definitely one way to go about her first day.

She pulled out her phone, ready to relay the events to her

friends who, at that point, had already sent her a barrage of "How did it go?" texts. Dania sent her replies, wondering why it was taking a while, before noticing the one bar flashing on her screen before disappearing.

"Great," she grumbled. *No signal.* The school was in the middle of nowhere, after all.

She begrudgingly got out of bed and wandered around the room, awkwardly waving her phone in the air at random corners. She opened a door, leading her into a bathroom which she definitely had not known was there.

"Wow." Dania had never had her own bathroom before. You couldn't get an en suite in the city without completely draining your wallet threefold. She stopped herself before entering, almost on instinct. For some odd reason, she half expected her mother to waltz in and start scolding her. Dania let out a heavy sigh and trudged back to her suitcase, pulling out her designated "bathroom slippers" before continuing her exploration, leaving the bag wide open.

Immediately upon entering, she noticed the shiny mirror cabinet hanging over the sink. She pulled it open, trying her best not to leave any fingerprints. Inside was practically empty, save for a first aid kit and a small travel toothbrush set. Dania took it as a sign to properly start unpacking. She went back to her closed suitcase up against the wall. She pulled out her clothes and other items, stashing them in the wardrobe and drawers provided. She was organizing her toiletries in the mirror cabinet and had barely shut it before her heart leapt out of her chest.

Its glowing yellow eyes caught her first.

In the reflection behind her, stood a figure. It was completely grey-black, almost crumbling, with bright orange lines running through it like veins of fire. Dania gasped and spun around, facing nothing.

What?

A sensation rose in her throat, and she started violently hacking.

She grasped at her neck, trying to calm herself before she passed out, and stumbled toward her bottle. Cool water sloshed down her throat, soothing her as she knelt by the dresser. Dania glanced back at the bathroom, staring at where she'd seen the figure. The sun was setting; it must've been a shadow or a reflection. Most likely both. She was still probably in shock from earlier, so it was no surprise she was a little jumpy. Slowly, she got up. The Headmistress was right, she needed to get some rest.

Her first day as a teaching assistant went as normally as one would expect. Handed out a few sheets, answered a few questions, caught some rumors about an old reverend. Apparently, the title of "head teacher" was passed through the Thorne family. However, amongst all the chatter, not one person had even breathed a word about yesterday's events. You'd think a student attacking a teacher would make the school gossip headlines. Yet nothing. Mr. Garcia must've told them to stay quiet about it, at least when they were around her.

She got called in to oversee a science class—the usual teacher was off sick, and they asked her to act as a substitute. Dania agreed. Granted, she knew nothing about science, but it would be great on her resume if she got a whole class to herself. She let out a light cough before stepping into a classroom of chattering children.

"Ok, settle down now!" Dania set her books down on the desk at the front of the class as the children calmed. "I'm Miss Dalal. Miss Thomas is unwell today, so I'll be taking over." She had previously leafed through the instructions the last teacher had left her. The students were older, so they should be fine on their own. Yet, to her dismay, they were doing an experiment she knew nothing about.

Stay calm, they're school kids. They can probably smell fear.

"Titrations!" she said, hoping to God that she'd pronounced it right. "I assume you know the drill—gloves and goggles are in the box, lab coats are hanging at the back."

The students scrambled around, gathering what they needed. Of course, Dania tried her best, yet she still couldn't help but panic every time a student asked for help setting up their *burette*. Aside from that, Miss Thomas's binder was right. The kids seemed to know what they were doing. Besides, the Mallory Thorne School of Excellence demanded just that—excellence. And with exams this year, the students had no other choice but to buckle down and comply. Dania just had to spend the rest of the lesson making sure they didn't set fire to the blinds or whatever else could happen.

"Excuse me, Miss," a student said from behind.

Dania turned around with a matchbox in hand, lighting the student's Bunsen burner. She went to blow out the match, but couldn't. It wasn't for lack of effort, but she physically couldn't bring herself to snuff the flame. Instead, she watched as the fire danced above her fingertips. The clamor of the class all melted into one distant noise—it wasn't like they were paying attention to her anyway. The flame seemed to grow bigger, warmer. Gently caressing her skin and inviting her into its fiery embrace. She felt a tickle in her throat, yet that's where it stopped. Just a tickle. Dania couldn't hear the students anymore—just the crackle of the fire and the sound of the clock as it ticked away.

Tick, tick, tick.

The flame slowly made its way down the match, burning her fingers.

Dania gasped and dropped it, clearing her throat. It wasn't like her to zone out, even if it was for a few seconds. She was probably just a little tired. She looked around to see if any of the students noticed—but the room was empty. Where was everybody? The lights were out, and the tables were cleared with chairs stacked neatly on top of them. All that was left was the one match on the floor, its gentle string of smoke tickling her nose. Dania checked her watch.

6:00 p.m.

School was long over. It couldn't have been. It had been barely 1:00 in the afternoon a couple of minutes ago. But the sun had almost set, and there wasn't a student in sight. She must've not processed the rest of the day. That could happen sometimes. *Right?* Dania shook her head. It must've been that. She picked up the match and tossed it away before heading back.

Sleep had always been her one refuge. No matter how bad her day, at least she still had her sleep. Or at least, she thought she did.

A knock on the door woke Dania from her deep slumber. She pulled her duvet tighter, hoping it was a dream. But the rapid knocks came again and shattered her hopes. Dania grumbled, blinding herself as she checked the time on her phone. It was the middle of the night—what would anyone want now?

She slithered out of bed, shuffling to the door in her robe and slippers.

"Yes?" she said, opening the door.

The empty hallway greeted her.

Dania rubbed the sleep from her eyes and paused for a moment. Did they leave? She stuck her head out, looking down either side of the dark hallway. Still empty. Sleep had still taken over her mind, so much so that she couldn't bring herself to even try and make sense of the phantom knocks. All she could do was shrug it off. Dania turned to go back to bed when the glowing eyes and loud screech of a student, not even an inch away from her face, sent her stumbling back onto the floor.

The silence after was deafening. Her ears rang as she desperately looked around for the intruder. She was still sitting on the hard wood floor, not daring to move a muscle, trying to rationalize what she'd just seen. But the room was empty. She stood back up.

Sleep paralysis. She told herself. What other explanation could she give? With how tired she had been, it wasn't completely unbelievable. She had no choice *but* to believe it. She laid her head on her pillow once more and muttered those words to herself until she eventually fell asleep.

The events of the night before had not left Dania as she had hoped. Her attempts at logical rationalization had been futile. She didn't know why. It made perfect sense. But the moment she set foot down the stone halls of Mallory Thorne, doubt seeped in. Or not doubt—more so the feeling that something was watching. Like the very echoes of her heels were colluding with her long shadow behind her, whispering. Following.

She tried to push the thoughts from her mind while she did her job. Yet she couldn't stop her hands from shaking as she handed out worksheets to the class, while Mr. Garcia was teaching up front.

"Are you okay Miss?" one of the students, a sweet boy who rarely spoke, asked.

"Of course. Just a little tired."

She gave him a reassuring smile and turned to get a stapler. Yet when she turned back, her face became as white as the sheets she was handing out.

The students were gone. And in their place, charred, grey bodies. They had no eyes but instead, gaping holes of beaming yellow-orange that bore into her. Dania screamed and gripped the table behind her, banging it loudly against the wall. A familiar tickle rose in her throat, fully unleashing itself as Dania fell into another coughing fit.

"Miss Dalal?" Mr. Garcia's voice caught her attention. She snapped her head toward him, watching him rapidly approach. "Is everything all right?"

She turned, breathing deeply until the coughing went away.

"The kids, they—" She looked back at the students, only to find them normal, albeit confused, and in their seats.

"The kids are what?" Mr. Garcia asked.

At this point, what could she say?

"No, never mind. It's nothing," she babbled, fixing her hair and erratically looking around. The students were whispering about her, no doubt speculating all manners of things.

He gently placed a hand on her shoulder. "Why don't we visit Dr. Davis, hm? If you're not feeling well, he could help you with that."

Dania contemplated whether or not a school doctor would be able to help her. Though she herself didn't know what was wrong with her—whether she was going insane, or if Garcia was right and she was just ill.

"Fine, yeah. Let's…let's do that."

Mr. Garcia nodded, borrowing the teacher next door to watch his class while he was gone. He led her out of the classrooms. Dania went to turn into the next corridor, heading to the infirmary in the west wing when he stopped her.

"It's this way," Garcia said.

"Isn't it down here?" Dania pointed down the empty hallway.

"Ah, no. The infirmary in this wing is under renovation right now. Didn't they tell you that? We'll have to go to the one in the east."

She nodded and followed him. The journey to the east wing was longer than she expected. The way the school was structured, they had to go all the way around the courtyard. Dania had never been to the east wing of the school, at least not yet. Thorne had told her there was no need, and she was right. It didn't bother Dania much; from what she imagined they were all the same. And she was right, for the most part.

The hallways were bustling with students chattering and running between classes—maybe twice, even thrice the number of kids they had in the west.

"How come there's so many students here?" Dania asked, looking at the back of Garcia's head as they squeezed through the gaggle of kids.

"Younger years—always so many more of them," he said, without looking back.

The crowd thinned, and they reached the infirmary. Dr. Davis sat inside, almost as if he were expecting them. He greeted Mr. Garcia with such familiarity, she couldn't help but assume that they must be friends. The large white room was a stark difference to the gothic stonework of the rest of the school. Dania was almost afraid to leave a mark. Mr. Garcia explained the situation to the doctor, giving her a reassuring squeeze on the shoulder before returning to his class.

"New teacher?" he asked her.

"Hm? Oh. Yes, I am. Well, just an assistant," Dania said.

Davis nodded, running a hand through his neat black hair, which showed a few streaks of grey. "Makes sense. We see this a lot with new teachers. Just graduated, heading out for the first time. Brings on quite a bit of anxiety, doesn't it?"

Dania stuttered. "Well, I'm not sure about *that*. I mean, I'd say I'm a little nervous, but that's it."

He met her with a blank stare, not believing a word. "So I take it you're sleeping well? Eating well? No irregularities or hallucinations of any kind?"

Hallucinations.

Her eyes flickered at the word, which he caught. He raised an eyebrow, prompting her to speak. "How...did you know that?" she asked.

"Mr. Garcia, of course. Just now? When he caught me up on your situation."

"Well, I'm not sure he mentioned *hallucinations*—"

Davis cut her off. "He mentioned you babbling about 'the students' with some degree of distress. It's not hard to deduce the rest."

Dania remained silent. So it was true—she was going crazy.

And everybody knew it. Hardly an ideal way to start a new job.

"It's okay," Davis said, breaking the silence. "Like I said, I see this sort of thing all the time. Here."

He slid a bottle across the table. Dania picked it up and read the name, recognizing it as an anxiety medication of some sort. "These will have you feeling better," he said, standing up.

Dania stood, too. "Are you sure? How many should I take? For how long?"

He walked her to the door. "Just follow the instructions on the bottle, and if you have any bad reactions of any sort, come see me again. Okay?"

She was practically already out. "O-okay."

Dania was about to say something else when he gave her one last smile and shut the door. She was used to doctors speedily prescribing pills and pushing her aside for the next patient, but even by those standards—that was quick. She turned the bottle in her hands, heading back to the west wing.

After a few days, Dania returned to work. She didn't know how Dr. Davis could've figured it out so fast, but the pills he prescribed her worked. For days she hadn't had a single hallucination, and somehow, she was coughing less, too. How had no one figured this out before?

"Good morning!" she greeted Headmistress Thorne, who was walking by.

"Good morning! Someone's chipper," she said in her smooth voice.

Dania laughed. "Yeah. I don't know. I feel like I'm finally getting the hang of this place, you know?"

Thorne let out a light chuckle. "I'm glad. Enjoy the rest of your day."

She waved goodbye and headed to her class. For the first time since she arrived, the Mallory Thorne School had finally taken its claws out of her.

Oh, how she missed those claws.

A few weeks passed, and Dania was fast asleep when she heard a familiar knock on her bedroom door. She groaned and tossed, barely one eye open.

"Again?"

Unlike the last time however, a voice accompanied the knocks.

"Miss! Miss Dalal help!" the muffled voice of a child said from behind the door.

Dania's heart dropped. She jolted out of bed, nearly slipping as she flung the door open. One of the students—a young girl—stood in front of her, bouncing in distress.

"What's the matter?" she asked.

"Quick Miss, follow me!"

The girl took off into the darkness down the corridor. Dania quickly followed, her slippers slapping against the cold floor as she looked around for any other teachers who might have heard the commotion. Despite the adrenaline, she was still incredibly tired, finding herself barely able to keep her eyes open. Her vision blurred for a moment, and she lost the student in the darkness. Dania swiveled her head around, aimlessly wandering as she tried to find the girl.

"Hey, where did you go?" she called out, before someone grabbed her shoulder.

"Miss Dalal?" a voice, definitely not belonging to the student, said.

Dania blinked, trying to make out who she was talking to. It was another teacher—one Dania only knew by face.

She took a step back. "Oh, I'm so sorry, I didn't see you there."

"Miss Dalal, what are you doing?"

"Pardon?" For a moment, Dania forgot what exactly she *was* doing. "Oh right. A student…"

"A student?" The teacher looked at her like she was speaking a different language. "Miss Dalal, you were *sleepwalking*. I know you're not supposed to wake a sleepwalker, but you were muttering all kinds of things and talking to yourself. Plus you were headed right for the old infirmary—you could've gotten yourself hurt!"

Sleepwalking? But she was so sure. The knocks on the door and the girl's voice were as clear as day.

The teacher continued, walking her back to her room. "I heard you went to see Dr. Davis for help. Why don't you pay him another visit, hm?"

Perhaps she was right. Whatever he gave her last could've stopped working. She brought the idea up the next evening, as she sat in Dr. Davis's office after class. He sat on the other side of the desk, bored, and seemingly sick of her despite this being her second visit.

"So, you're sleepwalking now?"

"It was just once—last night," Dania said. She opened her mouth to speak again, to tell him about the strange feelings she'd been getting. How it felt like everywhere she went, someone was watching her. But something stopped her. Telling this man would be of no help. He completely caught that she'd had more to say, but did nothing. He did not care.

Davis upped her dosage and waved her away. Dania just rolled her eyes and headed to the door, walking past the other infirmary beds as she did. All of them were empty except one, which had the curtains drawn all the way around. She barely caught the end of a conversation coming from inside.

"—all in good time," a voice said. Dania stopped—that voice sounded familiar. It spoke again. "We can't let you out until I know you won't attack her again."

She moved slowly, trying to catch a peek at who was behind the curtain. Her suspicions on the owner of the voice were proved right when she caught the back of Headmistress Thorne, speaking down to none other than Stephanie—the student who'd attacked her on the first day. Dania slowly backed away, but her eyes caught Stephanie's, causing her to jolt back instead and scramble out of the infirmary, not stopping until she was back in the west wing.

There was nothing inherently odd about what she had seen. They'd told her that Stephanie was going to be treated. In fact, the idea that they wouldn't be letting her out until they were sure she wouldn't attack Dania again should've been something of a comfort. Should've. So why was the pit in her stomach, the one that she'd been ignoring from the moment she stepped foot onto the grounds, growing bigger?

She had to leave. She could get a job at an after school study club. She'd work as a private tutor. Dania didn't care. All she knew was that there was no other choice—she had to get out of there. Dania sped through the hallways of the teachers' dorms, almost hearing the paintings that lined the walls laugh at her as she took the coward's way out. She blocked her hands over her ears and slammed her door shut. Clothes, laptop, books—everything went in her suitcase in a chaotic heap. She strained trying to zip the creaking plastic shut, nearly pulling a muscle before she took a moment to breathe.

Okay, think. Imagine she left Mallory Thorne. What then? It was already pitch-black outside, the winter days getting shorter and shorter. There was no road. No cabs would come now, and like hell she'd go out into that forest of nothingness alone. What exactly was she afraid of? A kid? She could handle a kid. Headmistress Thorne, too. Maybe. She didn't know what was going on, but these were people. She could talk to them. Dania exhaled and fixed her hair, laughing at her own rashness. In the morning she'd tell Headmistress Thorne she was leaving, and hand in her notice. In the morning. Like a sane adult.

She put her suitcase by the door and got into bed, but she couldn't sleep. Instead, she watched out her window, just waiting for sunrise. Eventually sleep came, and she fell into a heavy slumber. Dania breathed gently under the blanket. Peaceful. Like nothing was ever wrong.

But her slumber was short-lived.

Dania's eyes flew open. That feeling was back. The feeling that something was watching her. She didn't dare move; she stared at her ceiling as if it would shield her from the reality that there was something *else* in that room. Something that didn't want her there. Slowly her gaze panned down, landing at a pair of eyes at the foot of her bed. She froze, barely letting out a strained gasp. Was it another hallucination? No. There was no yellow glow in the eyes, or cracking grey skin. The figure crouching at the end of her bed rose to stand. It was definitely a real human. A girl.

Stephanie.

Something long glinted in her hand, but Dania didn't dare break eye contact. Time stood still—neither of them moved. Dania slowly shifted her hands under the blanket, getting ready to launch herself at the door. But Stephanie caught the movement and lunged at her. Dania tumbled out of the way, just in time to see the crazed student jam her knife into the wall where Dania's head had just been. She scrambled to the door, fiddling with the handle. It was locked. Dania looked back. Stephanie stalked toward her, eyes blazing with fury.

"*It's all. Your. Fault.*" Malice laced the girl's every word as she came closer, slowly, savoring the moment.

Something clicked and the door unlocked. Dania had barely flung herself into the hallway before Stephanie pounced. Dania ran down the dark corridor barefoot, praying someone would hear the commotion and come out.

"Help!" she screamed. "*Help!*"

Mr. Garcia, Miss Thomas…anyone.

No one came. The entire teachers' hall was silent, save for Dania and Stephanie. Where was everybody? Stephanie ran toward her, letting out a feral cry. Dania kept running, spotting the open door of the out-of-order infirmary up ahead. She gave one final push and stumbled into the room, locking the door behind her.

She hunched over, heaving and trying to catch her breath—letting out a cough instead. She straightened back up, trying to come up with a plan. Was there a phone anywhere? Another exit? Dania tried looking around the infirmary, but rows of long sheets of plastic hung from the ceiling, covering the room.

Just what had happened here?

Her ears were ringing. Dania wandered through the sheets, looking around. The walls were stained black, as if they had been burned. And the longer she stayed in the room, the more she noticed the faint smell of smoke. The smell triggered her cough, causing her to hunch over as she hacked into her hand. There must've been a fire, and it must've been recent. It was then that she noticed the shadow.

Behind one of the sheets of plastic was an odd figure. The way the plastic was moving, it seemed like it, too, was swaying in the moonlight. Throat still sore, she headed toward it. Gently, she moved the sheets out of the way and approached the figure.

That was her final mistake.

The ringing got louder. Dania couldn't move. She couldn't speak. All she could do was stare in awesome horror and ignore the rising sensation in her lungs. In front of her was a twisted, mangled body, hanging. Its skin was charred and peeling away in some places; its limbs dangled awkwardly from strings attached to the ceiling. And its face. Its face struck her, so much so Dania took a step back. Because the face it wore was hers. It was her. Staring ahead, mouth hanging open and empty eyed on a half-intact head.

Dania clapped a hand over her mouth, gripping the table behind her for support. She could barely comprehend what she was seeing before her attention was taken, again, by what was *under* the corpse. A memorial of some sort. Flowers, cards, and teddy bears lined the table beneath its feet. Still shaking, Dania reached her hand out for one. She picked up the largest card, which seemed to be signed by an entire class. Her eyes darted around, reading the messages.

The students we lost will never be forgotten. - Thorne

Taken too soon. - Jacob

Dalal will rot in hell for her mistake. x Anna

I'll make it right, Mark. I promise. - Stephanie

Dania couldn't comprehend what was happening. She recognized these names. They were students in *her* class. Anna, Jacob, *Stephanie.* Come to think of it, where was she? The ringing got louder and louder—morphing into something else. Something she recognized. The ringing changed into a choir of screams that she knew all too well. The sensation in her lungs changed into a deep, sizzling burn that spread through her whole body. The smell of smoke choked her—she couldn't stop it anymore. Dania collapsed to her knees, feeling her lungs jolting as she violently coughed into the ground. Her veins were on fire, incinerating her body from the inside out. Searing her flesh. Through agonized screams she remembered what it was. Her sin.

"I'm sorry," Dania barely whispered her last words before her soul was finally set ablaze by an invisible flame, and she disappeared into the quiet night.

The birds chirped outside the window as Headmistress Thorne stood by, peering down at the clumsy stranger in the green coat outside the gates. Of course, it was no real stranger. Thorne knew exactly who she was—the entire west wing did. The same face they never got sick of seeing—no matter how many times they watched her burn.

DEDICATION

MARY ZAMBALES

"Desiree Aquino."

The loudspeaker boomed my name, making me jump out of the bottom of the stairwell I was sitting on. The choir room was locked during auditions, so I had to wait outside. Despite getting startled, I welcomed the announcement. It was much better than trying and failing to shut out everything leading up to this moment: catching Ethan Harrison, my now-ex, cheating on me with my roommate; the viral video of me slapping aforementioned ex; the rumors that I only had this audition because of that video; and, most importantly, the rumors about the auditioners themselves.

They were called The Sirens, the elite chamber choir. I was already part of the greater Mallory Thorne Chorus, but if you were a member of The Sirens, you were guaranteed center stage.

So what if people thought their singing had the power to kill?

I entered the room, walking past the rows of empty chairs and toward the microphone stand by the piano. I tried not to look above the panel of mirrors in front of me. The portrait of Gabriela Thorne, renowned prima donna of her time (and rumored to have a Filipino mother), hung there, and it always freaked me out. Her cold gaze intimidated me, as if no matter how well I sang, I was never good enough.

Then I realized: there were no power outages elsewhere on campus. So why was this room dim?

Three members of The Sirens were sitting in the front row. The one I recognized was Amor Ramos. Not only did her appearance stand out with her angled bob with chunky highlights, her combat boots, the tattoo on her wrist, she was also the one who recruited any potential members…or crushed their dreams.

"Hi, Desiree." For a moment, she almost seemed nice. "Congratulations on the invite. Keep in mind, though, the little viral video you starred in is not going to work here."

I nodded. That video wasn't going to help anyway. I was letting off steam from the whole Ethan debacle by doing open-mic, and he had the nerve to be in the audience. Seeing him threw me off, and my voice cracked during my finale. He followed me after I ran out, blubbering some fake apology or whatever. I was so pissed, I slapped him for all the pain he had caused me. Little did I know I was being recorded.

"What're you going to sing?" Amor broke my thoughts.

"Um, 'Back to Black.'" Ethan hated Amy Winehouse, so it was another fuck-you to him.

She merely nodded but said nothing. After a beat she said, "Face the mirrors."

"Huh?"

"Turn around." She did a circling motion with her finger. "You sing to the mirrors. Do not take your eyes off them. And whatever you do, do not stop singing until you are finished."

I knew Mallory Thorne had more than its share of weird, but in all my six years here, I'd never witnessed nor experienced anything weird first-hand in this particular room.

Until now.

For starters, I didn't know where the background music was coming from, because no one was at the piano. Also, as I began to sing, my feet took root on the floor the moment I held the mic. I noticed it more when I tried to walk but couldn't; I usually like to move around while performing.

Then my reflection in the mirrors started to disappear, and in its place was me dressed as Amy Winehouse—beehive, winged eyeliner, black dress—in black and white. The background was parts of the "Back to Black" music video, specifically the funeral scenes.

Special effects at an audition? Cool.

And then the mirrors changed again. The black-and-white background dissipated, and now it was plain darkness. My Amy Winehouse reflection remained, but instead of my face, it was *hers*.

Not Amy's. Gabriela Thorne's.

I winced.

Gabriela motioned for me to continue. At least she wasn't menacing, and then she appeared to act out the lyrics.

At first, I shrugged it off as another quirk, until the mirror flashed several random scenes. The first was Gabriela catching a couple in bed, which triggered my own experience seeing Ethan with my roommate, Genevieve Chu. I grimaced thinking about her betrayal, but the mirror continued to show two other images: Gabriela bloodied and dead. A boy and a girl looking downward with sneers on their faces, presumably at Gabriela.

Then their faces morphed into Ethan's and Genevieve's.

I almost lost focus, but Gabriela showed up again and gestured for me to continue, this time with more force.

The scenes didn't stop there. The mirror showed someone falling out of a window. It cut to Gabriela-as-Amy standing over a grave, like in the video. She tossed a flower inside, but instead of a small box full of ashes, it was an open casket.

And Ethan was the deceased. Dried blood and bruises marred his once beautiful face.

Gabriela's face morphed back into mine, and "I" was sneering at him.

I may have hated Ethan, but I didn't want him dead.

"So you keep telling yourself."

Those words were spoken to me, as in *someone was actually talking.* Or rather, whispering. I didn't know where the voice was coming from, nor did I recognize it. I wasn't going to turn around and see if Amor or her colleagues were playing a prank—not that my frozen feet would let me, anyway.

"He broke your heart. He deserves to pay. Both he and your roommate that he impregnated shouldn't get away with what they did."

Impregnated? Was that why she transferred out of our dorm? And how long had he been seeing her behind my back?

My Amy Winehouse reflection morphed back into Gabriela, this time wearing the dress in her portrait, as well as the disapproval in her face.

Despite everything, however, I finished my audition. Good thing I picked a song that didn't require much range, so despite a few jarring moments, I stayed in tune. The mirrors went back to normal, Gabriela disappeared, and I saw my reflection in my own clothes once again. The lights in the choir room turned on all the way.

"Impressive," Amor commented as she stood up. I turned around to face her and her fellow Sirens, drawing back slightly at the realization I could move my legs again. "You're the only one who didn't freak out at the sight of our esteemed alumna," she said as she approached me.

Possessing the mirrors was part of everyone's auditions?

Amor raised a brow. "That was a compliment. Say thank you."

"Um, thank you." It sounded more like a question.

She sighed. "You're through to the next round."

My eyebrows shot up. "Really? I'm in?"

Amor held up her hand, her wrist tattoo in full view. It was the four suits in a deck of cards, and they were in black, grey, white, and purple. My eyebrows shot up. Amor was asexual?

Like me. Or at least, I thought I was. Unlike me, however, Amor was out and proud.

"That's not what I said." Once again, she broke my thoughts. "You're through to the next round. Get through the callback, but more importantly, get through the days leading up to it. If you do those two things, you're in."

My brows furrowed, but she continued. "Callback's this Friday night at six." She turned toward the other Sirens, signaling that they were finished, but I knew she was still speaking to me. "And no songs about heartbreak, please."

When I returned to my dorm, I was still riding the high from my successful—if bizarre—audition. What did Amor mean by "get through the days leading up to" the callback?

Apparently, that included overhearing and reading about my crappy love life on social media. Not to mention kids turning away when I saw them staring, or whispering amongst their friends about how I had a "vendetta" against Ethan. I did my best to ignore them and the cruel rumors about The Sirens. If I wanted a career on West End or Broadway, being a Siren was my best bet.

Then came the nightmares, all of them involving Ethan's and Genevieve's deaths. Probably didn't help that I had been watching *The Craft* and *Glee*, though in my dream, I caused Ethan to fall out of a window. As for Genevieve, I pushed a very pregnant version of her down two flights of stairs. Blood gushed out of her, and I ran toward her with an ax.

I forced myself to wake up before Dream Me hacked her into

tiny pieces.

Since I couldn't sleep, I spent most of my free time after classes picking and rehearsing songs I planned on singing. Taking Amor's advice, I rehearsed more upbeat music. I also practiced rangier songs, like "Defying Gravity," which paid off during choir practice. Guess who started getting more solos?

But when Friday came, a dead body was found outside Mallory Thorne's Creative Arts Wing, where the choir room was located. Official cause of death: defenestration. When I read that in my socials, my heart clenched. Was Ethan—

I looked at my phone and fortunately, it wasn't him. It was the star player of the football team everyone was gaga over.

Students and staff had crowded the scene, most likely wanting to see his body, all bent in unnatural angles, in his pool of blood. I couldn't have seen it myself, even though I was on my way to the Arts Wing. I didn't get a text saying the callback was canceled, so I figured it was still on.

Unfortunately, security had blocked all the entrances. Too many onlookers.

I sat by a tree in the quad area some distance away from the building, setting my knapsack on the grass. Maybe I could wait for the crowds to clear in the meantime. While scrolling through my phone to see if there were any updates from The Sirens, someone walked up to me. I jerked back when I saw him.

Ethan, or rather, a poor shell of the boy I thought I had loved, stood over me. His cheeks, one of them still carrying my slap mark, were sunken, and he had dark circles under his eyes, contrasting against his deathly pale skin. Once well-built because of his hours of swim practice, his body now struggled to fill out his uniform.

"What happened to you?" I gasped.

"Don't do it," he pleaded, sinking to my level and grabbing my shoulders. The look in his eyes made me want to run. "Don't do it!"

I wrenched myself away from his grasp. Yet, he reached out,

and I was under his hold once more. To think I once swooned being in his arms.

"Look at me! My life is shit! I am off the swim team. Genevieve is gone." I cringed at her name, but he continued his ranting. "And you hate my guts so much that you wanna join those singing freaks!"

"How dare you!" I shoved his chest, and he easily fell back on his ass. "All I'm doing is moving on with my life, and if you can't handle that, that's your goddamn problem!"

"They're killers, Desiree!" Ethan scrambled to get up. "Don't you get that? I can't eat, I can't sleep because all I hear is your fucking singing in my head! You and your fucking Amy Winehouse!"

I froze. Until he brought it up, I had never mentioned The Sirens, much less told him who I had sung.

"Don't blame me for your guilt, Ethan," I said finally, despite wanting him to explain. "It's *your* fault we broke up. As far as I'm concerned, you. Are. Dead. To me. Everything that's happening to you, you brought it on yourself. Now piss off!" I stood up, taking my knapsack with me.

"Is there a problem here?" As if out of nowhere, Amor and the same crew of Sirens from the audition had shown up. "Creating more viral video content again?"

"I'm sorry." I quickly turned away from Ethan's direction. "I was going to DM you because of all the security guards here, un-til—"

Amor held up her hand. "No explanations needed. Come now." She motioned for me to follow her. To her friends, she added, cocking her head toward Ethan, "Make sure he won't bother us ever again."

Something in her tone unsettled me, and the sounds of Ethan screaming and begging me not to go as Sirens dragged him off didn't ease matters one bit.

"I thought we were going to the choir room." Amor and I were walking through a dark corridor, a path I had passed whenever I headed to practice but never knew existed. The room was downstairs, but I didn't know there was another underground route.

"We are." She was using the flashlight function on her phone. "Just another way."

After climbing a dizzying spiral staircase, we stopped at a door. Amor shone her flashlight on the knocker, and if I wasn't mistaken, it was an engraving of Gabriela Thorne. If her portrait in the choir room wasn't intimidating enough, this one definitely had the capacity to kill.

"You scared?" Amor smirked, grabbing onto the handle and giving the door five distinct raps.

"Who goes there?" a ghostly voice boomed. My skin prickled with goose pimples.

"Amor," my schoolmate answered calmly, as if she'd been in this situation several times. "I've retrieved our last hopeful."

The door flung open. It was the same choir room I've always attended, same layout, same furniture, but with bright lighting this time, and with more students hanging around and socializing, as if there were an actual choir practice.

As I looked around, I realized we'd entered where the mirrors were, right underneath Gabriela's portrait. The microphone I used for the audition was still there, but I made sure to stay away from it. The last thing I wanted was to unleash something weirder than getting my feet stuck on the floor.

"Have a seat," Amor told me, gesturing to the crowd. I sat in the first empty chair I saw, which was in the front.

"Welcome, everyone," she greeted from the mic stand. "Thank you for coming tonight. As you well know, we have three callbacks trying to be the newest member of our humble little singing group. But first!" Amor tapped the mic. "A performance from our esteemed advisor."

I'm not sure if the lights in the choir room dimmed so much as the mic stand glowed, so brightly that it overpowered everything else. Everything, except the intro to "Cell Block Tango."

Spirits started flying out of the mic stand and moving in a procession in front of the room, carrying their chairs like in the stage production of *Chicago*. As much as I love this musical, I was looking for this so-called advisor Amor was talking about. Yet, something else caught my eye: the ghosts were maimed in some way. One had blood stains around his mouth; another had a missing eye; a third had a gaping hole where their stomach had been. There was even a ghost who had her face blown off.

As I shifted my gaze to the right, I saw *her*. There, sitting with her legs crossed in all her otherworldly glory, wearing Velma's bob and little black dress, was Gabriela Thorne. She and her fellow Merry Murderesses began to sing, relishing in each partner's demise.

When the song was over, everyone gave a standing ovation. I had no choice but to go along, but yes, their performance literally sent chills down my spine, and not just because the performers were all ghosts. Their voices sounded like some of the living choir members, and I could have sworn I heard my own.

The lights went back up again, and all but Gabriela disappeared. "Good evening, everybody," she greeted in a far friendlier tone than I would have thought she was capable of. "What? So many of you look like you've seen a ghost."

A smattering of forced laughs came about.

"Okay, okay, I can take a hint," Gabriela replied. "At any rate, this night is not about me for once. It's for our three Siren hopefuls." She gestured toward the audience. "If you heard us singing in your voice, come to the front, please."

So I hadn't imagined it. I went to the front of the room with two other girls. "Congratulations on making it this far." Gabriela wove her way among us three.

"Out of those who auditioned, I feel you have the most potential. And yet, only one of you can make it," she continued. "You've already gotten through the first audition, as well as the days leading up to tonight's callback. That in itself was a lot to endure, so kudos."

Endure? So the nightmares were part of the test?

"Tonight our theme is *dedication*, which you have to some extent. But your next two tasks will be the true test." Gabriela gestured toward the door behind the audience. Two men wearing the security guard uniforms from outside entered, carrying something long and wrapped in what looked to be dark canvas. They placed it at our feet. A loud scream tore through the room as soon as one of them opened the bag.

It was the dead footballer.

"What is he doing here?!" the girl standing farthest away from me shrieked. "Get him away from me!"

This time, Amor came forward, nodding at the guards to leave. When they had shut the door, Gabriela reappeared.

"Was he not the one who had placed a tracker on your phone, your laptop, to make sure you were not lying to him when you had to be elsewhere?" Gabriela's voice was even. "Was he not the one who stealthed you the first night you spent with him, getting you pregnant, punching you in the stomach repeatedly so you'd lose the baby?"

The girl gasped and shook her head. "I didn't want him to die!"

"You didn't kill him," Amor assured. "He did it all on his own."

The girl rounded on her. "And how would you know? You saw him jump out the window? Or did you and your Sirens push him out?"

"*Enough.*" Gabriela's voice silenced the entire room. She faced the three of us. "Your next task is to make this terrible excuse for a human being disappear." She gestured toward the corpse as if it were garbage. "And you will do that through your singing. If your song, called your Dedication, disintegrates this...body, you will go through. If not, you'll go back to your dorm, with no memory of tonight ever happening. And..." She paused for a beat. "Whatever singing talent you may have will disappear forever."

I straightened up. "Disappear? As in—"

"You'll be out of the chorus," Amor finished. "If you can't sing, there's no point in you being here. You wouldn't even be able to sing backup."

I blanched. Singing was the only thing I enjoyed, the only thing I was good at. My grades were nothing to wow top-notch unis.

"Fine." The girl who freaked out over her dead abuser boyfriend started to walk toward the door. "So the rumors about this group *are* true: you all are a bunch of murderous weirdos. I'm outta here."

There were a few gasps in the audience as they watched her go. However, she was halfway through when a whirlwind coming from my side of the room surrounded her, circling her several times. The whirlwind then broke into the same ghostly figures who'd performed with Gabriela. I recognized the one with the gaping hole in their stomach, but before I could fully process what had happened, they disappeared.

Amor walked to the girl, who stood there as if the ghosts had sucked the life from her body. Her eyes were glazed over, her skin drained of color.

"I am very disappointed in you. You had so much potential, and yet would rather throw it away." Before I could realize that Amor's voice had changed, she placed her hand on the girl's throat. For a moment I thought she was strangling her, but a visible gust of air emanated from the girl's neck as Amor absorbed it in her hand. When Amor had finished, the girl vanished.

"Anyone else?" Gabriela emerged from Amor's body as she rounded on us. I immediately shook my head, too shocked by what I had just seen, and in response Gabriela pointed to the other girl standing next to me.

"Go to that mic stand and sing," she commanded. "Remember the advice Amor gave you. And remember that being a Siren is an honor. Not only do we sing, but we sing for the greater good." To me, she said, "Have a seat."

The other girl sang "Defying Gravity," and my heart sank. That was my song! I wanted to showcase my range. What's worse, this girl's rendition was amazing, and surely Gabriela and Amor didn't want to hear the same song twice.

Yet, in the end, the song did not disintegrate the body. "I'm sorry," Amor said. "You won't be going through."

My competitor flinched. "But, but, I did everything, I–"

"*But nothing.*" Gabriela hissed. "You may hit all the notes, but *you did not do what I asked.*" She zoomed toward Amor, possessing her, who then approached the other girl to take away her voice. This time, the girl's own hands flew to her neck.

"Leave," Amor commanded, and the poor girl had no choice but to obey.

Now I was the only one left, confused as to why she was spared.

"I'm disappointed in your recruits, Amor," Gabriela remarked as she reemerged. She looked straight at me and cocked her head, telling me to go to the mic.

"You better make the right song choice," she warned.

After frantically sorting through songs in my head, especially those that had range, I announced that I'd sing "No Good Deed." At least it was still from *Wicked*.

Taking a deep breath, I began as the intro played. Everyone and everything faded away as I took the words to heart. Wanting to take a risk, I personalized the song, changing Fiyero's name to Ethan's. Murmurs came from the audience. From the corner of my eye, Gabriela looked surprised, though whether that was a good thing, I had no idea. Amor, on the other hand, remained neutral.

I'll admit I was nervous changing the lyrics, but if I didn't take any risks, I'll get dinged for being safe, or worse, a possessed Amor would take my voice away. Or make me vanish forever.

Near the end, though, I saw the body starting to crack.

I'd be lying if I said I pulled off the final note cleanly. The ending was a little weak because I ran out of breath. Yet, none of that mattered because the body turned into a pile of dust by the time I finished.

"Bravo." Gabriela materialized in front of me. "You did what I asked. Well done, though your ending needs work. But what you lack in polish, you more than make up for in your emotions. I've sensed it since your last audition."

I raised my brows. "S-so that was you, in the mirrors?"

She nodded. "The voices you heard? That was me. I look deep into the hearts and souls of Siren hopefuls. What separates you from the rest is that you're not afraid of facing dark truths, about you, anyone, or anything."

"Dark truths?" I frowned.

Gabriela gave me a chilly smile. "Most of what you saw in your audition *is* in your heart. Like you, I was betrayed by love, and murdered in the process."

The images of Gabriela seeing that couple came flooding back. Not to mention my sneering at Ethan's dead body.

"You and I are similar, Desiree," she continued. "But I refused to cross over. If I can't get my own revenge, I'll get it for everyone, if only for us musically inclined."

"What do you mean 'get it for everyone'?"

She shook her head. "Why do you think your trash ex-boyfriend's a mess right now?"

My eyes grew wide. "Y-you've been haunting him?"

"With your voice, I might add. If you are to be in this group, you take responsibility as well. That first girl did not want to dispose of her boyfriend's body, and so she was severely punished. As for the second one, she had no heart in her song, and so at least her life was spared. Whether she still wants it, on the other hand, is a whole different story.

"But don't worry," Gabriela continued. "The Sirens don't kill, not technically."

"Not technically," I repeated, confused.

"Anyway." She waved me off. "Face the mirrors. This is your final task. Complete it, and you're in."

These godforsaken mirrors again.

Various images flashed: dead girls rotting in ditches, girls with eyes wide in fear, boys and men with sneers on their faces, these same boys and men being lauded by the masses for some accomplishment, one of them being the footballer whose corpse I had disintegrated. There were a few male victims as well, along with female perps.

Then I realized: all those victims were the ghosts I had seen.

"We only target those who deserve it," Gabriela said. "They have it coming."

The mirror stopped as Ethan's picture.

"Oh, yes, this one." Gabriela's voice boomed throughout. "Aside from his infidelity, let's see what else he's done."

The mirror scrolled through various tweets, messages, social media posts of Ethan making racist and sexist comments and being part of sketchy online chats. The one that struck me the most, though, was his dating history. All of his ex-girlfriends were Asian.

"Isn't this you?" Gabriela's voice echoed.

An image of me shimmered in the mirror, a picture I had given him once. Another tweet popped next to it: *"My latest. A little darker than I'm used to, but she's sweet. Has such a great singing voice."*

What in the actual hell?? All this time, I was hurting over someone like *that*?

"It was probably for the best, never checking his socials beforehand," were Gabriela's next words. "So trusting of you. And of course, he tires of you and goes to his next target: Genevieve Chu."

Despite learning of Ethan's Asian fetish, hearing my ex-roommate's name still made me bristle. Even though she was likely a victim as all his others, I couldn't bring myself to sympathize.

"Now for your final task. To show your true Dedication, pick a song you know will break him. And don't hold back: if you fail, not only do you lose your voice, but you'll get the fate *he* deserves. Do you understand?"

My blood chilled. This choir was going to kill me if I didn't pull it off?

"You'll get everything you've dreamed of," Gabriela assured me. "You know that everyone in this school who ended up at West End was a Siren. Is that not what you want?"

West End. Me, headlining a major musical. Perhaps even an original production.

"And you'll be ridding this place of racist, abusive assholes," Amor spoke finally. "If the school's too chickenshit to do it, we will. And the best part: they can never trace it back to us. Our voices may haunt them, but they do the deed themselves. You've come so far from being the victim to almost being the victor, Desiree. Do NOT screw up your chance."

I woke up in my own bed, unsure whether I dreamed it up or if it really had happened. Did I really audition in front of a ghost, and did I actually dispose of a corpse with a song?

Reaching for my phone on the nightstand, I wanted to contact Amor. I jolted when I saw the date: *it was already Sunday???* I had slept through all of Saturday?

As soon as I was able to gather my thoughts, I sort of remembered traces of Adele's "Rolling in the Deep" playing in my head and thinking how threatening the background vocals had sounded. Was that my Dedication, or was that a dream?

Dedication? Where had that come from?

Going through my apps, I didn't get any messages about being the newest member, or even being rejected. And if I were rejected, I realized, I'd be dead. I plopped onto my bed; maybe I did dream it all up.

I got out of bed. I didn't want to have to wait too long to use the bathroom. Grabbing my toiletries, towel, and a t-shirt and jeans, I left my dorm.

"You bitch!" The moment I opened the door, Genevieve flew at me, causing me to drop my things. I fell on my ass on the cold hardwood floor. She probably would have attacked me further had it not been for one of her friends.

"You killed him, didn't you? DIDN'T YOU?!" she screeched.

I looked up at her, her pregnant belly fully pronounced. Guess she and Ethan *had* been sneaking around long before I found out. "What the hell are you talking about?!"

"And she fucking denies it!" one of Genevieve's friends spat.

"Ethan is dead, and it's all your fault!" Genevieve threw her phone at me. It hit my forearm as I tried to protect my face. I yelped in pain.

"You deserve more than that, you murderer!" Genevieve continued her tirade. "Look at it!"

Not wanting her to keep yelling at me, I did what she asked. My jaw dropped as I read the blurb:

The body of an eighteen-year-old student was found at the swimming pool of the Mallory Thorne School of Excellence. This was another unfortunate death at our school. Previously, our prominent Year 7 footballer was found dead outside Mallory Thorne's Creative Arts Wing. Investigations are still ongoing as to whether this recent passing was a suicide or if there was foul play.

I scrolled down and saw Ethan's school picture in the article. Indeed, my cheating, racist ex-boyfriend was dead.

At first I thought it was some twisted prank, but I saw the URL came from the school itself.

"You're gonna pay for this," Genevieve seethed.

"No, she won't." A familiar voice rang through my dorm. Amor.

"Who the hell are you?" another one of Genevieve's friends called as they rounded on her.

"You wouldn't talk to me like that if you knew, you uncultured lapdog." She made her way through the clique to get to me.

"Get up," she commanded.

"Uh, we're not done here," Genevieve cut in. "So get the hell out."

Amor gave her a once-over. "Shouldn't you take care of yourself and your baby?"

Insulted by her question, Genevieve's friends attempted to grab Amor when Amor let out a yell. Or rather, sang a pitch-perfect note that was loud enough to be a yell. I covered my ears, but the rest of the clique fell on their knees, tortured by Amor's singing. They all passed out when she had finished. Briefly, I worried about Genevieve with the way she thudded on the floor, but then I remembered this was Ethan's kid, so whatever.

Amor held out her hand and cocked her eyebrow. I scrambled up and let her take me wherever she was going to take me.

"I was about to change," I started to say, but Amor waved me off.

"There's no time," was her curt reply, not looking at me.

The route we took felt familiar, and before I knew it, we were underground. We were going to the choir room.

I entered to the sound of cheers. The first face I saw was Gabriela's, who was leading the applause.

"Congratulations," she greeted, though I didn't miss her judgy glance at my pajamas. To the crowd, she announced, "Everyone, welcome Desiree Aquino, our newest Siren."

My jaw dropped. Seriously? I made it?

"I don't see why you're surprised," Gabriela commented after the cheers died down, "considering your ex-boyfriend's dead. Good job, you passed all the tests. You could have at least dressed for this occasion, however."

I was about to explain what had happened, but she cut me off. "Your life is forever changed, Desiree, hopefully for the better. But, you must still put in the work. Starting now."

Suddenly, memories of last Friday came flooding back the moment I saw the security guards enter with another body bag. Another dead body, which I would have to decompose through song. Even before one of the guards unzipped the bag, I knew the corpse was Ethan's.

Even after everything I'd found out, I winced at seeing his drowned body. Ethan Harrison, one of Mallory Thorne's best swimmers, dead from drowning—or so I kept telling myself.

Yet, he was no angel, and I had a job to do.

As if on cue, the mic stand was ready for me.

A month later.

During rehearsal, where I was playing my dream role of Velma Kelly, I received a link from Amor. Clicking it, I saw Genevieve's picture with the headline: *Eighteen-year-old student found brutally murdered near Lake Gracia.*

I was too shocked to read the whole article, but I did see the words "decapitated," "butchered," and "fetus taken."

Then I made the mistake of checking the comments, all of them accusing me of killing her.

"Come to the choir room after practice," Amor texted.

I nearly dropped my phone. She wanted me to disintegrate Genevieve's body, something I hadn't done in a month because, aside from the callback, you only disintegrate the bodies your voice had driven to suicide. I never targeted Genevieve once. Hell, I hadn't even thought about her since she and her friends ambushed me at the dorm.

"Control that voice, Velma. That's a powerful gift you got

there. Almost *too* powerful." Amor punctuated her latest text with a winky-face emoji.

A comment popped out at me: "All Genevieve could hear was Desiree Aquino's voice before she died."

That was a goddamn lie! I. Never. Targeted. Her. Never made a Dedication toward her. Also, butchering and decapitating were not in The Sirens' vocabulary.

But what did Amor mean about controlling my voice? That it didn't matter whether or not I Dedicated a song, as long as the victim heard me sing? Did Gabriela—

"Velma, you're up!" One of the stage crew members interrupted my thoughts.

I sighed. Velma Kelly was my dream role, and if I wanted to enjoy the privileges of a Siren, I needed to do *all* of the work. No matter how unpleasant. Or unfair, even.

Besides, it's not like Genevieve was a friend anyway. I took a deep breath and headed for the stage.

BEHIND THE EYES

ASHLEY DENG

Early morning, and the bells of the new term rang out in the halls of Mallory Thorne. It was the start of Year 7, the beginning of the end for their time together, buzzing about preferred majors and ideal universities. Izzy felt the thrum of the same routines, this time tinged with the smell of blood: breakfast, class, class, lunch, nap, class—yelling, knives, blood, and viscera. How many others knew? She sure as hell didn't know.

They were a group of best friends—well, no, all of them except for Izzy, who had been taken in by them—who knew each other before they started here at Mallory Thorne, knew each other's work ethics, each other's interests and shared hobbies. Izzy Wong was new (the "Wong" kind of Asian, as Irena called her), and they accepted her like an act of charity, homed onto her potential, saw the barest beginnings of what they all had, and absorbed her into their group. She was grateful to have friends help her navigate her school life and commiserate when things went bad; shame how it went, really.

She was one of three in their friend group who wasn't aiming for medical school, though she still planned to pursue the sciences. (June and James set their sights at business; Izzy later swapped science for English after her first year at university, but if you'd told her this in Year 7, she'd have buried her head in the shame instilled in her by the others.) The rest were Christine, Irena, and Emily, a smattering of immigrant kids with built-in ambitions, thanks to a mix of familial and societal expectations. Izzy hadn't experienced those until meeting them and she suddenly felt obligated to follow, until the reality kicked in their last semester and started to make her sick. It was lonely, now. She felt better about it.

At the start of Year 7, Izzy found June in their usual meeting place before class, under the vaulted ceilings of the science wing, where they usually sat in the crooks of the pillars with their morning books at their feet. June sat alone, freshly returned from her family trip and buzzing with an energy that Izzy hadn't seen before. June was generally the quietest of the group, the one who talked like her life depended on it, but only when the room had come to a hush or with company smaller than three. Normally, she only showed her excitement when asked. Normally, she wasn't clutching her bag so tightly her knuckles went white. Her ears burned red, almost matching the color of their uniform. She wasn't smiling, either. There was almost a fear in her eyes.

Izzy sat next to her. It was going to be a few minutes before anyone else showed up. "Are...Are you okay?" She pointed to the bag.

June let the words tumble out, a rapid, post-anxious ramble that left her breathless: "So y'know when you visit family and they make you tell them all about your school shit and how your classes are going and what your plans are for the future and you kind of just mutter your rehearsed lines because your Chinese isn't really good enough to go in depth and they just nod along and criticize you?"

Izzy didn't, but she muttered a "Sure," anyway. "I'm guessing the visit to China was bad."

"Sort of?" June shrugged. "I got some new clothes and years' worth of laisee money."

"Brought back a shit ton of red envelopes?"

Here, June grinned. "You bet."

"Okay, but like—" Izzy pointed to the bag.

"It's a surprise," June replied. "Let's call it a good-luck charm for now. I think James and Emily will appreciate it most."

"Why?"

"Because they're try-hards! You'll see. The important thing is, we'll have a meeting about it over lunch."

Her bag seemed innocuous enough, but whatever was in there was big enough to fill the whole thing. She had her arms around it, clutched closely to her chest, but Izzy didn't even question the idea of holding an entire meeting for a good-luck charm. Instead, she asked "Why not get it from your room at lunch, then?"

June replied with a distant voice. "My aunt told me I should hold onto it until we were ready. Also that it'll be good for me. Good luck from Buddha. Apparently." There was a pause as June stared at the floor, a sudden and empty quietness washing over her. People passed them in the hall; none of them looked. There were stranger things that happened at Mallory Thorne, and some girl having a breakdown in the middle of the hallway was on par for Year 7s at most schools. Izzy wanted to say something but couldn't think of what. They waited in silence until the bell rang.

Izzy had math with Emily and James, and she hated that fact more than she probably should have. Class with friends was supposed to be fun—the little chatter in the pauses between the teacher's lecturing, the notes passed, the plans made for between and after class. There's a conspiratorial atmosphere when you have class with friends, a gleeful conference of minds, plotting, plotting, always plotting—that was where the fun was, after all. But Emily and James didn't care to indulge in the fantasy. Maybe after class, if they didn't have homework. They'd get in a few playfully snide comments when the moments came, but mostly, Emily and James had their heads glued to their assignments, studying, too focused on beating each other for the top grades in the class. It was tempting to blame their upbringing, but Izzy reminded herself constantly that they were a group of Asians and one white girl, and their experiences were as varied as any other group with different demographics. Instead, it meant that they were a self-selecting group of highly-motivated, highly-driven, socially awkward teenagers carving a hole to belong in and forcing themselves to fit, even when the hole was too small. Not that anyone noticed. They were too busy enjoying each other's company.

Izzy finally had the chance to talk to Emily and James once class wrapped up, all too eager to put her notebook and calculator away and not think about numbers for the next couple of hours. Instead, Izzy was thinking about June and whatever was in her bag. Had her aunt given her some sort of Buddhist talisman for academic success? Did those even exist?

Emily walked over and put an arm around Izzy's shoulders. She grinned and said, "I called my parents last night—well it was more like they called me—but guess who's got tickets to the K-pop fest next year?"

James, not far behind her, tsk'd. "Aren't you going to be too busy?"

"No!" she snapped, almost biting at James. "I know how to manage my time."

"So do I," James sneered.

"Whatever. Look, it's conditional, okay? My parents said they'll let me go only if I keep my grades up and get into my top choices.

Y'know, med school track."

Izzy shrugged out of Emily's arm and got out of her seat. She never understood why Emily involved her in these things. They listened to very different genres of music. But, she supposed, it was a way to include her. A small gesture, even if Izzy was less than interested. She feigned a polite smile in return. "You sent all your apps already?" She hadn't. Izzy thought she knew what she wanted, but the whole ordeal scared her.

"Of course!"

"Same here." James replied almost immediately after and, in hindsight, it was hard to tell if they were friends or dedicated rivals. He continued, drawing out his words into a sneer: "Except I'm going to make my money elsewhere. You know, not as a doctor."

That won James an outburst from Emily, who slammed her fist onto Izzy's desk, her jade bracelet clanging loudly against the wood. Definitely rivals. "What's wrong with med school? What kind of Asian are you?"

Cringing, Izzy slipped between them, heading for the door. "Let's, uh, let's go get lunch. June's got something to show us."

Lunch was always a spectacle. Between the excited shouting and the parry-ripostes of light but mean-spirited comments, the entertainment lasted the entire hour. Currently, they were in the middle of an extended joke, lasting days of small jabs, rolling into a cacophonous picture of the various barely-teenager-appropriate exploits of Irena. From flashing her lab partner to making out and fondling behind the backs of the librarians, she took the comments in stride, even if they never happened. It was like a badge of honor, the dare that went too far, the excitement of risk that played out only in their heads. Izzy didn't know why she loved it, but they all did—it was exhilarating, a fantastical break from the hells of school.

The dining hall, lit in a way that exaggerated all the shadows of its crevices, was packed with students and their chatter. Christine sat on Irena's lap and waved them over at their usual spot, a table at the far corner, claimed by the group unofficially but never contested. June was already there, her arms wrapped around her bag, which sat on the table itself. Trays of food were set aside, forgotten more than anything. Christine piped up once she saw James and Emily converging at the table:

"James—or Emily, whichever of you—do you think I could get your help for chemistry before my parents find out and kill me? Y'know, before they make me spend my holidays with a tutor."

Izzy felt a tinge of regret. Her grades weren't nearly as good as Christine's, and *she* didn't feel like she needed a tutor, nor were her parents pressuring her whenever she gave them updates in school. It was belittling in a way, and Izzy wanted to change the subject, fast. "So, what's the surprise?" she asked June, interrupting James before he could reply.

June's grin grew, slowly and steadily, sparking a fire behind her eyes. "I don't know," she said, unzipping her bag and reaching into it. "But it feels... special."

What June pulled out could only be described as an idol, a miniature statue that could have been mistaken for a Buddha, if you didn't know what Buddha looked like. It was a fat, jolly man, whose face was obscured by his round cheeks, and whatever features might've been left were wiped off, leaving only a smooth, rounded head behind. Its ears were long, even for a Buddha, and its hands were covered by cloth, hiding whatever gesture it had from the eyes of the world. The sight of it made Izzy queasy. It was wrong but alluring, a presence she wanted no part of yet could tell that it tasted sweet, like clarity and knowledge, like wisdom and fear—

It was the fear that made her jerk away, the sweetness turning metallic, like blood. She looked around, but no one else seemed to have noticed.

June was still talking. "My aunt found this in her village. Apparently one of the old ladies gave it to her when she found out I lived abroad. She said it'll bring us success—academic success specifically. But only if we provide a sufficient offering. I don't know if I believe her, but it couldn't hurt, right?"

"Depends on the kind of offering," said Irena, grinning. "Does it want blood? Hair? Teeth, maybe?"

"It's Chinese, so probably food," Izzy muttered. "That's probably enough." The thought made her uneasy; she sure as hell didn't believe a thing, but her head bristled with anxiety anyway. There'd been enough weird shit happening at school that she couldn't pretend like it wasn't a possibility.

"Food it is, then!" said Emily. She placed a napkin in front of the idol and set an apple slice on top of it.

James was the most openly skeptical. He eyed the table, his face twisted into a disapproving glare. "You're actually doing this shit? It's fake! There's no magic!"

"Why, are you scared?" taunted Emily.

"You say magic's fake and all," said Christine, shrugging, "but remember what happened to the Year 4 girls in the library last year? How else would you explain the pockets of fire and shifting walls of books?"

James shrugged. "Gas leak." Still, he plucked a carrot from his lunch and placed it next to the apple.

Christine and Irena both gave up a small piece of their meals— chips, broccoli. That left Izzy and June, and Izzy did not want to join, the thought further making her nauseous. June did it, though. She dropped a few berries onto the table, most of which fell onto the dark wood and not the napkin, and they scrambled to pick it up before they rolled onto the floor. Thinking quickly, Izzy swiped one and passed it off as her own, setting it next to the others. If anyone saw, they didn't say.

There were only two months left of the semester before final exams, which meant final projects and presentations, throttling Year 7s toward the grades that determined their very futures. Izzy hated thinking about it. Her grades were mediocre but passable, and her vision of the future was engulfed in an empty void. She felt like she was writing test after test, paper after paper, treading in a black sea at night, ready to give up and drift away. Whenever she thought she could see the light, she was met with that idol's face, the bulbous cheeks and grinning mouth staring back at her from the darkness.

The others, though, they didn't seem to care. Emily and James finished their calculus tests with a higher than perfect score, thanks to the usually-impossible bonus questions Mr. Kent threw on tests; Christine and June aced their debates, scoring higher than anyone had ever been known to do in Mrs. Ingoldt's Politics and Civics class; Irena handed in her English final paper late—something that usually came with a penalty—and was marked perfect, despite the red of the teacher's pen marking the pages with strained crit-icism-turned-compliments (incredulous and proud, Irena let Izzy flip through it, and there were smudges of red that Izzy swore wasn't ink).

One lunch, James, with a wide-ass grin on his face, patted the idol on the head whilst Emily rushed up to the table to fawn in front it, half-jokingly bowing to it a few times. James caught June's eye, that same grin stretching the skin of his cheeks.

"Worth it," he said.

My grades didn't change for shit. The words almost fell out of Izzy's mouth but didn't; she wanted them to like her, wanted to be their friend—but she didn't want to be around *that*.

It was Christine who pulled it out from under their table, plac-ing it gently next to her meal. Izzy felt that regret rise in her chest again, a remorse over having cheated this thing, that her grades weren't going to benefit from whatever magic it possessed like her friends' grades were. But that thing freaked her out, stared at her, daring her to give it an offering to join them, too.

She thought she'd heard something, words from a veil not yet explored, bright, bright like the stars and sky—it spoke in tones of gold and red as the idol taunted her, whispering words she couldn't understand in her ear. When the hum simmered down around her, she realized the others were planning something. A pact, the details of which Izzy'd missed. Irena cried out, "Oh, you're fucking *on*, James! I will personally see your arse kicked from here to the Headmaster's office, and you can clean the blood with your dissertation yourself."

James cackled, his face twisting with some dark glee. "Good luck, you indignant wench."

"If there's anyone who'd win," June started, giggling, "it'd probably be Christine, I mean *look at her*, she's been studying the anatomy books for weeks now." Christine, in response, gave a wide, beaming grin.

"We shouldn't be competing against each other!" exclaimed Emily. "This is for our uni acceptances."

"With limited seats," said James. "Of *course* we're competing against each other."

"I think we should work together. We can help each other out," continued Emily.

Irena pulled Izzy and June into her, wrapping her arms around them. "I call these two!" she said, with a glee pointed at James.

Izzy leaned forward and whispered to June, "What are we competing for?"

June smiled sheepishly, that same feverish excitement in her eyes. "For who could get the most out of the idol," she said. "To see who makes it out at the top at the end of the semester." There was a quiver in her voice, and Izzy could taste the fear the idol showed her, rising up her throat with bellowing tones of gold and red.

Irena took them back to her and Christine's shared room, carefully navigating the papers and final projects and literal student bodies scattered across the common areas and the hallways. People were studying if they weren't sleeping, with the rowdiest among them shunted to their rooms or the greater common areas of Mallory Thorne. Izzy kept her eyes on the ground as she walked to avoid stepping on anyone's essay drafts or worksheets, the pages upon pages of white and black slowly blooming with red spots as they approached Irena and Christine's room. Meanwhile, next to her, June was growing increasingly anxious. She pulled at the sleeves of her uniform, her eyes darting all around the hallway.

"We—We should—I—" she stammered right as Irena reached for her door. "I need to leave," said June, turning on her heel. She didn't quite run out of the dormitory, but she left with enough haste that the students in the common area lifted their heads from their work to watch her go.

"Well," proclaimed Irena as she swung the door wide. "You'll help me, right Izzy?"

Inside the room was dark. The curtains had been drawn and their desk lamps flickered with dying lightbulbs, letting in barely enough light to make out the features of their room. The dark pools at their feet merged into something bigger, and Izzy flinched when Irena flipped on the light switch, her eyes hurting from the sudden brightness.

By the time Izzy's eyesight adjusted, she was faced with Irena removing her blazer and undoing her shirt. She had her back faced to Izzy, who could see, now, where the blood had come from: Irena's shirt had been stained red, the color hidden by the shared color of their school jackets. Along her back were delicate lines of freshly-cut skin. In Irena's hand was a scalpel, probably lifted from the science wing. She held it out for Izzy to take and said, "I'm worried about my physics final, but he told me what to do. I can't reach by myself, so c'mon, Izzy—I'll tell where he's instructed me to cut."

Izzy didn't want to—she didn't want to help, didn't want to cut into her friend, make her bleed more than she already had—but Irena slammed the door closed and grabbed her by the wrist, her eyes wild and bloodshot. "I'm worried about my physics final," she repeated, her voice a hollow imitation of what she once was. "I can't reach—"

"...so I'll cut where you tell me," said Izzy, scared. Her ears burned, and she could hear her heart beating against her eardrums.

She took the scalpel and, following Irena's instructions, she began to cut.

She ran to the girls' lavatory as soon as Irena told her they were done. She wanted the blood off her skin, wanted to scrub it out from under her nails, wanted to erase the memory of Irena's widening grin as she cut and cut and cut into her back, through the layers of skin and its interfacing as blood blossomed up and out to reveal the muscles beneath. Izzy remembered her hands shaking; somehow her lines were clean, sharp, and smoothly instinctive. It felt like she had been scratching an itch with every cut, and she hated it, hated that that idol had wormed its way into her head even if she wasn't yet fully under its spell. Whatever that spell even was. She could still hear its brightness, loud against her own thoughts.

The lavatory was, fortunately, empty except for one other person, and inside, Izzy found Christine, sitting up against the wall near the sinks. She had what looked like a paring knife in hand. Her skirt had been hitched up and her stockings hitched down to reveal the markings on her thighs. Blood dripped down from her legs, and Izzy felt that same wave of nausea rush over her. How long had Christine been here? How had no one else seen her? "What the fuck are you doing?" she said aloud.

Christine traced the markings on her thighs, digging in deeper this time. More blood gushed out as the blade all but disappeared into her flesh. Izzy noted that the markings traced along her quad muscles, down the length of her thighs to her knees and back up again. She must have hit bone with that latest cut, and yet Christine didn't flinch. Instead, she said: "My parents think I need to see a tutor? Not if I do this. Not if the secrets are in my favor."

Izzy's nausea subsided only to be replaced by a haze, the lingering fog of when she'd helped Irena. She had the urge to take Christine's hand, help her apply more pressure to the knife, help her carve out the muscles of her legs whilst the idol beneath their lunch table hummed sweet notes of academic success. She got as far as putting her hand atop Christine's before the smell of blood shook her out of it. She pried the knife from Christine and held it to her face. "Can you even walk?! Do you *hear yourself?*" she cried. Her voice echoed through the empty lavatory. Water dripped from a leaky tap. "There's no way this is worth it."

What came over Christine's face wasn't pain, at least, not in the way that Izzy expected it. It was more like anger, a pained rage not at the wounds she'd inflicted upon herself but rather toward Izzy, toward the fact that she stood in the way between her and her goals. "Fuck off!" Christine shrieked. "Give me my knife back—I won't see a tutor, I won't, I won't I won't I won't!"

Izzy forgot about the blood on her hands and clothes and ran. This was all June's doing—where was June?

Another thought occurred to her: *James and Emily.* The tryhards. The perfect-isn't-good-enough faction of their group. If *this* was what they meant regarding their challenge, then she dreaded to imagine what those two could come up with. Or did it work some other way? Did the idol dictate their fates? Whisper to them the exact sort of blood it desired? Give them dreams of mutilation and high test scores?

Someone grabbed Izzy by her arm and pulled her out of the hallway. The door slammed shut behind her, and she was alone with June, whose face was tear-stained, her eyes red, cuts adorning her face and neck like the line work of an illustrator.

"I didn't mean for this," she whispered. Her hands were shaking, but there was no knife nor scalpel in sight. "I-I need to tell you."

"I don't think it matters anymore," said Izzy, scowling. "Whether you meant for this to happen or not. Not that you could've known, your aunt—"

"It wasn't my aunt who gave it to me." June pulled herself onto a desk and wrapped her arms around her knees. "It isn't from China. I found it whilst looking for a book deep in the library. It...it spoke to me. It still speaks to me."

Izzy didn't know what to do with that information. She just wanted her friends to be safe. She would worry about the idol later. "Do you know where James and Emily are?"

June shook her head, wincing at the pain from her cuts. Then she paused thoughtfully. "The lunch table? They sometimes work there during their spare period. You know...sneaking in when it's empty."

It was hard not to be self-conscious about all the blood on her, though Izzy was grateful for the color of their blazers masking the worst of it. She still garnered a few stares, though she ducked below the worst of them, weaving her way through the student body of Mallory Thorne, lethargic from their late nights and end-of-semester stress. The crowd dissipated around the cafeteria now that the day had moved on from their midday meal, and inside the lights had been dimmed to conserve energy. There were only two others in the cafeteria—each of them brandishing a long, thin stick, sharpened to needlepoint.

The hum of the idol filled the air, causing Izzy's words to get caught in her throat. She felt it rage red at her, as though it also sensed her distrust and indignation at its power. Slowly, she approached James and Emily.

On their table was their math homework, pages after pages of calculus problems, all covered in splatterings of blood. They were more red than they were white at this point. They had taken off their jackets, rolled up their sleeves to their elbows, and carved lines all along their forearms. Izzy saw a severed finger on the paper and tried to work out, through the dim lighting, which one of her friends it belonged to. And then she saw the other parts: another finger, an ear, a tooth—James was bleeding down the side of his face, Emily was missing both her pinky fingers, and Izzy couldn't yet tell who was missing a tooth.

Emily and James raised their needles to each other's heads, pointed at the space between their eyes. "See?" said Emily, gleefully. "I told you teamwork was better."

"I'll give it to you this once *if* it works," snapped James. "We aren't through yet—you can hear it, though, can't you? You feel it too?"

"Yeah," breathed Emily. She rubbed the spot on her forehead. "Right there. It's *itching*."

Don't, don't, don't—Izzy dove for the idol beneath their table, climbed onto a neighboring one, and held it high above her as James and Emily (and June, who'd finally decided to approach from the sidelines) clambered at her in response. "I can't let you!" Izzy cried. "Look at yourselves! Holy shit, what are you doing?!"

In her hands, the idol beamed. She felt an overwhelming sense of stability, a shining light of success; she wanted to feed it the blood from her wrists in exchange for the guaranteed praise of her teachers and her peers. She could have it if she wanted to. A way to join in their studiousness, to share the highs of their success; imagine how proud her parents would feel, how proud *she* would feel with perfect grades and a perfect entry scholarship, a university life that would make others envious—but, then, did she care?

Her friends cared, and she cared about her friends. But school... she didn't derive pride from her academics. She wanted to do *well* of course, but she had other priorities, other places that were near and dear to her heart. And none of that was worth all the blood.

Izzy threw the idol to the floor and her friends cried out in shrieking despair.

"How could you do this to us?!"

This was the first term in many years that Izzy sat alone, waiting for class. Winter holidays had come and gone, and Izzy had been especially quiet in her time at home. She hadn't had the chance to hang out with her friends, because they didn't offer, and when they arrived with their belongings in the halls of Mallory Thorne, they passed each other with the barest of acknowledgements, outright ignoring Izzy when she tried to say hi. They were recovering, slowly, barely. The resentment was incomprehensible, but Izzy felt it almost as strongly as she'd felt the idol's call.

She should've been sad about it. She was, for a bit, at first. But by the time the first week of the new term passed, she'd felt better about what she'd done. She'd never been one of them, and she'd made peace with that. It was liberating, more than anything. Time to find her own priorities, without their influence crushing her in place.

BREAKING INTO FINALS

KAVYA VENKAT

Anjali faced the wall and tried again.

"The political environment that India faces…" No, that was stupid. She needed a better hook than the dry opening to a textbook.

"India may have the biggest population, but does it have power on the world stage?" No, starting with a question was a cop out. It lacked any semblance of authority.

"India is a failure on the world stage." Yes. Yes, that was controversial enough to grab an audience's attention.

Anjali didn't believe what she was saying, but she didn't need to believe anything for this competition. She could say whatever she wanted about India and not sound racist, and the old white judges would eat it up with post-colonial fervor. Anything to get those ten thousand pounds. Anjali didn't *need* the money.

But she wanted to win.

She wanted to win purely to win, because her parents expected her to do well, because she had placed her self-worth on being *good at this*. She was Anjali Narasimham, the smart kid, the smooth talker, who worked half as hard to be twice as good.

The older she got, the harder it was to pull it off, the more time she actually had to put into doing the work. But Anjali had never learned to work hard, so now she was stuck working for twice as long, getting half the work done.

"India's population, diversity, and myriad political neighbors—" Myriad. Who even said myriad? Pretentious bullshit.

She had written the speech's outlines already, but phrases that sounded good on paper didn't necessarily sound good spoken aloud. Plus, Anjali had to flesh the bullet points of the speech into proper paragraphs. She always did best when she spoke impromptu, when her nonsense flowed without the restraints of forethought, but the scholarship expected a written transcript.

In two weeks, she was expected to give a seven-minute speech about the changing global stage. There would be three rounds. The first was open to anyone who wanted to compete, the second consisted of the top fifteen, and the last would consist of just the top three. The lucky trio would then repeat the speech in front of the scholarship committee in a private event.

Anjali took a deep breath and stared at the off-white walls, yellow and distorted with age. She had gotten used to saying what she didn't believe in. With these kinds of competitions, truth didn't matter: just the appearance of conviction.

"India is a failure on the world stage." It didn't matter if it felt vaguely self-destructive to say. Anjali had gotten very, very good at pretending conviction.

The demon king was clothed in gold, but he cradled the corpse of his brother. All the wealth in the world could not stave off death. "How could you do this to me?" he asked the gods. "He wanted the world, and you killed him for it."

The gods did not answer, because necessity needed no justification.

The demon began to pray.

The clock ticked quietly above her. "India is a failure on the world stage. Though hailed as a future superpower…"

She faced the corner of the room, where a decade-old motivational poster poorly covered a constellation of peeling paint. Her eyes always focused on the crevice in the brick just underneath the poster. The shadows there flickered in time with the overhead light that threatened to give out. In the moments between speeches, Anjali looked down, deliberating. She knew the exact geometry of the coffee stain on the linoleum tile that repeated cleanings had never gotten out.

The deadline for submitting the written draft had closed five minutes ago. She had submitted it six minutes ago. It was…fine. Not her best work, but she never turned in her best work. Anjali didn't even know what her best work looked like—when she didn't *need* to put in her 100% to get 100%, what was the point of trying harder?

(Nowadays, though, that grade was starting to slip lower and lower. Half effort didn't get full credit. It barely got passing credit.)

Thankfully, the performed speech didn't have to be the exact same as the written speech, so she could smooth out the details through practice. She had one week.

For the seventh time, she repeated, "India is a failure on the world stage."

Who is a failure on the world stage?

Anjali paused. That didn't quite sound like the whisper of her conscience, or any voice from down the hallway. It was neither internal nor external, quiet nor loud, male nor female.

Clearly, Anjali had been doing this too long already. She needed a break. So what if she'd planned on practicing for another hour? Anjali was clearly too tired to be productive. But if she spent a little time on the internet, maybe she'd find her energy restored. (She never did.) Anjali opened her laptop and tried to lose herself in the mindless flow of information.

The demon king prayed for years. He foreswore all pleasures of the mortal world: no food or water passed through his lip—with each inhale and exhale he spoke the name of Brahma. He sat like a stone at the top of a great mountain peak.

Moved by his devotion, the god of creation appeared before the demon and promised a boon.

Anger fermented inside her. Anjali wanted to smash her laptop on the ground, but her anger was passive: it encouraged stillness, not movement. She hadn't won first place. Instead, Susan had taken the metaphorical crown. *Susan.* She wasn't half as smart as Anjali was. But Anjali knew that Susan's speech was *better.*

Yes, Anjali had still placed second, which meant that she'd continue into the second round. The small bitter part admitted that Susan needed the scholarship more than Anjali did. Susan was already a scholarship student to Mallory Thorne, and there was no way she could afford to pay for uni without outside funding.

Anjali's parents were wealthy enough. They were both engineers, brought to the far shore with the most recent diaspora, and they had saved enough money that Anjali had never considered where her college funds would come from.

But did that really matter? If the world revolved around what people *needed,* then nobody would get any help. She still went to the doctor even if she wasn't the sickest person in the world. Why shouldn't she try to get the scholarship?

It wasn't about what she deserved. It was about what she wanted.

"India is a failure on the world stage," she said again. "This nation of...of..." God. "India is a failure on the world stage." The tone was wrong. "India is a failure on the world stage." Why couldn't she get this *right*?

Anjali, we see your penance.

What?

Anjali, we see your tapasya. *We wish to reward your devotion.*

It was that voice again. She started looking around, stepping closer to the speaker to see if someone had played some demented prank.

We are pleased with you.

She peered through the window in the door, looking for someone in the hallway that could be the source of the hallway.

We are pleased with you.

Anjali pushed the door open and, struck by some impulse she couldn't vocalize, ran.

The demon king asked for immortality.

"No. I cannot grant you that. What lives must die."

"Then promise me this: I will not be killed by a mortal, demon, or god. I will die neither on the earth nor in the sky. I will die neither inside nor outside, by human nor by beast, at day or at night. No weapon nor spell will do me harm. Promise me dominion over flesh and magic and illusion."

"So be it."

She returned to the room the next day.

Anjali had done nothing in the meantime besides sleep the day away. To be fair, she did nothing on most days, but she normally went to bed past midnight: most of her daylight hours were spent whittling away time by doing neither what she enjoyed nor what she should do. Then she spent the hours from twilight to early morning finishing what she had to do in her cramped dorm room, forced by the immense pressure of an upcoming deadline.

But Anjali was afraid that sleep deprivation was catching up to her. That was why she had heard the strange voices, right? The voices telling her about devotion, stories she remembered from her childhood in front of incense and flame—it had to be some unconscious hallucination.

The word *penance* rattled around in her head. In the English translations of old myths, clunky attempts to bring the children of immigrants back into the fold, they usually translated *tapasya* as *penance*. And with the completion of a penance came a boon: a reward for devotion, regardless of the price. She had rarely heard those two words anywhere else.

Perhaps there was something Freudian about it. Some unconscious calling, some guilt she felt for never being Brown enough for her parents. Sure, she knew the myths. She just didn't care. Anjali's parents had sacrificed so much to get her into the school—as they liked to remind her, and she was wasting it—as they also liked to remind her.

That was why she had heard those voices. Sleep deprivation and Freud. Nothing more.

Anjali took the same corner. This time, she held a notepad and pen in her hand, clicking it on and off as she read the transcript and rephrased words. The introduction was nearly perfect, but it lost steam toward the end.

"India is a failure on the world stage." After the fourth time, she started rushing through the rest, and words lost their meaning and disintegrated into their component parts. Another breath. She tried again.

She lost herself in the flow of the words. She wasn't supposed to do this: she was supposed to pay attention to each sentence, the tone and intonation, the facial expressions she made, each breath. The goal was to have the speech memorized so she could be conscious of *how* she said it, not what she said.

What she was doing now was entirely counterproductive. Anyone could recite a speech. But not everyone would perform it. This chant felt like doing work without actually doing work.

It was soothing. It was *easy*.

And that was the problem, wasn't it? She always went for what was easy rather than what was better or right.

Anjali wished that she had an excuse. She wished she had something she could point to, some tragedy or trauma or neurodivergence that she could point to and say, "If only…" or "It's because…" During her worst moments of self-imposed despair, Anjali silently wished for some minor inconvenience to strike her and give her an excuse. Maybe a minor car accident, or a quick stabbing, or—in her worst moments—a family member would be struck by a serious but recoverable illness.

She knew the thoughts were cruel and nasty and wrong, but they bounced in her head regardless of how much she hated herself for thinking them.

She would never say it. As silly as it was, her mother's superstition of *tathastu* had caught into her mind and throat. Only speak good, never malice: So be it—*tathastu*—the gods would say, if you spoke your wishes out loud.

So instead, Anjali would wish for determination or self-discipline and victory as she procrastinated and half-assed everything she did, even as she spent hours and hours grinding her fingers against the plastic desks.

Anjali just didn't want to try her fullest and still fail.

Ask your boon.

She stopped halfway through the conclusion of her speech. It was that voice.

Ask, and we shall grant your desire.

"Who…are you?" she asked, her voice cracking.

We are the spirits of hunger and need. We who come from the waters of creation and are born of the creator god's ancient impulses. We are those who wish to bestow a reward for your penance.

Rakshasa.

Yes.

Demons, but not quite. In the stories, they tended to villainy. But there were few absolutes in Hindu mythology. Not all rakshasa were evil. She couldn't distinguish anything about these voices: intent, gender, emotion...they were nothing but a steady whisper in her mind.

"What's the catch? What do I have to do?"

The debt has been paid. Your self-recrimination is punishment enough.

She didn't believe it. Boons could be given for tasks already performed, but what had she done besides speak half-heartedly at the wall? What had she really done to pay for her victory? But...she wanted it, right? She really wanted it? Maybe that was enough.

Ask.

"I want to win." It was the truth. She did want to win.

We will grant your desire. Leave your offering by the altar.

Her eyes immediately darted to the crevice in the brick.

The shadow wasn't flickering in time with the light anymore.

None of this was real, but if it were, was it cheating to take the help of a rakshasa? Did it matter? It wasn't like she could get caught and punished for consorting with demons. This wasn't the 1800s anymore. If this voice was real, then she'd win. If it wasn't, then she'd just feel a little silly for talking to the wall and expecting a response.

Well, it also wanted an offering. Anjali looked down at the pen in her hand, and then she wedged the cheap plastic into the wall.

"I accept."

The king of rakshasas waged war on the heavens, and the roots of the earth shook with his might. No corner of three worlds was left untouched by his conquest. But in his very home, his son had turned away from the face of power to seek divinity. His son worshipped the god of protection, he who held the universe in his hands, he who killed the king's younger brother.

The king begged his son to turn back, but he refused. They were both set on their paths. He could not bear to raise his hand against his son, so he ordered his guards to draw their blades.

––––––––––––––––

Anjali sat in the desk, her legs wedged underneath. The clock had broken last week, stuck perpetually at 9:43 AM. She should start saying her speech. Any time, she would start. Anjali had made it to the last round along with Susan. There was a third participant—Edward—but he wasn't close to threat.

Despite becoming sick in the middle of round two, Susan had still made it to finals. What kind of monster still qualified after throwing up in front of the judges?

Anjali bounced her right leg and it hit the top of the desk. Not hard enough to bruise, but the stimulation settled her. Why did she feel worse now that she had a guaranteed win? Maybe she just felt bad because she was going crazy. She felt crazy. Did people who were going crazy feel crazy? Maybe practicing her speech would help her feel better. But did she even need to practice? The deal had worked, right?

You have done penance. Victory is guaranteed.

Her legs stilled when she heard the voice, and Anjali sighed with a mixture of relief and anxiety. Was victory guaranteed, though? Was it?

You have done penance. Victory is guaranteed.

What if she forgot her speech, or Susan performed her speech at her highest level? Anjali *knew* it was better than hers.

You have done penance. Victory is guaranteed.

"I know!" she screamed.

It echoed in the dingy room, and Anjali was hit with the mortifying self-awareness that she was yelling at a crack in the wall. She smacked her knee against the top of the desk, hard enough to bruise this time. It would join the collection of dark patches coloring both knees: the pain was grounding.

Why did she feel so bad?

Her grades were starting to get worse. Her barely-As were now barely Bs. She couldn't get herself to complete her assignments, and the lectures couldn't keep her attention anymore. Anjali didn't have to do anything but study, and she couldn't even manage that. Meanwhile, Susan worked a part-time job and still aced every exam. Susan barely slept five hours a night and still did all her work. How was it fair that even with everything working against her, Susan still did so well?

You have done penance. Victory is guaranteed.

This time, Anjali let herself believe it.

"I have done penance. Victory is guaranteed."

He who was swathed in gold, the king of rakshasas—Hiranyakashipu—tried to kill his son. Blades broke against his flesh. Beasts refused to trample him. Fire flickered merrily against his skin. No longer could the king let others try and fail.

Hiranyakashipu would act himself.

The king summoned his son to the throne room. His son stood between the pillars, as defiant as he was silent. Finally, rage overcame his love, and the rakshasa picked up his mace.

"Your god will not save you. Your god is not here. I am here. Acknowledge that I am your father and your lord, and I will spare you."

Unafraid, his son said, "Our god is everywhere."

"Is your god in this pillar?"

Hiranyakashipu raised the mace above his head and brought it against the marble column.

"Yes, I am."

Anjali set the trophy on the desk.

She had won.

Susan's mystery illness had taken her to the hospital. Finals had been just Anjali and Edward, and that had been no competition at all. Even in the hospital, Susan had texted her "Congrats!" Anjali still hadn't responded yet.

She didn't feel any different in victory.

Anjali stared at the clock's reflection in the trophy. Facilities had come and fixed the clock, but they hadn't corrected the time: it was now two hours too fast.

Susan would have felt different. Ten thousand pounds was enough to let her quit her part-time job. Ten thousand pounds was enough to stop factoring tuition and scholarships into her choice for university.

It hadn't really changed anything for Anjali.

Should she feel bad about this?

Should she feel bad about winning?

Anjali turned the trophy around in her hands, the metal cold and sharp like teeth, the gold engraving of her name glinting in the fluorescent light. Seeing it, she felt a little thrill.

No.

No, she shouldn't feel bad.

Some people were lucky. Some people were naturally better. It wasn't Anjali's fault that fate had given her this opportunity.

So be it.

She looked up. The shadows spiraled across the cracks of the brick wall, denser than they had any right to be. The pen she'd left as offering had disappeared, and in its place was an expanding crevice—one large enough for the trophy in her hands.

"The debt has been paid," she said to the empty air.

So be it.

This trophy was hers.

So be it.

Anjali stepped forward. The light flickered in time with her step, which echoed the tick of the clock, which pulsed with the growing shadows. She placed the gold trophy in the crevice, and a hand reached out.

Vishnu, the god of protection, the eternal, the omnipresent, stepped from the pillar. He came as an avatar, cloaked in flesh, neither god nor mortal. He was half-lion and half-man, and with a massive claw, he dragged Hiranyakashipu to the balcony by his cloth of gold. The sun had dipped below the horizon, but his light still filled the sky.

The god pulled Hiranyakashipu into his lap and cradled his head.

Teeth tore into flesh.

"So be it."

WRITING WITH BITE

NATHANAEL BOON

From one lonesome corner of her computer screen, the clock stared judgmentally at *Su. 5:00pm, 21/10/2020*, it read.

"*Crap, crap, crap,*" she muttered. Pushing away several errant strands of hair, she typed away furiously at her final year essay. It would soon be closing time at the Grand Hopkins Library—the library of the Mallory Thorne School of Excellence—and she would have to vacate the premises.

As if right on cue, a massive figure motioned to her. At nearly one hundred and ninety centimetres tall, Mr. Firman, the librarian, cut an imposing figure. Tapping the face of his very antiquated looking wristwatch, he indicated a "six" with his right hand, before motioning to his nose.

"Oh, right. Sorry, Mr. Firman," Su mumbled, pulling up her mask. With a slight nod in assent, the librarian stalked off, resuming his patrol of the premises for other "unruly" students rushing out their essays in the final hour before the library's closure. She quietly wondered how she was doing compared to them, being halfway toward her estimated word count of three thousand words. In lieu of the university placement examinations that had been scrapped under current Headmaster Melthrope Thorne two years prior, every final year student of Mallory Thorne would instead be graded on a "Petit Thesis," demonstrating their expertise and passion in any subject of their choosing. This would then be graded by an independent committee of subject matter experts gathered from as many fields of study as possible. For Su, it was herpetology—she had decided to concentrate on venomous snakes.

As the minutes ticked by, so too did Su's patience. Her phone, sandwiched in between the pages of her book, was vibrating with unread notifications—mostly from her dorm-mate Alix and their video game-related ramblings. *No*, she reminded herself, no entertaining their musings at this critical juncture, much as she wanted to. A single picture of a black mamba glared at her with its jaw agape, as if to express dissatisfaction at being bound within its encyclopaedia.

"I'm supposed to want to study you for a living. What the heck?" she groaned.

Then, she froze. From out of the corner of her eye, she thought she had seen the snake subtly shift its head, mouth closed, as if watching her. In a blink, the vision was gone, and the reptile re-assumed its baleful expression.

Su rubbed her eyes.

"No, no, I must finish this now," she murmured.

She could not.

The school bells chimed six, and her heart sank.

The cavernous bellowing of Mr. Firman echoed from somewhere up the stairs.

"Students! Leave at once! Any of you caught in the premises after hours will be sent for disciplinary action!"

The remaining student body did not have to be told twice; Discipline Master McCann was not one known for his lenience, and that was saying something, considering the few authority figures at Mallory Thorne were pretty tough.

Then there was the other thing: the rumors. Rumors of the witching hour, that the school took on a whole new, paranormal nature at the dying of the light. Not that Su or Alix put much stock in them; they were too busy slaying eldritch monstrosities in *Dark Souls* to indulge in campus gossip. What was material to her right now was getting to somewhere quiet so she could work in peace. No games, no pesky librarians, and hopefully no snakes coming to life.

Noticing Mr. Firman's occupation with another student's query, she slinked under the second level balustrade into the place where he would (probably) least expect to find any errant student—his office. Clenching her teeth, she gently set the door latch in place and eased the tension off the handle. Behind the plain wooden door was a fairly typical librarian's office space, about twice the size of her single bedroom dorm. What unnerved ever slightly was the absolute neatness of the space. Returned books sat abreast in their cart like soldiers in a parade, separated by genre and then by author. Invoices and other documents stacked the shelves in orderly rank and file, while the works of Murakami, King, and Le Guin stood directly opposite in similar shipshape fashion. Beyond that lay a single, completely unremarkable desk, again with not a single paper or pen out of place. The only thing of note on the desk was a framed picture of an art relief—Su could not tell where it had been taken—depicting an enormous black dragon in flight. In a corner of that picture was a number: "1532," probably a lock or safe code of some sort.

A light breeze brushed her ear. Bizarre, for there were no windows in the office, and the ceiling fan had not been switched on. Su's eyes turned toward a corner of the room, where a black and yellow drape hung over a mirror. Intrigued, she removed the drape, beholding a mirror that took on the same unremarkable appearance as everything else in the room, save for its unusual polishedness. There, she considered her physical form. Her auburn hair, barely held together by bobby pins at the start of the day, had all but lost any semblance of neatness, drooping over black spectacles like moss. Her honey brown eyes, threatening to close a mere ten minutes ago, were now wide open, flush with adrenaline and intrigue. Inexplicably, Su reached out with her finger, and the Su in the mirror responded in kind.

What she felt was not the cold, unyielding touch of glass, but something much softer. Something fleshy. To her horror, she realized it was her own finger. The Su of the mirrored world stared right into her soul and smiled an impish smile, saying to her, "It's time that I came out to play." Realizing what she meant, Su backed away, an all too familiar ache growing in her chest. In a final moment of lucidity, she remembered to change out of her school uniform, recalling the numerous clothes she had ruined before doing this.

Su collapsed to the floor, her breaths coming in heaves. Rolling on her back, she whimpered as she allowed the transformation to take rein. Auburn fur sprouted from every follicle, and bony claws pushed through her finger and toe-tips. Her feet stretched in a sickening manner, not unlike a lump of dough. Her mouth took on the appearance of a short muzzle, and she coughed several drops of blood, panting vigorously all the while.

It was over. Su rose unsteadily to her feet after several moments. She looked in the mirror once more. Gone was the bespectacled, nerdy mouse of a student—the mirror had relieved her of that shell. In its place was a seven-foot tall, bipedal, wolf-like creature, half human, half dhole, complete with a long and bushy tail and eyes like amber. She held one giant paw to her skull and skulked to a corner of the office, instinctively licking her fur. The door pushed open, and she huddled against the corner in fear. Mr. Firman raised an eyebrow, surveilling the scene with imperiousness. To his relief, none of the books, *his* books, had been knocked over or otherwise eaten or urinated on. Neither had his other belongings been disturbed.

"Well, young lady, it seems we learned a hard lesson today about touching things that should not have been touched?" he boomed.

Su shrunk into the corner even further, issuing several warning barks. The librarian simply shook his head.

"I take it you *are* still able to understand me in your current state, yes?"

The half-dhole cocked her head slightly, eyeing him with suspicion.

"I have something for you, but I will need a while to procure it. Wait right here, and refrain from touching or chewing on anything."

The creature that was Su lay slumped in the corner, unaware of the passage of time. This was far from her first rodeo; in fact, she counted five transformations since she started getting them three years ago, and detailed what she could remember on her phone's notes application. There was no particular stressor or factor or common thread that united each occurrence—they seemed to occur completely at the whims and fancies of the animal that lay beneath. Was this some form of curse or hex? She could not think of any magicians or gods she had wronged. It could not possibly have been a hereditary condition—her terrified and bemused, yet doting, parents had never experienced anything like this, and were at their wit's end finding communities for her to fit into. She vaguely remembered getting nipped by a neighbor's terrier she had stroked the wrong way, but she reasoned she would have transformed into a were-terrier instead, not a dhole. Either way, she did not think she would be getting her answer tonight.

Just then, something slipped underneath the doorway: a long, grey, cylindrical shape that slithered across the floor in leisurely fashion. Su growled, and her fur stood on end. Even in this form, she could recognize what was staring at her now: a black mamba. The mamba reared up, appraising her for several seconds…and then, it spoke.

"What's all this then? Are you another...one of us?"

Its voice was low. Gravelly. Masculine.

Su gurgled a low growl, baring her teeth.

"Ahh, I see you have fiddled with one of old Phobos's toys. That mirror does no one any good. Not sure why he has not up and smashed the damned thing."

Phobos...? Su wanted to say, but it emerged as a snort, and she tilted her head.

"Phobos—or what does he call himself these days? 'Firman,' eh? Silly old sod. Oh, pardon me, I have forgotten my manners, The name's Deimos. Well met, fellow shifter."

The serpent locked eyes with the canine, not in hostility, but they had appeared to reach a sort of didactic understanding. She was curious, and he relished it.

"To be honest, me and Phobos, we have history. Baggage. Most of it was good, and I cherish our time together in my heart of hearts. However, I said some things, committed some acts, that I am not proud of to this day, even after all these centuries."

Su let out a small whine, clutching both paws to her face.

"I know, I know. You must be considering how this is germane to your current predicament. You see, Phobos and I were passionate scientists in times of yore. We ate together, we slept together, we would supervise all manner of alchemical reactions overnight. Most of all, we appreciated and critiqued each other's work, for we both wanted the good of our kind, and that, too, of mankind. That mirror was one of our more esoteric experiments."

Deimos glided along the floor effortlessly, and Su hopped aside, mildly startled.

"If you are a formshifter like us, and you touch this mirror in your human form, you will be transformed into any one of the aspects of nature that you embody, but you are unable to change back if you touch it again. For you, it is this canine form. For Phobos and I, it was serpents and reptiles of all sorts, both real and fantastical."

Su grunted. It was probably Deimos that Firman was looking for, in that picture on the desk with the dragon relief.

"Even I have yet to find any answers as to 'why us,' what cosmic force drives the creation of shifters, and who gets to live with this, but this mirror was a valuable insight into how to trigger a change, and dealing with said changes."

He sighed. "The experiment did not go as planned. After I touched this mirror all those years ago, the intention was to craft a device or potion to induce a reversal to human form. However, all our efforts proved fruitless, and..."

Deimos cast his face toward the ground in pensive thought.

"In 1532, we were captured by the witchfinders, and held in captivity separately. I was able to make good my escape, but not him. When they lit the pyre on which his original body rested, he metamorphosed into a giant wyrm, one that stalks the spaces in between dimensions. The form of Mr. Firman that you see is merely a projection of his old physical self. 'Twas only after reading some of his old notes that I was able to figure out how he did it and managed to replicate the same for myself. Which explains why you saw me in that book earlier, and I must truly apologize for giving you a scare."

Su crept slowly, inquisitively toward Deimos, sniffing him out. The serpent held his tongue and his nerve. Satisfied, Su settled down once more, watching him intently.

"To be perfectly honest, I do not wish to talk to him. I only came by to see how he was doing, because my heart ached ever so much at the thought of him growing distant, forgetting me."

"I doubt I could ever forget you, my love."

Su and Deimos whirled around, the immense figure of Mr. Firman towered above them. Only in her current form, Su saw not only Firman's physical human projection, but his real form: an immense purple wyrm whose body and tail reached the double doors to the library, fifteen meters away. *Phobos.*

"After all these years of mourning and grieving, I have come to meet you in the one place I was hoping you would not turn up," Phobos continued. "Do enlighten me, however. What would motivate you to say that you did not intend to talk to me?"

Deimos gulped.

"Well, after our whole debacle, I...felt guilty for everything. For suggesting the creation and study of this blasted mirror to begin with, the capture, being unable to rescue you in time. It's just too much for one soul to bear."

Phobos scooped him up and kissed him, the effect of which seemed to add some color to the serpent's cheeks.

"You silly nit. That was our job as scientists. It was our life's and death's work. We both should be well aware of the consequences of tampering with the things we did."

"Am I forgiven? Do you have—"

"Belay that. You are utterly and completely forgiven, and I could not be happier to have you back. Now, about our guest."

Mr. Firman reached into his coat pocket, pulling out a handful of what appeared to be sand.

"This is dream dust. After interactions with you and others like you of this generation, it dawned on me that what we need sometimes is a 'reset.' To switch your device off, and then on again, clearing any and all 'bugs' and imperfections. This will aid you in your sleep tonight, and you shall awake in the morn none the wiser."

Su turned in an attempt to run, guided by her canine instincts, but the cloud of dream dust overcame her, and she entered the domain of sleep.

"Su, wake up! Wake up!"

Su could barely lift her eyelids open. She had no idea how Alix had this much energy this early in the morning.

"Jesus, Su, come on, it's seven already. Half an hour till literature class!"

"Oh, crap! Okay, okay, I am coming!

"Don't forget to get some clothes on, ya cheeky!"

Oh, Su realized.

"Sure Alix, just a second! Hey, how did you find me nake—"

"I did not! I was too busy with that fortress raid stage on *Call of the Battlefield*. I figured you needed extra time to work on your thesis and came back late.

"Sure," Su admitted, "although I have not finished yet. Something about the Librarian. I can't remember."

Alix laughed audibly.

"You're dreaming about him? I guess we all know your taste in men now, huh?"

"Shhh, that's enough, Alix! He's taken, anyway."

"Wahahaha, even someone like him is off the dating market, who knew?"

"It's more complicated than that, to be honest."

Rubbing their hands, Alix exclaimed "Okay Ms. Complicated and hardly shares anything, who's dating who?"

Su smiled an impish smile at them, and for but a flash, her eyes glazed yellow.

THE HOUSEMASTER'S CURE FOR HOMESICK BOYS

CHARLIE JIAO

Term begins on a frigid sort of Monday, where mist leeches through young Hugo Lau's overcoat and wrenches warmth from his veins. He darts across the courtyard with chattering teeth, cutting a path away from the stone gazes of hulking gargoyles.

The new First Years arrived at dusk the preceding evening and marched across the courtyard to their residences. In the middle of the monochrome courtyard, even though statues cannot see, September's air grew colder under their icy expressions. The First Years exhaled hesitance where there had before been excitement, breath spinning silken webs of mist that quickly dissipated to nothing once again. New shoes, clattering, stumbled to a halt. In their wake followed the absence of echoes, for the flagstones swallowed sound greedily.

In the dwindling twilight, the First Years agreed cautiously that the courtyard was watching.

"How can that be," whispered one boy, the son of two talented botanists, "when not even weeds dare grow?"

Today, Hugo reaches the oaken door of the First Year Boys' dormitory. He removes one hand from its mitt to fetch his key. Though the air is lifeless, it bites at his fingers still as they curl, pallid and aching with cold.

It is a relief when he slips through the door. The First Year Boys' dormitory is warmer, if only because no malignant dread follows him inside. The walls are panelled in wooden squares, and the ceiling is painted a fading grey. The curtains are silken, the sort that should let light through in the summer, but for now the weather drizzles on, and any light does not seem to want to permeate their little haven. In here, nothing is watching.

Disagreeable to being trodden upon, the floorboards whinge as Hugo steps across. There are two bunk beds against two walls, simple wooden things with drawers underneath for belongings. A fifth bed is stubbornly squashed up against a writing desk, awkward, like it did not want to be moved. Huddled amongst its covers, Billy Huang is whimpering.

Billy Huang cried when they arrived at the school, and cried through the dinner held in their honor. This morning, after Hugo slipped into shining new shoes and wrapped his heavy woollen scarf around his neck, Billy hid in his bed. Hugo tried prodding him, but that only made the boy cry harder, and so Hugo left with the others.

Billy's absence went unnoticed for a long while. When the Housemaster, already exasperated, barked his summons, only Hugo offered to return.

Hugo is bigger than Billy, in stature and in mind. He does not think himself particularly imposing, but Billy shrinks as he approaches. It is a pathetic sort of shrinking, like Billy would much like to disappear from this world entirely.

Hugo stands in front of Billy Huang and fidgets. "The Housemaster says you should come to breakfast." Hugo is eleven, has short-cropped hair, and is very good at mathematics. His mother is an engineer, his father owns a corporation. Before Hugo, England snatched them from their homeland with whispers of excellence. Excellence always demands sacrifice.

Billy sniffles. "Not hungry."

"I think you have to." Hugo stands, awkward, and wonders what Billy has sacrificed.

The miserable boy mistakes Hugo's detached bemusement for kindness. "The Housemaster said I couldn't write to my mum." His shriek is on the verge of hysteria.

Hugo's mother has already sent him fifteen texts. He doesn't understand why anyone would want to talk to their mums when they've just started school. "You can borrow my phone," he offers.

Billy looks at him like he's the mad one. He keeps wailing. The noise is grating and annoying.

Hugo backs away. He casts his eyes around the room, at the scarred wood from years of boys clawing fingernails across walls. In the middle of the parquet floor there is a stain like the ceiling has been weeping, but above there are no signs of damp.

Hugo has the lower bunk and a basket of treats from his mother on the bedside table. He pulls the basket toward him, rifling between Haribo and M&Ms. He finds a sherbet dip and a packet of Skittles. Cautiously, he approaches Billy, holding them out.

Billy accepts the Skittles nervously, turning the packet between bone-thin fingers. His cries quiet to sniffly hiccoughs, self-pity dissolving away to fascination. Hugo's ears are grateful.

"I've not seen these before." Billy has a wispy sort of voice, weak and faraway.

Hugo rips open his sherbet dip and pours the powder straight into his mouth. "S'just Skittles," he says.

"They're so bright." He puts one on his tongue, cautious. And then another. He saves the red one for last, chewing thoughtfully.

Hugo licks at the lollipop that comes with his sherbet and decides that Billy must have a family who is rich, or perhaps he is related to the headmaster. *Ne-po-tism* is a word Hugo has heard his father snap to his mother, regarding a deadbeat uncle.

Hugo pours more sherbet into his mouth and promptly coughs a cloud of sugar into the air. Billy giggles. It's a pathetic girlish laugh that makes Hugo look over.

Through the sherbet cloud, Billy has faded. Hugo's gaze meets hollow eyes, sunken so deep into his skull they can't see light any more. The skin of his face pulls tight around his mouth, grinning teeth dripping crimson like blood.

Panicked, Hugo backs away. The stain on the floor sags when he steps into it, and he inhales, sharp. There's sherbet in his throat. He coughs again, and this time Billy does not laugh.

"Are you all right?"

Hugo coughs and coughs. Bony fingers reach through sherbet that stings his eyes. The grasp is stronger than Hugo could've imagined. Billy pulls him forward and out of the cloud. Hugo wonders if he is going to be eaten, but the boy, eleven years old, is a boy again.

Billy lets go of him and leans backward from where he is sitting. His face is normal, head cocked and expression confused.

Hugo wheezes, throat sore. "I think I coughed myself dizzy."

Billy is silent and concerned. Like Hugo's own, Billy's eyes are black, his dark hair cropped short. They both have skin darker than the aristocracy of this country, but that is where Hugo considers their similarities to end. Billy is *other*. His native Mandarin sounds foreign to Hugo's ears, worlds away from his Beijing aunties and uncles. He sounds more like Hugo's grandmother, and he can't speak a lick of Cantonese. His writing is atrocious, strokes wobbly in their slow uncertainty. As if Billy has long lost the country he left for the school.

And yet he doesn't suit England, not the way Hugo knows how. Hugo was born to this country, knows how to walk the line between worlds. Billy is a forgotten thing. It is no wonder he cries for his mother.

Hugo is growing impatient with the odd feeling their dorm is not free from the force in the courtyard. "We need to go to breakfast."

Whatever spirit haunts here does not watch, though. It does not care. It hangs in the air and engulfs their dorm in a listless arrogance that leaves stains on the floor and eleven-year-old boys sobbing in their beds, hearts aching for home.

Billy Huang untangles himself from the confines of his duvet and stands. He has his uniform on already. He follows Hugo out of the First Year Boys' dormitory, avoiding the stain in the floor as if he is worried it will swallow him whole.

The Housemaster slams down a greying bowl of porridge where Billy Huang is expected to sit. He is an ageless figure, somewhere between thirty and sixty, in the way eleven-year-olds cannot understand. The Housemaster has a name, but they do not use it, for a name is a familiarity not yet earned.

"Eat," croons the Housemaster, and he pushes Billy into his seat with pale hands and spider-long fingers.

Earlier, Hugo opted for cereal, but he does not remember the vat of porridge turning his stomach like it does now. Billy's bowl looks as if the milk is curdling. Smells like it is festering. Hugo is certain that he can see Billy's breakfast becoming rotten. But it is a trick of the light, for when he blinks the illusion is gone, alongside the stifling doom that he had not noticed was building.

Something is afoot within the walls of the Mallory Thorne

School. Hugo knows old schools have their quirks and their myths, their outdated rules. He knows one is not supposed to walk the hallways of the school at night, not from the underbelly of the ancient storerooms to the highest classroom in the Old School. He has heard whispers of wintry dorms where only candlelight is accepted.

Yet these traditions are no stranger than the traditions of other schools with histories drenched in colonial prestige. He knows of Winchester College, where the students still commemorate the death of their founder; of the King's School, Canterbury, where only pupils of status may walk across the grassy lawns of certain courts.

Churning, tumbling, like the great rushing of water, a storm drain at the height of the wildest of weather, time careens on. The Mallory Thorne School of Excellence demands everything, and there is not time to watch Billy Huang, who struggles against the tide which demands him.

He cries less now, and for that the First Year boys are relieved. He flounders against the mountains of homework, tongue numb against the Latin and French they are prescribed. Hugo cannot find a subject in which Billy flourishes, cannot name one thing that makes him excellent.

He drifts from classroom to classroom. He hangs like a specter at dinner. He barely eats, has not joined any clubs, and Hugo doesn't know what he does between classes and dinner and bed. At the end of each day, Billy creeps into the First Year Boys' dormitory with misery hanging off his bones. Each day he steps around the stain on the floor.

It is November. Half term, two blissful weeks of reprieve from school, has flown by. The boys jeer and laugh as they regale each other with stories of their adventures. Hugo himself had holidayed in Switzerland, though only because his father's work had taken them there. He shows off some photos of bears in an enclosure along a river.

Across the room, Billy Huang is a silent husk of a boy already huddled under covers. The other boys have given up on him. Sometimes Hugo thinks there is not enough of him to comprise a real boy. But Billy's dark eyes peer at Hugo, curious.

"What did you do?" Tommy asks. Billy blinks, as if the very concept of his own life, his own existence, is a foreign one. "Did you see your parents?"

They're the wrong questions. Billy's expression twists. "I didn't go home," he laments. "I wanted to. I wanted to see my mum, but she didn't send a ticket."

Hugo's parents picked him up on the last day of the half. He can't fathom his mother leaving him at school over the holidays. "Maybe she didn't want to see you?" he suggests, an ignorant unkindness only children could possess.

"I hated being alone." In his misery, Billy's strange accent grows stronger. Hugo knows something about being stuck in a world he doesn't belong. When his parents asked him about school, Hugo lied. The Mallory Thorne School produces children of excellence. It whittles away at the sort of child Hugo thinks he himself is. It destroys the sort of boy that is Billy Huang. "The school's haunted."

The boys glance around at each other, dubious. Hugo doesn't believe in ghosts.

"I went on a safari," says the boy in the bunk above Hugo, and Billy Huang and his allegations of the unworldly are quickly ignored.

Eventually they settle down. They brush their teeth and change into their pajamas and say their goodnights. Hugo, bare feet on creaking floorboards, switches off the light. He pads back to his bunk, stepping into the stain on the floor. The floorboards here don't creak, but they do sag, despondent and resigned. Across the darkness, Billy sniffles. His dead-eyed gaze bores through Hugo, his ghoulish mouth grins. Even though the image is only an illusion of a memory, Hugo hastens to his bed and wraps himself in his covers, squeezing his eyes tight so whatever darkness that looms cannot possibly see him.

In the hallway, the Housemaster prowls, ears vigilant for any semblance of a whisper after lights-out. To the rhythm of his precise footfall, sleep claims the boys.

Hugo dreams of a faraway land he knows only in the summer, of jubilant ruckus alongside boats shaped like dragons, of long days filled with carefully curated packages of glutinous rice. And he dreams of the quieter days with only his mother and father beside him. In his dream, it is not quite right. They should be speaking a language that, in the weeks leading to half term, he was worried he wouldn't remember. Despite his mother's smiles and his father's laughs, the words that come out of their mouths are wrong.

Billy screeches. Hugo's heart lurches. Panic forces him to his feet, into the stain on the floor. For a moment he's sure he is sinking. The whites of Billy's eyes shine, even though the world is doused in darkness.

Someone switches on a lamp. Billy is curled up underneath tousled sheets. Hugo knows he couldn't have seen his eyes. Billy whimpers, crying, and his body jerks. He is mumbling, incoherent.

The boy in the top bunk closer to Billy throws his pillow down. "Wake up!" Billy awakens with a jolt, scrambles into a ball in the corner. "It's just a nightmare!"

"The walls are coming for me. *They want me.*"

Hugo glances around without quite meaning to. The walls stand firm. "It was just a dream."

Billy shakes his head, frenetic. "The dormitory is haunted!" His shriek cuts through Hugo's ears and rattles around his skull.

The doorknob turns with a snap. The Housemaster pushes the door open, and for once it does not squeak. His shoes strike like hammers to nails as he walks. The boys are silent. Hugo doesn't dare move from where he has one foot planted in the stain on the floor. Doesn't dare breathe.

The Housemaster wears his tailcoat, midnight black from head to toe save for his bone-white shirt and chalky skin. His coaly hair is cropped short, thicker than it should be for a man his age, Hugo decides idly. Perhaps the Housemaster is younger than he thinks. Perhaps he is very much older.

Dark eyes cut across Hugo, disdainful, but the Housemaster does not loathe Hugo as he does the small boy bundled in the bed on the other side of the room. He grabs Billy, hauling him into the air between two tight fists. Billy hangs slack a few inches off the ground, softly choking on breaths he can't take. "Quiet," croons the Housemaster, low and dangerous.

Billy trembles in his iron grasp. It seems he is incapable of making a sound. He does not try. The Housemaster lowers him to the floor, where bare feet twitch on the hardwood.

With a cold elegance, the Housemaster passes the tossed pillow back up to the boy in the bunk. He looks to Hugo again. Hugo's right foot, the one planted in the stain on the floor, is beginning to go numb. The Housemaster regards Hugo Lau with an opportunistic interest, like he is a plaything ready to be shaped. "To bed," he instructs.

Hugo dips his head in his subservience and hurries to comply, lying down and squeezing his eyes tight. He does not believe in ghosts, but if there were such a thing, he's certain the Housemaster would be it.

The Housemaster is otherworldly in the way he commands obedience with an uncanny omnipresence, at least in the eyes of First Year boys. "Come," he murmurs to Billy Huang. Beneath his eyelids Hugo can see this scene playing out; one thin hand against sharp shoulder blades, Billy's passive face too scared for fear, how the young boy avoids the stain in the floor like it is the cause of his hauntings, but the Housemaster steps through it and for him the stain does not sag, the strike of his heel as cutting as ever. Hugo thinks he sees Billy as he did that one morning, with sunken lifeless eyes and skin that does not want to stay to his bones. He thinks he sees the outline of the Housemaster ripple like a phantom. Hugo's heart is loud in his chest, racing as he is lured in by the scene in his imagination, and it must be all too real, for he misses the bit where the door opens and the pair leave, the bit where the light is turned off and the boys cross the line between the waking world and the slumber of night.

Hugo returns to dreams. He begs his parents to talk to him in the language they made him learn as a child. His mother smiles, kind and sad. Her fingers wrap around his face, and she presses a kiss to his forehead. When she opens her mouth, she answers him in the language of her heart, he recognizes, but he cannot understand a word she says.

Hugo spends his time between worlds. When he speaks his tongue catches on the English he knows and the raw meaning of the Chinese he is trying to convey. He can speak English as well as any-one—better, even—but there are words and concepts that simply do not exist in the language of the country he calls home.

The Mallory Thorne School looks upon imperfection with de-rision. To wield the power of knowledge *is* power. To hesitate is almost as bad as not knowing at all. Hugo knows he cannot lead with his heart if he wishes to thrive.

Come the morning, Billy Huang is not in his bed. None of the other boys acknowledge the lingering malevolence Hugo can feel.

"Do you believe in ghosts?" Hugo asks after hours, or maybe days. Time exists asynchronously within the walls of the school, secluded from the rest of the world. The other boys only give him blank stares. They do not answer the question at all.

When he thinks back to the weeks following Half term, Hugo is not entirely sure if Billy is in them. He can't remember the boy's presence at all. Most days he doesn't notice the absence.

He lets himself into the dormitory with his huge iron key from an old world, shies away from the nipping frost that has settled across the school outside. Billy Huang stands in the middle of the room, staring at the blank wall across from his bed. Hugo thinks he hasn't seen him in a long while. That can't be the case. Billy must have been in classes, in meals, and in the dormitory every night.

"There's something scrabbling in the walls." His voice is dull. "It wants to go home."

Hugo comes to stand next to Billy. He stares at the wall, cocking his head and listening in shared silence. There is nothing to listen for, only scarred wallpaper, pitifully old.

He turns his head, opens his mouth to say this. Instead, he catches the dark and blurry patch that wraps across Billy's cheek, like someone has hit him over and over, fingerprints sitting a little differently with every strike.

"Did the Housemaster lay his hand on you?"

Billy blinks, and then his head turns too. Neither of them have moved their bodies away from the wall. "I told you," Billy says, faraway. "This school is haunted."

"Is the Housemaster a ghost?" Hugo cannot believe in the supernatural.

Hugo thinks Billy laughs then, but he's not sure, because he doesn't think he has ever seen Billy laugh before, nor does he think he sees his mouth move, even though they are staring into each other's dark eyes. He is not sure if something happened or something did not, like the last few seconds have been erased from his memory, or perhaps they occurred not in this world but instead one existing alongside his own.

"Look." He raises the hem of his shirt, showing Hugo the side of his ribcage. Hugo inhales, sharp. Atop every prominent bone is a layer of black and purple, like ink or wine, vicious and painful and indelible. He does not think them the sort of marks the Housemaster could have made. "And the walls call to me." He shows off blunt, broken fingernails, fingertips raw and cracked in greens and greys.

Billy Huang has been tearing at the walls.

"I think it's you," Hugo says, certain he believes in no spirits. "I think you must be hearing voices in your head."

And Billy wails a great dissonance, like there are ten of him and none of him. The walls close in. The First Year Boys' dormitory is suddenly stifling, and the cacophony from Billy Huang grows.

Hugo runs. He slams shut the door to the dormitory and bolts into the center of the lifeless courtyard with its watchful gargoyles. But the courtyard isn't quiet. It whispers, insidious and incoherent in the back of Hugo's mind. It is restless, like it knows Billy's screeching howl. Ghosts do not exist, but there is something in the Mallory Thorne School that is not quite alive, yet breathes into every crevice nonetheless. The School takes root in the pride of its past; it clings to the foundations of intolerance it thrives upon.

The hallways feel empty, like it might have been this way for years. Hugo can't see his classmates or teachers, or any other pupils, and he hurtles through the school at a desperate pace. He flees under limestone archways, elegantly adorned, through hallways where his shoes echo thunderously. Hugo runs through the school and feels a bit like he has never seen its walls before.

The Housemaster alone sits in his office, and he stands and invites Hugo in as if he is expecting him, like the entire school knows what Billy Huang sees. The school has sequestered away its pupils, shuttered its affairs, and it waits with bated breath for a moment it knows will come, a moment that has come and will come and is as much a part of the school as the foundations it was built upon.

"I think Billy Huang is sick, sir," Hugo bites out, hardly out of breath in his adrenaline.

The Housemaster's cruel eyes fix upon him with lazy interest. He is more interested in Hugo's fretfulness. "Bring him to me," he says with a voice of ice. "We shall see he stops this nonsense."

Hugo stumbles back outside and understands the world is waiting for him to deliver Billy Huang to the Housemaster. He thinks of destiny, of fate. Billy Huang is destined for something Hugo does not yet understand, something he fears. It is Hugo who is fated to guide him, he thinks, one foot in front of the other. Hugo thinks of a red thread and wonders how far from these empty halls it would take him. Would it take him home?

These walls of stone warp destiny. This aching desire for excellence suffocates. Hugo does not know if excellence expects him, or if the path he forges at the hands of those like the Housemaster cuts out too far from his personal destiny.

He knows the gargoyles above the courtyard watch for evil. He wonders if they would understand the language of his own guardian lions. He thinks the two would tear each other to pieces.

The door opens, welcoming, and Billy Huang is standing, staring through Hugo and through the courtyard beyond.

Neither boy utters a word, for they both know what is happening. Destiny cannot be rejected.

Billy cringes under the oppressive eyes of gargoyles. Barely a wisp of a figure, he disappears in timeless shadows that linger under limestone archways. Hugo wonders if it is the sort of time where shadows so dark should be possible. Time has disappeared altogether in these walls.

They return to the Housemaster's office. It feels ceremonial.

Hugo thinks perhaps he should have gone to the nurse first. The Housemaster has never shown Billy anything but vicious unkindness.

The Housemaster draws a cane from beside his desk.

"I want to go home." Billy Huang's voice is dull, like they are words he has to say. "I just want my mum."

It is Hugo who cries out, whether in horror or terror, when the cane comes down across Billy's knuckles. Billy's skin bursts. There is no blood. His flesh is grey, his bones stained in black.

Hugo gags as the smell hits him. The Housemaster looks up at him sharply. "Are you not made of sterner things, Lau?"

"I think he needs the nurse, sir," says Hugo, knowing at eleven that boys should not rot.

"Billy didn't meet the school's expectations for excellence." The Housemaster talks as if Billy is not here, as if he is already gone. "Run along now, back to your dormitory. It is nearly time. Billy Huang won't bother you much longer."

Hugo Lau sits on the edge of his bed with his pencil case open beside him. He pulls out the scissors he stole from the art classroom and presses the blade to his thigh. He scores, hard enough to tear through his trousers, to leave a line of red beneath the paler flesh of his thigh. It is a morbid curiosity that has taken hold of him. He pulls apart his trousers, pushes at his skin so blood dribbles out of tiny invisible cuts. His blood bleeds a brilliant red. With the scissors he pushes deeper, with the desperate need to see for himself that his muscle is red and his bone white.

The door opens. Billy clutches his hand, and the sour stench of decay fills the room. He is limping. He approaches Hugo with great hesitance, right up until he sees through torn sinew and down to the core of what separates them.

Hugo glances back down to the sliver of white that is quickly pooling crimson and wonders what he has just done.

Billy's face, ghostly pale but for the blooming bruise on his cheek, drains of any remaining color. He cries out weakly, as if this is worse than his festering body. Billy backs away, turns to run, and in his panic forgets to sidestep the stain on the floor until the very last second where he missteps. He trips, hurtling into the corner of the writing desk. Any ordinary person would be fine. But Billy's body makes a noise like a stomach gurgling and the smell increases tenfold.

"Ah!" gasps Billy in a high-pitched squeal, almost human. He whirls around, mouth open as he looks to Hugo, as if Hugo could help. His good hand goes to his stomach and comes away sticky with fluid, and then both hands tear at the fabric of his shirt. The hand that is already rotted fails, tendons to fingers giving out, neither skin nor muscle left to hold onto his bones. His fingers hang by rotted sinew, dangling as he paws at his chest. Where he pulls his shirt out from his belt, he pulls sloughed skin too. His good hand bursts buttons, but his efforts have worn away the skin on his palm and on the top of his fingers, oozing black blood. His greyed shirt plasters itself to his body with the ruin he has made.

The boys stare at the mess of Billy's abdomen. And *oh*, the smell.

Billy drags fingers across the map of his ruined torso. His nails catch on skin, tearing like wrapping paper, scraping at sludge like sewage beneath. He whimpers. Pushes into his ribs, softened with decay. His fingers grasp at the maw of a wound he has created, curling to hold himself together. But his bones are exhausted, and they cave against the little strength Billy has. He rots from the inside out.

Billy stumbles forward, lands with a squelch in the stain on the floor. The stain on the floor welcomes him like a friend. Like it has expected him. Like it had before and will again.

The First Year Boys' dormitory rots. Buried beneath the floor, Billy howls.

"What are you?" Hugo whispers.

Billy whimpers with what little he still is, sunken eyes and skin that clings desperately to his bones. "I'm homesick," he murmurs, in a voice that is distant not in space but perhaps time. Billy's fate has long been written. Long has passed.

Billy Huang crumbles into the floorboards beneath the stain.

Hugo lurches forward, ignores the weeping of blood from his leg as he sinks to his knees. Frantic, Hugo pulls at the stain on the floor. His fingertips tear on splintered wood and he bleeds, crimson. The wood gives way.

There are bones. Bones so old they are beginning to crack and crumble to dust. Billy Huang has for half a century sat beneath the floor of the First Year Boys' dormitory, bleeding his soul into its walls.

The Housemaster watches. Hugo doesn't know how long he has stood there. Does not recall his entrance. Hugo cannot remember the name his mother calls him, from a country so far away. "Let this be a lesson to you, child. Don't you come mewling to me again."

There is a lesson in rot and ruin for little boys who whine and whinge, for little boys who have been bestowed the opportunity for a greatness they are too weak to achieve.

A MEMORY LEFT FIGHTING

M.K. SARRAJ

It stormed the night Jonathan Pensworth was called back from Hell. He stood in the dark corner of the room, watching as the young girls that summoned him chewed on their lips and fidgeted with the hems of their skirts, their eyes darting around the room. It amused him to think these four girls, clueless and naïve, had pulled him out of the infernal flames. To what end, he wondered? Perhaps they had meant to call on someone else.

His lips pulled back, splitting his face into a Cheshire grin.

Four little girls, dressed in black. What a nice reward for the Butcher Jack.

Ghosts don't want to die. They don't want to be torn from this plane of existence, yanked toward whatever afterlife waits for them. It's hard to tell which ghosts fight back the hardest—usually it's the malicious spirits but, on occasion, it's the quiet ones. The ones you thought made their peace with moving on.

My grandfather was like that. We had always thought he'd pass on peacefully, being a spirit soother and all. So, we were surprised to find him haunting my parents' apartment. How he'd even gotten there, we didn't know, since they lived an ocean and a continent away. But he must have taken a ride on one of his old pocket watches.

Anyway. We thought it was fine, at first. He had never seen my parents' place before. Maybe he wanted to make sure his daughter was really okay before he moved on. Except he didn't leave, and what's worse was that he wouldn't tell his kids how to help him pass. They had never wanted to learn while he was alive, so why start now?

That's why they called me home from boarding school. Because I was the only one who had taken up my grandfather's mantle; I was the only one who could soothe his spirit.

You're probably wondering why my parents didn't just call someone else—why traumatize their seventeen-year-old daughter by having her exorcise the spirit of her favorite relative? Well, it's because there aren't a lot of us. You could call a hunter, of course, but they tend to be a bit aggressive, and my grandfather could get, uh, rough when angry. We didn't want him to bring the house down. Literally.

And I'm probably not that traumatized, anyway. Maybe only a little, but who makes it out of their teen years without a little trauma? No one. So, I'm probably fine. I *am* fine.

Mallory Thorne is the kind of boarding school you send your kids to when they don't quite fit in anywhere else. I've been here for five years—since I was thirteen—and I'm not the only hyphenated transplant, either. Plenty of kids from all over the world are sent here, because while there are plenty of other imitators, there's only one Mallory Thorne. Normally, admission to the school is difficult. You have to be deemed "special," or know people who know people, or be a legacy kid. I'm none of those things. Just a spirit soother, one of the few practitioners of a dying craft.

Not many people can see spirits anymore, which might be a good thing at Mallory Thorne. If the students could see how many souls wander these haunted halls, they'd never be able to focus on class. Especially if they knew about the creepy ghost in Classroom 212 that reads over students' shoulders. Or the occasional Peeping Toms I've had to forcefully exorcise out of the girls' dormitories.

Unfortunately, this also means that there are a lot of skeptics out there. Skeptics who don't understand the extent of what'll happen when they mess with spirits. Or worse, the witchy wannabes, who think that Ouija boards are harmless fun, or that they can cleanse a place of bad spirits with only some sage purchased online.

There are a handful of us "supernaturally inclined" students (as Headmistress Thorne likes to say), so we're often left to help clean up after students who have accidentally unleashed something on the school. It doesn't happen *that* often, and it's usually pretty harmless.

Anyway, it's one of the reasons that we have Nurse Fairweather and Ms. Cole, the resident school psychologist and hunter of the supernatural. She's here so that we "gifted" students (another term Thorne likes to use) have someone to talk to about things we can't really discuss with other people. Cole's also a teacher, in charge of our middle-of-the-night lessons on everything spooky-scary.

I've been back from exorcising my beloved grandfather's spirit for about forty-eight hours now, so of course Cole calls me into her office. It's a pretty nice office, if I'm being honest. Thorne's clearly let her do whatever she wants with her space, as she's painted it a calming sage green. I can also tell that she's one of the millennial plant moms—she's got several different plants propagating in little jars on the windowsill, and has a whole wall made up of flora. I'm not a plant person, so I avoid sitting on the loveseat by that wall. It's not that I'm against the idea of plants, I just really hate bugs, and bugs like plants. So instead, I sit on one of the vintage up-holstered chairs across from Cole's desk. It's not the most comfort-able chair in the world, but at least I won't spend the rest of the day fidgeting and feeling like I've got insects crawling all over my skin.

The essential oil diffuser lets out a puff of air—lavender scented. The relaxing colors and scents in the room are mostly for her, not the students she's counseling. Millennials seem to exist in perpetual anxiety, and honestly sometimes I wonder if she's more intimidated by us than we are of her. Cole adjusts the blue-screen glasses on her face before deciding to take them off. She folds them carefully and places them to the side of her meticulously organized desk.

I stifle a yawn from behind my hand. It's too damn early on a Saturday for counseling, but this was the only time Cole was free. Still, I wish I could join the rest of my classmates back in the dorms, taking advantage of a weekend morning by sleeping in.

My yawn, however, attracts Cole's attention. "How are you feeling, Arzu?"

"Fine."

Cole raises her eyebrows. "Just fine?"

I shrug. "I mean, I sent my grandfather's spirit to…well, wher-ever ghosts go after we kick them out of here."

"And how did that go?"

My lips press together as my grandfather's ghostly screams echo in my mind. "About as well as you'd expect. Which is to say, not well at all."

"I'm sorry to hear that."

Again, I shrug. "It's fine."

Cole cocks her head to the side as though she doesn't believe me. Which is okay, I don't really care one way or the other. I don't really want to talk about exorcising my grandfather's ghost with a hunter. She straightens up, ready to say something more, but we're interrupted by a frantic knocking on the door. Cole doesn't even finish the words "come in" before the person on the other side stumbles inside.

Elizabeth Canton, the dormitory supervisor, practically falls into the room. She's panting, blond hair plastered to her sweaty forehead. "You're needed in the girls' dorms. You too, Arzu. The headmistress is already there, and the police are on their way. There's been a murder."

Murder is not condoned at Mallory Thorne (it says so: on their website, in their brochures, and in the legal paperwork you have to sign before admittance). However, murder happens a lot here. No one has been able to figure why yet, but my money is on the atmosphere. The dreary English weather and the buildings' Gothic architecture really lends itself well to the occasional homicidal urge.

So, like, I get it.

Still, the murder of four Seventh Years is cause for alarm. Especially since their door was locked, according to what Elizabeth told us. She had been the one to find them and had run to get Thorne before doing anything else. But rumors move fast through the spirit vine. The hall is crowded by ghosts, all a titter with the news. In fact, it's so congested that as I walk down the corridor, I pass through a bit of almost every spirit; it's impossible to bypass them all. Elizabeth and Cole, of course, don't seem to notice much except for the drop in temperature, judging by the way they rub their arms.

Outside the door is Headmistress Thorne, who sighs in relief when she sees us. "Oh, thank God."

Wow, no one's ever been that glad to see me before. I'm not sure I like it.

"What happened?" I ask, craning my neck to peer into the dorm room. The door is cracked open, but I can only make out a smear of blood on the floor. Like someone was dragged across it.

Headmistress Thorne shakes her head. "It's a horrible murder. The police have been notified, of course, but I don't believe they'll be much help."

"Why not?" I ask, watching Cole from the side of my vision.

Presented with a crime scene, Cole's demeanor shifts. She sidesteps Thorne and slides into the room, careful not to open the door too widely. Students begin to step out of their rooms to see what all the noise is about, but more staff members arrive to keep everyone in their rooms.

"It doesn't seem as though a person could have done this," Thorne says. "I want you and Cole to take a look—Aref will be joining us soon."

I want to argue that I can do it on my own, but Thorne sighs, her shoulders sagging with the weight of exhaustion. "Those poor girls," she says.

"They might still be here?" I offer, a little unhelpfully. "Their spirits, I mean."

It's unlikely—I've personally never heard of people murdered by ghosts who then also became ghosts. It's possible, but for some reason, it just doesn't really happen.

"If they are, that makes our job easier," Cole states, coming out of the room. She doesn't look too well and leans against the wall of the hallway. She takes a few breaths before speaking again. "I want you and Aref working together on this, Arzu." I open my mouth to argue, but she shakes her head, cutting off my protest before they can start. "No. This is serious. If this is a ghost, then we need someone who can also see them there with you."

I scowl. "Fine. But I'm not going to like it."

"You don't have to," Thorne says. "But this is an all hands on deck situation."

I purse my lips, knowing she has a point. "Okay, but if you think something supernatural did this, what are you going to do about the police? It's not like they're going to be able to help."

"I don't expect them to. But these girls have families, and if we didn't call, then they'd hold us accountable for that. Leave the police to me—the sheriff and I have an understanding."

Thorne's gaze moves to behind my shoulder. I turn to see Aref approaching. It's hard to tell if he dressed in a rush or not—he's pulled on a leather jacket over a beige sweater, with dark black jeans underneath. His face is grim as he walks up.

"We're sure it's murder, then?" he asks, mostly toward Cole. As a hunter himself, Cole is his mentor here at the school.

"Sadly." She nods to the door. "You two should take a look as well. I know you don't have a lot of experience with scenes like this, Arzu, but—"

My cheeks heat up. For some reason, I'm embarrassed to feel a little deficit to Aref, even though a healthy human being would probably be glad they've never encountered something like this before. "I'll be fine," I almost snap.

Two things happen in pretty quick succession.

One: Aref and I are not the only people in the room. Technically.

Jasper the brooding ghost stands in the middle of it, taking the scene. As we enter, he turns to us, a lock of curling dark falling over his pale blue eyes. He pushes it back with the palm of his hand. I know Jasper pretty well—weirdly, he's probably my only friend here at the academy.

I don't really have the chance to ask him why he was here, though, because of the second thing that happens: I do *not* take it fine.

The stench of iron is so thick, my stomach lurches out of my throat. I barely make it out of the room in time to throw up bile into the awaiting bin, held up by Headmistress Thorne. The woman has a sixth sense for students in distress. She crouches down next to me, stroking my hair. "You don't have to go back in there, if you don't want."

I shake my head, and pull off the scarf around my neck, wrapping it over my nose and mouth. "I'm fine."

This time, I am.

Sort of.

Both boys turn to me when I enter the room again. "Are you okay?" Aref asks, his brow furrowed.

"I'm..." My voice trails off while I look around. I swallow hard, wrapping my arms around my waist. Thorne was right—no human could have done this. And if they could have, I certainly don't want to meet them.

Calling these girls murdered is putting it lightly.

The room is one of the cheaper, four-person rooms. To the right of the entrance is one set of bunk beds, with the other set on the wall across from it. In between them is a Ouija board, splattered with blood. Blood is splashed all over the place, and if it were only that, it would be gruesome enough.

The girls were brutalized. One is laid out on her back on the closest bottom bunk, her long blond hair completely rusty with blood. Another sits at a desk, her head barely hanging off her neck. The third is slumped against an armoire, her head missing. I spot it a moment later, placed with intention on the bookshelf in the corner. The fourth roommate is stuck to the wall between the bunk beds, impaled on a leg that broke off from one of the desk chairs.

I don't linger too long at each body—only enough to see the extent of their injuries. It isn't hard to spot, though. They are all disemboweled, their intestines scooped out and decorating the room like garlands. In each of the girls, a heart is placed in the mouth. Other organs are placed on desks and bookshelves, like garish interior design pieces.

"Oh God," I whisper, breaking the silence.

"He's no good to them now," Jasper says bitterly.

Aref sighs. "All right, I've seen enough. I'm heading out."

I nod in agreement, following him out the door. Thorne is no longer there, but Cole is. She looks between the two of us, not seeing Jasper standing behind. "Any thoughts?"

"A lot, but nothing that really makes me think I know what happened there," I say. "Did you notice the Ouija board? There are ghosts all over the place. I can talk to them, see if they might have heard or seen anything, but I wouldn't be too hopeful. They usually stay out of the dorms if they can help it. You know, to give us privacy."

More because I threatened to rip them out of this plane of existence by force if they didn't. Generally, soothers like to wait until the spirit makes that decision for themselves—unless they're a risk to others. It's rumored to be pretty painful when it's done against their will, so the spirits of Mallory Thorne complied pretty quickly.

Well. They did after I made good on my promise by getting rid of a particularly pervy ghost, who screamed the entire time. Screams that only I and the other spirits could hear. But anyway.

Cole nods. "Yes, questioning them could be useful. Not here, though. Once breakfast is over, have the spirits meet you both there."

It sounds so simple when said like that.

"Most of them might not show up," Aref warns. "And there isn't really an attendance sheet of all the spirits on campus."

"Just do what you can," Cole says, rubbing her face. "Everyone on this floor is already down at breakfast—I'm just waiting for the police now. When they're here, stay out of the way."

It hadn't taken Jack long to hear about the girl. Spiritualists had flocked to her kind back in his day. Not him, though. He had never believed in that stuff and was never more pleased to be mistaken. Jack had been given a second chance to continue his life's work. The work had always made him feel alive. Made him feel like a god.

However, the spirit following her around gave him cause for concern.

Most of the ghosts didn't notice him as he drifted among them. They wouldn't—even those that looked as though they might have been from his time had no chance of recognizing him. He'd never been caught. He had simply moved from place to place, making sure to keep his kills quiet. As much as he liked the attention some of his kills received, he much preferred being able to continue his bloody profession.

Had Jack known there was a spirit soother nearby, he would have thought twice about killing four girls in one go. From now on, he'd have to move carefully.

Jack moved along with the other spirits, following them through the dimly lit corridors of the school. A fully covered stone bridge connected the girl's dormitories to the main building—Jack overheard a chatty, matronly ghost talking to herself about how many ghosts had been stuck in their original haunts before these bridges linked the other buildings to the main academic structure. Now, they were all free to move about as they pleased. She was grateful because now she was no longer stuck in the school's infirmary and could socialize.

Through the arched windows of the bridge, Jack saw the police cars drifting onto the road leading up to the school. They would soon be making a mess of his art. The fact bothered him more than just a little.

The dining hall teemed with spirits. Judging by their dress, they had all died in various times across the centuries. They clamored around the spirit soother from earlier, who was accompanied by a young man with dark sandy skin.

"Where's your boyfriend?" the young man asked her.

She scowled. "First, he's not my boyfriend. Second, he's at the crime scene, eavesdropping. The police aren't exactly going to talk to us, so he's going to see gather whatever information he can for us."

The boy grunted. "I guess that's something."

The spirit soother rolled her eyes but didn't bother to respond. Instead, she turned her attention to the ghosts gathering around. The two soothers separated to question the spirits on their own — Jack could tell there was no love lost between them. He wove through the noncorporeal bodies, listening in to the conversations. It was crowded — it seemed that many spirits had come out to help, or at least snoop.

Should he interact with the soothers? He didn't want them to be aware of him, but by approaching them himself, he would prevent himself from seeming suspicious.

The young man got to him first; Jack had been too busy watching the girl. He always did like to watch pretty girls.

The boy was already suspicious of Jack. He spoke to him with narrowed eyes. "Sorry, who are you? I don't think I've seen you around before."

"I like to keep to myself," Jack replied with a smooth smile. "The name is Jonathan. And you?"

"Aref. It's nice of you to come out and help, Jonathan. Did you happen to see anything odd last night?"

Jack pretended to think. "No, I don't think I did. Are there any details on what happened? Perhaps something I should be keeping an eye out for?"

"Just let me know if you overhear anyone, I don't know, confessing to killing four students. Or behaving strangely." Aref ran a hand through his mop of curly dark hair. "Sorry, this is stressful. If you have anything unusual to report, please find me."

Jack inclined his head amiably. "Of course."

If this was the kind of investigation he was up against, Jack had no reason to be concerned. These were simply children playing dress up.

Boys aren't allowed in the girl's dorms—Aref's examination of the crime scene was an exemption—so Aref and I reconvened outside, under a birch tree in the courtyard under my dorm window. Aref isn't happy about this, citing that ghosts can listen in on us if they want—not very stealthily though, as we'd be able to see them. He wanted to meet somewhere warded against them, but then Jasper wouldn't have been able to join us.

And if Jasper hadn't joined us, I wouldn't currently be tortured by the retorts volleying between the two of them.

I rub the bridge of my nose. "Can you two stop? We're already here, so we don't need to keep fighting over where to sit. And, also, four girls died, so maybe we have more important things to think about."

That shuts them both up, thank God, because I can only handle one disaster at a time.

"Did the police have anything interesting to say?" I ask Jasper, while Aref ignores us.

"Some of them threw up like you did," he mentions, a little amused. "Mostly, they were horrified."

"Not surprising," I murmur.

He nods. "Not at all. But, out of curiosity, I followed the sheriff to Thorne's office to see what they talked about. Apparently, he's an academy graduate and isn't surprised by some of the goings-on here. They've got some kind of agreement that the sheriff ensures his cops fumble the case while Thorne has her people take care of everything."

If Aref is disturbed or impressed, he doesn't give it away. Instead, he's busy typing away on his phone. I snap my fingers in his face. "Hello? I'm sorry, is there something more important than a gruesome ghost murder?"

"You know," he starts, his yellow-green eyes moving slowly

away from his phone to meet my perturbed gaze, "you're lucky you're cute because otherwise you'd be insufferable."

Cute? I'm so taken aback that I'm still struggling to find a biting response when he shows me his screen.

"Oh. Oh shit." I take his phone from him without thinking.

He was reading a blog post by UnsolvedCrimeBitch detailing a series of murders that spanned the late 1880s to the early 1900s. All the victims were young girls, all were disemboweled to varying degrees. Whoever UnsolvedCrimeBitch is, they connected a string of possible deaths as well, tracing the murderer's kills back to here—the town Mallory Thorne is nestled beside.

"Are you thinking they brought this guy back?" I ask, looking back at Aref as I show the screen to Jasper to read.

"Nothing like this has happened on campus before," Aref points out. "A new spirit is the only thing that makes sense." Looking at Jasper, Aref's forehead crinkles. "You okay, Casper?"

I shoot him a scowl, knowing he got Jasper's name wrong on purpose. But fury is twisting Jasper's face into an expression I have only seen once before—on my grandfather's spirit, when I forced it to move on. "Jasper?" I ask, concerned.

"I thought the murders were familiar," he growls. "It's Jonathan Pensworth."

Aref raises a brow. "And how do you know him?"

"He was a student here around the same time as I was."

His cold tone makes me think he doesn't want to discuss it, but Aref is either unaware of that or doesn't care. "So, what makes you think it's him?"

"Because I saw him kill, right before he murdered me."

Aref shoots me a glance that I avoid. Generally speaking, we like to keep the spirits of the murdered and their murderers from meeting. It never really goes well. Angry masses of spiritual energy tend to get...explosive. Hell, they get explosive enough on their own if they're pissed off enough.

Aref shifts the conversation. "I'll contact my dad, see if he's ever dealt with something like this."

"Why?" It seems a bit unnecessary, since I am a spirit soother and Aref is a hunter. "Can't we send him back the way we send back all ghosts?"

"Not really. He's not stuck here—he was called back. I want to make sure we cover all our bases." Aref doesn't even wait for me to reply before calling his dad. A deep voice picks up, and he glides off the bench to take the call farther away.

I'm not excited about the idea of a serial killing ghost loose on campus that I might not be able to send back to Hell on my own. And, of course, that he might continue to kill while we're scrambling to figure out what to do. Thank God for Jasper, though. I know when people say, "everything happens for a reason," they don't usually mean murder, but if Jasper hadn't been murdered, then who knows how long it would have taken us to figure out this ghost's identity?

Aref is going to want us to keep Jasper away from Jonathan, but I know Jas won't go for that. Besides, what if this is what he needs to move on? My heart constricts. What if it is? I mean, I have other friends than just a grumpy 19th century ghost but...not many more. People seem to find me off-putting, for some reason.

It would suck if Jasper moved on, especially so soon after my grandfather. I'm a spirit soother, though. The whole point of our existence is to help ghosts. I can't be selfish.

No matter how much I want to be.

Jack should have known Jasper would come back to haunt him.

He watched the trio from the window—the spirit soother's window, in fact. It seemed a fitting irony, and he had always loved twisted symmetry. Jack recognized Jasper as soon as he laid eyes on him. He remembered all his kills, but Jasper's death stood out amongst them, a vivid tableau against the others. Jack had never meant to kill him. Necessity dictated his death, unfortunately, for he had seen Jack kill his first victim.

And Jack had no intention of stopping. Not then, and not now.

However, he knew the clock ticked against him. Jasper would have recognized his work by now. It was only a matter of time before he was stopped.

Butcher Jack had to get to work.

The school is in lockdown. Now, the students of Mallory Thorne are no strangers to weird shit. We're kind of used to it, honestly. But we've never seen a murder on this scale—at least, not in recent memory.

But here's the problem with a lockdown when the murderer is a ghost: walls don't exactly stop them. Kids who watched way too much TV have grabbed salt from the dorm kitchenettes and lined their windows and doors with it. Staff members are assigned to roam the halls, keeping an ear out for things like screams of murder.

Meanwhile, Aref foils my efforts to go back to my room to research Jonathan Pensworth. He refuses to let me go without fortifying me against a possible possession.

"There's a specter roaming around, possessing people, and you want to go back to the scene of the crime without any kind of protection? I don't know how you're not already protected," he says, shaking his head with amazement.

I shrug. "It's never come up. No one in my family's ever been possessed, and possession isn't something we've dealt with. We usually get called before that happens."

"Must be nice," he mutters.

We trek down the cobblestone pathways toward the center of the school. Jas has disappeared without a word which, even for him, is unusual. I get it, though. It can't be easy to know your murderer is back on this plane of existence.

Aref leads me through the side entrance of the main building. It's dark in this portion of the school—we must be in a corridor used for maintenance and storage. Aref clearly knows where he's going. He reaches immediately for the door to the right, which opens to reveal a long, stone staircase leading to the basement.

Lovely.

"Are you sure you're not the one who is possessed?" I ask, carefully following him down.

Aref chuckles. "The threshold is warded. If either of us had been possessed, we would have been thrown against the wall."

"Oookay."

We don't even stop at the basement—yet another set of stairs go into something more akin to a dungeon. Which is really one of the last places I want to be with Aref.

"What exactly are we doing down here?"

"I've got a bit of a set up here. Well, it's Ms. Cole's set up that she lets me use. It's a hunter's cache, essentially. We keep our shit here."

I side-eye everything. The stakes stacked up like wood for a fireplace. Axes, swords, and crossbows hanging on weapon displays. There are lockers, one of which is open to reveal leather and light chainmail clothing. Aref crosses to the table on the other side of the room and pulls out a needle and ink.

I step back. "What are you planning on doing with that?"

"A protection tattoo. It's to prevent possession."

"I'm not getting a tattoo."

"If he possesses you, I won't hesitate to kill you. I won't enjoy it, but I'll do it."

I take another look at the needle and shudder. "I'll pass. There has to be another way."

Aref groans a little, tossing the equipment across the table.

"I think we have an amulet around here somewhere. Just so you know, though, a ghost could be able to get it off you."

"I'll take that risk."

I meander around the room, keeping my arms crossed over my chest. There is a history of distrust between spirit soothers and hunters—we don't usually approve of their methods. Or their tools, so I keep my hands to myself. Don't want to accidentally touch something that'll cause gradual petrification of my limbs, or something.

Dramatic? Maybe.

"Found it," Aref announces, fishing something out of the bottom of a chest. At first glance, it looks like a dazzling emerald but, when the light refracts off it, I can see a symbol carved into the stone, right in the middle. The emerald is surrounded by yellow gold and small diamonds.

It seems excessive.

My opinion must be written on my face because Aref clears his throat. "Usually, pieces like this come from old families who lost their ties to the supernatural and donate items like this, not knowing what they're for. Look, you don't have to wear it but—"

"It's fine," I say, taking the necklace out of his hands. The clasp is stuck, but I manage to loosen it at the expense of my right thumb nail. The necklace is almost unbearably heavy—the stones and gold weigh it down.

"So," I start, toying with the amulet, "what exactly is our plan?"

"Cole and my dad have put in calls to get some hunters down here for security—the staff are just as vulnerable as the students. Cole is warding the main hall so that Thorne can send for the students. I think she's putting something together to keep everyone in there while we take care of it."

It's a shame we can't bring them down here, where it's already warded. But there's no way this dungeon could fit everyone, and definitely not without people asking questions.

I sink into one of the chairs by the table. "So, it's just going to be the two of us against a serial killing ghost?"

"Probably not. I imagine Ms. Cole will come by as soon as she's done helping escort the rest of the students. Until then, it's you and me."

"And Jasper."

"Right." Aref straightens up, having packed a motley of weapons into two duffle bags, and sits across from me. "We need to talk about Jasper."

I swallow hard. "What about him?"

"Don't play dumb. You have as much experience with ghosts as I do—probably more, honestly. What do you think is going to happen if Jasper faces off with the man that killed him? Nothing good. Nothing safe. So, I want you to do me a favor."

"What?" I ask, suspiciously.

"Keep Jasper busy while I get rid of the Butcher."

The sound coming out of my mouth is a cross between a laugh and a scoff. "I'm not doing that. You said it yourself; I have more experience with ghosts than you do."

"General experience, sure. But I have more experience killing them, so to speak. And Jasper is definitely not going to listen to anything I say."

"First of all, I just got back from 'killing' my grandfather's ghost, as you put it. And second, Jasper isn't as unreasonable as you think he is. If we explain things to him, I'm sure he'll understand."

Aref arches an eyebrow, and I ignore the fluttering in my stomach. "Somehow, I doubt that'll be the case."

Jack stalked his new suit: a large, muscular cop who had stayed behind as his colleagues—confused and upset over the murders— left to work from the station. This man hadn't joined them, insisting that he wanted to speak to the students. Hear their own stories.

A mistake, of course. One that would be his last.

Jack neared him when a voice rang out.

"Jonathan. I know it's you, and I won't let you harm any more of them."

Jack turned to see the young man, his face twisted in a scowl. The Butcher tsked. "Now, now, Jas. Didn't you learn the first time? Don't interrupt me while I'm working."

Jasper moved quickly—Jack had barely blinked before the spirit was in front of him. He hadn't even processed it when Jasper's fist came hurtling for his face. Jack stumbled, his hand on the side of his face. He hadn't expected it to *hurt*. What the hell was the point of being dead, then?

Jasper chucked. "There's a lot you have to learn about being a ghost, Jonathan. And I've got loads more experience than you."

With an angry roar, Jack launched himself at Jasper. He wasn't going to let him ruin his fun with his interruptions anymore.

The cavalry (re: Aref's dad and his hunter buddies) decide to bring Jonathan Pensworth to them, rather than track him down. And while it makes sense, I still can't help feeling uneasy as they paint a summoning circle in the auditorium. It's a risky move, calling a dangerous spirit to you, especially one that is already wandering around. There is always a chance it could stop you before the ritual is complete.

But then again, that's why Aref and I are there—we're the glorified lookouts. The hunters keep telling us how "great" we're doing, even though the only thing we're doing is using our eyes. I guess their aging corneas find that impressive, I don't know.

"All right." One of the hunters gets to his feet, rubbing the chalk residue off his hands and onto his red checkered flannel. His American accent reminds me of home. "Let's get this show on the road."

Aref and I don't join—his dad's orders. Apparently, we're only good enough to hold down the fort until the "real" professionals arrive. Aref's brow has been furrowed since we got our commands, and he hasn't even bothered to make a single snide remark.

It makes me wish his dad was a permanent fixture of Mallory Thorne. I'm not supposed to be watching the ritual so closely, but I can't help it. I've used spirit traps before—like on my grandfather—but never like this. Never with so many people. Granted, there are only three other hunters, Aref's dad not being one of them (he stayed behind to guard the main hall with a handful of others). But the summoning circle doesn't just work to bring the spirit to you. It also makes the spirit within the circle visible to everyone else. At least, as long as it's trapped.

The hunters' voices harmonize as they recite the incantation to call the spirit. At the end, they each light a summoning ingredient, one by one, in brass bowls. For a moment, there is silence. All that can be heard is the lapping of the flames against metal.

And then, chaos.

A pair of energies appear in the circle. It takes a second for them to come into focus. My heart sinks when I recognize one as Jasper. He's wrestling with the other, an older man with a tall hat. Jonathan Pensworth, it's safe to assume. Even though the ritual was only meant for one of them, Jas must have gone along for the ride if they were in physical contact at the time. Or whatever counted for physical when you're a ghost.

"Jasper!" I run for the circle, only to be tackled to the ground.

Aref is on top of me, pinning my flailing arms down. "Stop it," he growls in a way that would have been attractive in any other context. "Arzu, if you break that circle, you'll kill all of us. It's too late for Jasper, but it's not too late for you."

Of course, this is the only time he gets Jas's name right. "He's my friend," I shout back, glaring up at him. What I don't say is that he's one of my *only* friends.

"I'm sorry." Aref's expression softens. "But I'm not letting you die for him."

I struggle against him, trying to force him off me but he's too strong. "You don't get to make that decision for me."

"I'm a hunter, so yes, I do."

A part of me knows that he's right. But a larger part of me is in pain. "Aref, please," I whisper. Tears sting my eyes, and I know he can see them, but there's no way for me hide them. To hide my vulnerability. "I just lost my grandfather. Please don't make me lose my friend too."

From the corner of my eye, I see Jasper and Jonathan wrestling. The hunters don't quite seem to know what to do—they had only prepared themselves for one spirit. One of them—the American—decides to go ahead with the banishing spell. But I can tell it won't be necessary.

The ghosts are tearing each other's spiritual energies apart.

Aref can see it, too, and his grip tightens. Smart, because I was just about to make another escape attempt. "I really hope you can forgive me for this," he says, mournfully. "But if you can't, I'll understand."

I'm only half listening. My head is turned, watching the circle. The masses of the two spirits combine into one, growing in intensity. Goosebumps prickle my arms, and I wonder if we're all going to die here, anyway. I don't really want to die. Especially not with Aref on top of me.

And then the mass explodes.

The circle lights up, an illumination of pale green as bits of energy hit the barriers and disintegrate. The Butcher is gone. My friend is gone.

Aref gets up, and I quietly let him help me to my feet. I don't have the spunk to fight him, not even verbally. "Arzu?" It's funny, but he sounds as vulnerable as I feel. "Are you okay?"

I shake my head. "Leave me alone," I say before I walk away to find a private place to cry.

Two weeks have passed since the murders. Thorne and Cole have left me alone, although I'm one of the only students still on campus. I assume Aref told them about Jasper. Everyone else was allowed to go home to have four weeks of remote classes while they spend some much-needed time with their families.

And while the biohazard team cleans up the crime scene.

Aref is also still on campus. I avoid him, of course. On some level, I understand that he was just doing his job. But still. Jas was my friend, and now I'll never see him again. Just like I'll never see my grandfather again.

And both of those losses are on me, regardless of whatever Cole or Aref might say.

I'm sure Cole has a lot to say, since she's summoned me to her office. The rain patters against the windowpanes behind her desk. "We haven't really gotten a chance to talk about everything that's happened. How are you doing?"

"I'm fine."

She pauses. "You've been through a lot lately. No one would blame you if you were a little less than fine."

"If you already know that I'm not fine, then why even bother asking? You're only setting me up to lie to you."

"No, I'm giving you an opportunity to share your feelings. Your dishonesty is your choice."

Okay. Well then. Clearly, we're both tired of the bullshit script we've been following.

Cole's head is cocked innocently, but her eyes say, "checkmate bitch." She's not going to stop calling me in here, so I have a choice.

I can be sullen, uncooperative, and completely alone. I can float through this hall like a living ghost, or I can pull myself together. I can recognize that I've lost my two confidants—my grandfather and my friend—and that unless I start coping with it, I'm never going to make any other friends.

I sigh. "All right, fine. Where should I start?"

"Wherever you'd like." She settles back in her chair and spreads her hands wide open. I don't want to find it comforting, but I do.

AUTHOR BIOGRAPHIES

MAY SELESTE (EDITOR)

May is a South Asian Muslim author from London, and a psychoanalysis Masters graduate. She writes gothic fiction and dark fantasy, and has previously appeared in *When Other People Saw Us, They Saw the Dead* in 2022. She is currently querying her personal masterpiece—her gothic, dark fantasy novel. Her literature preferences lean more towards the dark and sometimes literary, with an unusual affinity for eerie tragedies or the viscerally uncomfortable. Bonus points for psychological elements—particularly anything referencing Jung.

Other than that, her hobbies include not leaving the house, caring for her bonsai, and admiring new K-pop videos. Whichever one requires the least talking. You can find her on social media at @Writermay_S.

KATALINA WATT

Katalina is a Filipino-British author of speculative fiction and gothic horror, represented by Robbie Guillory of Underline. Their work has been published in *Haunted Voices, Unspeak-*

able, *Extra Teeth*, and forthcoming in an eco-horror anthology *To Root Somewhere Beautiful: An Anthology of Reclamation* from Outland Entertainment. She was longlisted for Penguin Write Now 2020 and a 2021 Ladies of Horror Fiction Writers Grant awardee. They are also Founding Audio Director of khōréō magazine, and won the 2022 Ignyte Award for Best Fiction Podcast. She's also run writing workshops and appeared at events for Cymera and FIYAHCON.

M.K. SARRAJ

Marwa is a Turkish-American hijabi writer, and has a short story out in *When Other People Saw Us, They Saw the Dead* with Haunt Publishing. She writes primarily SFF with gothic elements, and has two cats.

NATHANAEL BOON

Nathanael (he/him) is a Chinese Singaporean with a long-time passion for creative writing. He has written mainly fanfiction on and off for close to ten years, and this is one of his first forays into creating an entirely original story and characters. He excels at high action sequences, particularly in techno-thrillers, but has no qualms with dipping his toes into the horror/supernatural genre.

His other primary interests include heavy metal and punk music, prehistoric wildlife, and left-wing politics, all of which have been or will be featured in his writing at some point.

MARY ZAMBALES

Mary Zambales is a 1.5 generation Filipino American living in the Bay Area. Her hobbies outside of reading and writing include baking, watching K-dramas, and dumpster-diving social media. While not sticking to any one genre or age group, all her stories center Filipino main characters.

MOACHIBA JAMIR

Moachiba Jamir is from Kohima, Nagaland. He is the 2023 fiction winner of TOTO Funds the Arts in English Creative Writing. He is an alumnus of the University of Iowa's International Writing Program, Summer Institute. He has also been a part of Write Beyond Borders, a transnational creative-writing project funded by the British Council. His work has previously been published in *Inverted Syntax*, and the anthologies *Exodus*, *Swansong*, and *Olio: Obscure Writings from Nagaland*.

KAVYA VENKAT

Kavya Venkat is an Indian American writer and medical student who lives at the intersection of science and creative writing. She also physically lives in Florida, where she works on speculative fiction in between doing flashcards about everything that can go wrong in the human body. Her work often focuses on queer and South Asian themes about family and the changes brought by technology. She also enjoys drawing on Hindu mythology as inspiration. Kavya particularly loves writing about how traditions change and grow; one of her favorite Indian rituals is the blessing of cars and motorcycles, something which originated in the blessing of horses and carts. She is an avid gardener who takes advantage of the subtropical Floridian climate to grow a variety of vegetables, and she firmly believes that cold watermelon at the beach brings one along the path to enlightenment. Kavya can be found on Twitter with the username @sage_thrasher.

AUDRIS CANDRA

Audris is a queer Chinese-Indonesian writer, editor, and co-founder of #APIPit, the first Twitter pitch event created to elevate Asian and Pacific Islander creators. As a klenik (something akin to a shaman), they're too haunted for their own good so they find refuge in being a certified weirdo who loves their IKEA shark maybe a little bit too much.

MIRHA BUTT

Mirha (she/her) is a Kashmiri Muslim, currently living in London and studying toward a Geography degree alongside writing unapologetically desi novels with diverse casts, important social issues and a lot of love (and pain). Her greatest joy is being able to put mental health perseverance, nuanced female characters (intersectional feminism FTW!); and religious characters in her work. When she's not coloring in maps or typing away, she can be found watching Bollywood films, swapping identities with her identical twin-sister, and seeking out academic validation.

ARCHITA MITTRA

Archita Mittra is a writer, editor, and artist, with a fondness for dark and fantastical things. She completed her B.A. (2018) and M.A. (2020) in English Literature from Jadavpur University and has a Diploma in Multimedia and Animation from St. Xavier's College (2016). Her work has appeared in Tor, *Strange Horizons, Locus Magazine, Anathema: Spec from the Margins,* and in the Bram Stoker-nominated *Human Monsters* anthology, by *Dark Matter Magazine,* among others. Her stories and poems have been nominated for the Pushcart and Best of the Net prizes, and long-listed for the Toto Award for Creative Writing in 2020. When she isn't writing speculative fiction or drawing fan art, she can be found playing indie games, making jewelry out of recycled materials, baking cakes, or deciding which new tarot deck to buy. She lives in Kolkata, India, with her family and rabbits, and can be found on Twitter and Instagram @ architamittra.

CHARLIE JIAO

Charlie is a twenty-three-year-old amateur writer and Chinese adoptee. As a fun fact, they have a sister and two cousins also adopted from China! They're obsessed with putting Lee Kum Kee char sui sauce on things, and is sure their housemate is sick of their one cooking style: questionable fusion. They have a 360 day streak in Chinese on Duolingo and despite their parents' best efforts, the owl has taught them more Chinese than any laoshi. They currently live in Cambridge, England, mostly found coffee shop hopping along the Cam, or exploring the poppy field that's suddenly appeared on their usual run. Digitally, they're @halcyonwritings on Twitter. Their projects tend to be contemporary thrillers across YA and NA. All of them involve found family, and recently they've been writing a lot around the subject of adoption. They've got huge brainrot for an NA wip on the back-burner featuring Chinatown, magic, and lesbians. Of course, they've first got to finish any of the other WIPs they've jumped into.

TEHNUKA

Tehnuka (she/they) is a Tamil writer and volcanologist from Aotearoa, New Zealand. She likes to find herself up volcanoes, down caves, and in unexpected places: everyone else, however, can find her online at www.tehnuka.dreamhosters.com or as @tehnuka on Twitter. Some of her recent speculative works appear in *Reckoning*, *Apex*, and *Uncanny*. She is the 2023 winner of the Sir Julius Vogel Award for Best New Talent in New Zealand science fiction and fantasy.

ASHLEY DENG

Ashley Deng is a Canadian-born Chinese-Jamaican author of dark fantasy and horror. She holds a BSc in biochemistry, specializing her studies toward making accessible the often-cryptic world of science and medicine. When not writing, she is a hobbyist medical/scientific illustrator and spends her spare time overthinking society and culture. Her work has appeared at Nightmare Magazine, Fireside Magazine, Augur Magazine, and others. Her climate horror novella, *Dehiscent*, is available from Tenebrous Press. You can find her at ashedeng.ca or on various social media as @ashesandmochi and @baroqueintentions.

L CHAN

L Chan hails from Singapore. He spends most of his time wrangling a team of two dogs, Mr. Luka and Mr. Telly. His work has appeared in places like *Clarkesworld, Translunar Travellers Lounge, Podcastle, the Dark,* and he was a finalist for the 2020 Eugie Foster Memorial Award. He tweets inordinately at @lchanwrites and can be found on the web at https://lchanwrites.wordpress.com/.